Lighthouse Point

Lighthouse Point

Lisa Poston Murphy

ISBN: 098964460X
ISBN-13: 9780989644600

For my Nana,
Thank you for marinating me in love
and introducing me to Sanibel Island.
March 18, 1924 – April 16, 2013

Acknowledgments

I owe a debt of gratitude to those who were so generous with their time and expertise:

Sergeant Jimmy Garrett and FTO Colin Lane, who led me through the details of a crime scene investigation. The expertise in the book belongs to them, any errors are mine.

Amanda Sauer, my editor and friend, for the countless hours spent tweaking this book—you are extremely talented. Thank you for your honesty, suggestions, and comic relief lunches.

I would especially like to thank my husband for supporting my obsession with writing this book, for the poetry and romance he has pervaded throughout our years together, and for driving five hours out of the way to let me stick my feet in the ocean at Lighthouse Point.

As in the soft and sweet eclipse.
When soul meets soul on lovers' lips.
—*Percy Bysshe Shelley, Prometheus Unbound,*
Act IV

Prologue

Six was a hard age for patience, and it was hard not to look up as I heard the sound of the waves crashing on the shoreline.

"Don't peek, keep your head down," Nana said as she held my hand. "This is our tradition."

Carefully stepping through the path of the thick sea-grape hedge toward the beach, I continued along the sand with my head down.

We were almost there, just a few more steps until I could run into the water.

"Let's count to three and then open our eyes. Ready?

"One . . . Two . . . Three!"

I looked up to see the blue water, its waves crashing onto the sandy beach. "It's so pretty, Nana. Can I go play now?"

"Yes, darling. Let's get some lotion on before you go," she persuaded, as she coated me with sunscreen before I wriggled away to get in the water.

I played in the sand making castles, stopping only for trips to the ocean to fill my bucket. Every six-year-old knew that all good castles have moats. Sifting through a mound of shells that had washed up during high tide, I was very choosy about which ones were worthy of my masterpiece.

My castle was almost finished, with shells decorating the walls and bridge, when I heard Nana call.

"C'mon, Emma, time to go."

"I don't want to leave." Tears streamed down my cheeks.

"I know, little love." She picked me up and held me on her hip. "But don't worry, we'll be back in March. I'll help you mark the calendar and we'll count it down together."

I wiped the tears off of my cheeks onto her shirt and with my tiny sand-encrusted hands, pulled her face around to look at mine. "One day I'm going to live here so I don't ever have to leave."

She kissed my forehead and straightened my ruffled bathing suit. "I have no doubt in my mind that you will, my little island girl."

One

I've never been a fly-by-the-seat-of-your-pants kind of girl, packing my things and traveling fourteen hours away from my comfortable, neatly-organized life to an island that promises sanctuary and a fresh start—until today.

Something had to change. The dark circles under my eyes solicited too much attention and questions I wasn't ready to answer.

As I drove over the Causeway onto the island, memories of my Nana and I making Key lime pies in our beach cottage years ago flooded my mind. I must have looked ridiculous, giggling through tears as I recalled our time together. She had been gone for six years now and I missed her. *"It has eggs and fruit,"* I could hear her say, trying to justify our decision to have a slice for breakfast.

My daydream was shaken as a song came over the radio, the relaxed melody instantly transforming my mood. I sang along until my thoughts returned to the reason for my escape. Would the nightmares cease once I was safely ensconced by Sanibel's refreshing waters?

Would the island be the same after all these years? Fear and excitement of my unknown future filled me. I didn't know how long I would be able to stay, I would have to find a job before my money ran out and settle somewhere.

I rolled the windows down, letting the fresh, salty air permeate the inside of my silver Volvo C70—a practical car for a sensible woman—but all that was in the past now. Certainly traveling eight hundred miles to seek refuge from the past was anything but sensible.

All doubt vanished as the lighthouse came into view, and I allowed the thick, sweet air to warm my skin and soul. When I reached the cottage I had rented, I pulled into a long gravel driveway lined in overgrown shrubs and cabbage palms that hadn't been trimmed in years. The small cottage was a light shade of blue—it reminded me of periwinkle. Inside, paintings of pelicans and egrets hung from the cream walls lending a bright cheery feel to the place. I knew right away my favorite spot was going to be sitting in the oversized paisley chair by the large picture window in the living room. I couldn't wait to unwind there with a cup of Earl Grey and a good romance novel.

Eager to get to the beach, I grabbed my black swimsuit out of the suitcase in the car and ran back in to change. After setting the air conditioner to a cooler temperature, I skipped to the car.

As I pulled out of the driveway, I realized I hadn't eaten a solid meal since breakfast. My stomach growled, but I ignored it, imagining sticking my tired feet in the cool ocean water.

While most things on the island were thankfully unchanged, one small change threatened to delay my beach reunion: pay parking. After an extended search through places in the car where money seems to hide, I was able to satisfy the self-serve parking machine. I tied my hair in a ponytail and wrapped the ends back into the rubber band, making a messy bun.

Walking along the sandy trail, I carefully stepped through the path of the thick sea grape hedge toward the beach. It was so hard not to look up as I heard the sound of the waves crashing on the shoreline, but this was our tradition, something I had done since coming here as a little girl.

Almost there, Emma, just a few more steps through the path and onto the sand. I could hear Nana's voice in my head as I counted to three and then glanced up to behold the emerald water. The most glorious sight, even after all these years, it still brought tears to my eyes.

The sun was setting, not a cloud in the sky to block my view of the descending orange ball. When it finally disappeared below the sea-line, everyone on the beach clapped and headed to their cars.

My stomach reminded me again that I had not eaten. Famished, I drove to Jerry's Foods, a local grocery store, and picked up a deli sandwich and a bottle of Pinot Noir.

Trying to get the key in the door, while holding as much luggage as I could carry, and balancing the bag from Jerry's on my knee, I finally stumbled into the cool cottage. It was dark, and I dropped my suitcase, patting the walls inside the door to find a switch. I found one that turned on a lamp next to my soon-to-be favorite chair.

After scarfing down the delicious deli sandwich and a couple glasses of wine, I headed to the bedroom. As I drifted off to sleep, I remembered the sound of waves crashing against the beach.

* * *

I woke up in my bed back home. Suddenly, coarse hands held down my wrists. The rank stench of alcohol mixed with sweat assailed my nostrils. I tried to move but I was pinned. I tried to scream. No sound escaped my lips. Hot tears slipped down my temples, wetting my hair. Gasping, I sucked in a deep breath and yelled, "No!"

I wrenched upright in bed. Disoriented, I looked around wondering where I was. Finding the lamp on the nightstand, I switched it on. I saw that I was in the rental on Sanibel, alone and safe. It had just been another nightmare. I searched my purse for Motrin and took a swallow of water from a little cup in the bathroom to wash the pills down, wishing I had let the doctor write me a prescription after all.

"No. I can do this without medication," I said, trying to convince myself I could heal on my own. I heard my subconscious scold me . . . *By running away.*

* * *

As the sun filtered into the room, I awoke and rubbed my sore eyes. I hadn't gotten much sleep and could've used some coffee, but I never cared for the taste of it. Instead, I made a cup of hot tea with honey and headed to the back porch. There were several fruit trees—orange, lime, grapefruit, and star fruit. I picked a grapefruit the size of a softball, peeled it, and ate it like you would an orange. It was much sweeter than the grapefruit back home. The star fruit tree was also full of ripe pickings, so I plucked off one to taste. The skin had the texture of a grape, and the flavor of the fruit was hard to compare to anything—simultaneously sweet and tart. I decided this would make excellent jam and maybe I could make a sauce to go over grilled pork.

As I finished my tea, I planned my first full day on Sanibel.

Two

*S*heldon

Sheldon Barringer packed his windsurfing gear on the truck, secured the board and sails, and headed home. If it weren't for his parents and the busyness of his fast-growing company, he would have slipped into a deep depression. He had tried to fill the empty void with women, but tourists always left and he found the local girls unadventurous as well as either boring or snooty. His mother had hoped he would marry Victoria Preston, a beautiful brunette, both smart and ambitious, who came from a wealthy family. His mother harassed him about her almost daily. He'd dated her for two years and had planned to propose, until he realized she was sucking the life out of him and had almost convinced him to give up his passion of windsurfing.

Sheldon ran a hand through his light brown hair as he drove behind a couple on a scooter. He was eager to get home and let the hot water of the shower soothe his sore muscles and the stress from the day. After showering, he called his father. "Okay if I stop by and bring a couple of beers?"

"Sounds good, son, your mother's at bridge, and I'm watching the tennis tournament on ESPN. I have beer in the fridge, just come on."

While he sat watching tennis with his father, Sheldon popped open his beer and took a long drink. As the ice-cold fizz slid down his throat, relaxing him, he heard his mother come in.

"Can I get you something to eat?" His mother, Helen, was dressed in her navy pleated shorts, white polo, and a pale yellow sweater.

He stifled a chuckle at the sight of her. She was always trying to feed him and care for him, and continually worried about him. "I already ate, Mom, but thanks. Just watching tennis with Dad."

"There's plenty of food in the fridge if you get hungry. You boys enjoy yourselves."

When Helen left the room, Sheldon's dad turned to him and asked, "So how's the business?"

"It's going really well. A huge deal fell through today though. You know that property I was telling you about in Boca? It was a steal and I had it in the bag until the Ross group came in and made a higher offer. Win some, lose some, I guess." Sheldon finished off his beer and cleaned up his empties as well as his dad's.

"Sorry, son, you would've made a profit on that one for sure, but the way the market is around here, another one will come along soon."

Bill had aged well—his gray hair and gray-blue eyes were distinguished against his tan skin. He stood and stretched his arms over his head. "I'm going to have to call it a night, son. Early tee time in the morning. Wish you could join us, I'm playing with Bart and Fred."

"Sorry, Dad, I have an early meeting tomorrow." Sheldon left his parents' house and drove down Sanibel-Captiva Road toward home.

As he climbed into his king-sized bed, he set the alarm for 6:00 a.m., which wouldn't leave any time for a morning run, but he needed the extra sleep.

* * *

Sheldon's meeting went on for a dreadful two hours as he sat with the board members around a large wooden table with coffee, tea, danishes, fruit, and yogurt. They went over each property that was on the market and talked about which ones were the best investments.

"What about this one in Naples?" Hannah asked.

Hannah Vaughn was tall and thin with straight shoulder-length brown hair and too much makeup.

Sheldon looked up at her after viewing the file on the Naples property once more. "No, it has great curb appeal, but Brady and I looked at the property personally last Tuesday and it needs too much work. There's also a question about the foundation. We might break even, at best."

After the meeting Sheldon decided he just needed a day devoid of decisions and responsibilities, just him and the sea. He peeked his head in Charlie's office. "Hey, I'm taking the rest of the day off, can you handle things here?"

"Sure, everything okay?"

"Yeah, I just need some time to unwind. It's been a hard week."

"Sure, bud." Charlie Cooper and Sheldon had been friends since sixth grade and both shared the passion of windsurfing. Charlie was shorter than Sheldon, about 5'11" and had a stocky build. His crystal-blue eyes and wavy blond hair made him look like a surfer caught in a business suit.

Sheldon headed home to get his swim trunks on and grab his bike for a long ride down the beach.

Low tide made for an easy ride because of the firmer wet sand, but he had to weave around a few people shelling. They all had the same pose, bent over at the waist, famously dubbed the "Sanibel stoop." Most of the diehard shellers had the net bag hanging off their waist or a netted shell shovel.

When he made his way past Casa Ybel Resort, the beach became less crowded. He climbed off of his bike and made his way into the water for a quick refreshing swim. Low tide left the sea calm, and the water felt like silk on his skin. Before getting back on his bike, he took a long pull of water from his bottle and looked out across the ocean. He smiled to himself as he watched two dolphins play about 100 yards out.

Sheldon rode his bike farther down the beach and enjoyed the sun and the sound of the ocean, blocking out any thoughts of his business when he saw three girls, probably eighteen or nineteen years old, scream as they eyed something on the water's edge. He made his way over to see what they had found.

"It's just a horseshoe crab, can't hurt you," he said, only slowing down on his bike but not stopping.

"Wait!" one of the girls said. "We've walked too far and don't know where our other friends are. Can you help?"

Sheldon was exasperated but agreed. "Where did you see them last?"

"Um, they were lying out on the beach, near the fishing pier."

He was sure that they knew exactly where their friends were— the fishing pier was right around the corner. The flirting was way too obvious and he wasn't sure which emotion was stronger: being so turned off by their forwardness, or worry for these young girls looking for trouble. He debated on pointing in the direction of the pier, but he was going that way anyway so he said, "Follow me, it's just around the corner."

As they were rounding the corner Sheldon saw a woman coming out of the water in a coral bikini. She was wringing the ocean water out of her hair as she looked down, carefully watching where she stepped. He took this opportunity to steal a few more glances to take in the sight of her. She looked like a goddess the way her long blond hair fell down the middle of her back. Her arms and shoulders were toned but not buff, and that flat hard stomach told him she liked to work out. Looking at her figure he judged she was in her early twenties. Her body was curvy, and her big brown eyes revealed innocence yet they were sexy as hell. He couldn't remember the last time a woman had caught his attention like that and all he could think about was how he was going to approach her.

"Pier's right up there, girls." Sheldon pointed and then turned his bike around. He sped off as the girls tried to start another conversation with him.

As he got closer to the woman in the coral bikini, his heart started to race. *Why am I nervous? I've never been nervous around women. Just say hello, dude, what's the worst that can happen? Just say hello.* Sheldon rode his bike past the woman and chided himself for not saying hello. "Idiot, turn around," he said under his breath.

Three

I stuffed the necessities in my bag—sunscreen, towel, a small net bag for shell collecting, and a couple of water bottles—and headed out to the car to drive toward Lighthouse Beach.

Finding a spot to lay my bag down, I made my way to the edge of the water to get my feet wet. Looking down for shells, every now and then I glanced up to take in the scenery and did a little people watching.

A family of four was building a sandcastle, while a young couple held hands and walked at a vacationer's pace in the opposite direction. They looked at each other lovingly and I made the assumption that they were probably on their honeymoon. Two older gentlemen sat in beach chairs under a red-and-white-striped umbrella watching their wives, who both wore big floppy hats and dark sunglasses, do the "Sanibel stoop" near the shore.

The sun was beating down on me and I had become too hot, so I set my orange net shell bag on the sand and walked a little deeper into the water, dipping down low enough to get my shoulders wet, and lingering there a bit as I checked out the surroundings. I could see part of the lighthouse peeking out over the lush tropical landscape and found myself reminiscing about my vacations here with my family. Those were such happy times. I always felt safe and carefree here on Sanibel, never worrying about death, loneliness, money—heck, I had never even seen a jellyfish here—it was my perfect paradise, free of anything sad or malicious.

No one here knew the troubles that I had left behind. I was free to be whomever I pleased. The people surrounding me were strangers, and for all they knew I was as happy and contented as they were. It seemed like an easy enough task—putting on a mask for the world—but it was my mind and heart that wouldn't play the game of foolery. My mind refused to trust and made me look over my shoulder every time I heard a noise.

My daydream was cut short as I focused my attention on a tall, bronzed, sandy-haired man riding his bicycle on the sand. There were girls on both sides of him and I wanted to roll my eyes in disgust, but I kept my head down and concentrated on where I was stepping. I came here for peace and healing, not to worry about the choice those girls had made to hang out with a conceited player. I made my way out of the water and continued my venture for more shell treasures.

Glancing back up the beach, I spotted the man again. He was pointing toward the pier and seemed to be annoyed with the girls. I almost felt sorry for him as he politely tried to get away from them. I chuckled to myself wondering if he had learned their age. *Yeah, jerk, you better pedal away!* Focusing my attention back to the sand, I hit the jackpot near a piece of driftwood stuck deep in the sand on the edge of the water. Shells must have gotten stuck there during high tide. I found lady slippers, turkey wings, and a small whelk. As I reached in to grab a bright orange scallop shell, I heard a male voice right behind me.

"Hi there."

This area of the beach was crowded and I could hear the low murmur of people in the background, but this was close, too close. I tried to ignore the voice behind me and wondered why he wasn't respecting my personal space.

The voice spoke again and this time I was fully aware that it was directed at me. "Um, if you could just pretend you know me for a moment and say

16

'hello,' maybe everyone staring right now won't think I'm trying to pick you up. I just wanted to talk to you." He laughed uncomfortably.

His voice was kind, a little shy and seemed to be sincere, so I turned to look up at him and realized it was the creep on the bike. I mustered up my flattest voice and replied, "Hello. Not interested."

"What kind of shells have you found so far? I can show you where to find the best shells if you like?" He was so smooth and I wondered if he could actually see my skin crawling.

"I came here to be alone, not to be picked up. Looks like you were doing fine with those three girls," I said a little too snippy and regretted the fact that I had just let him know I had been checking him out earlier.

In a defeated voice he answered, "Yeah, that's not the kind of guy I am." His tone had suddenly gone from happy to irritated. "I'm sorry I bothered you, but you should know I was just helping those girls find the pier."

I could hear him getting back on his bike and I felt like a real jerk. *Who have I become? I used to be kind and trusting and now I am suspicious of everyone and full of hatred.*

"Hang on, I'm sorry. Can we try this again?" I said apologetically as I stood up to face him.

17

He paused but conceded. "Sure. My name is Sheldon, Sheldon Barringer." He held out his hand to shake mine.

He was tall, a little over six feet if I had to guess. His thick sandy-brown hair had been heavily streaked by the sun and was messy and windblown. His smile revealed perfectly straight white teeth and a few laugh lines around his striking blue eyes that I was sure could see right through to your soul if you held their gaze long enough. I felt myself starting to blush so I looked down at my shells for a moment. When I finally caught my breath, I stuck out my hand to shake his, realizing it was full of my little treasures from the sea. I giggled as I closed my fist back around the shells and told him, "My name is Emma. Nice to meet you."

It was obvious that Sheldon took care of himself. His arms were well defined along strong broad shoulders and he had incredible abs. Orange swim trunks sat low on his hips and complemented his tanned body. I tried to steal glances of this Greek god standing in front of me without being obvious. He was definitely the hottest guy I had ever seen. We stood there for a moment and I could feel the blush start to rise in my cheeks again.

Thankfully he broke the awkward silence, "Can we go for a walk?

A walk down the beach seemed innocent enough—we were in public and surrounded by people. I didn't see the point of getting to know him as I knew it wouldn't benefit either of us in the future. We were both on vacation, coming from different worlds and would eventually part ways. The best we could hope for was a friendship. *Pen pals—wouldn't that be fun? You could tell me about your adventures back in Idaho, or South Dakota, or wherever you come from, and I could tell you about my gypsy travels while trying to find a new life for myself. So sweet. I'm sure as hot as he is, he won't get any better offers than that!* I laughed to myself and had to turn my head as I rolled my eyes. "I guess so, but can we go this way toward the pier? I left my things over there." I had no idea how far I had traveled away from my belongings. You could really lose track of time and distance searching for shells.

"Of course, it's not far at all. We're at Lighthouse Point, just around the corner from the pier," he informed me.

"Lighthouse Point?" I said as I looked around and saw the magnificent lighthouse. How did I miss it, it was right behind me the whole time. "I wanted to get some shots up close with my camera."

"Do you have it with you?"

"No. I'll just take some shots later," I sighed.

"So you've been here before?"

"Yes, I've been vacationing here since I was a little girl, but it's been a few years since I've been back. Doesn't look like too much has changed. How about you, ever been here before?"

"Uh, yes, I live here."

Great, I thought to myself, *I've gotten hooked by a local and am not sure if I can shake him off. It would have been so much easier if he had lived in Idaho, and he's probably a model instead of the CPA that I had him pegged for. Good grief, how do you get yourself into these situations, Emma?*

"Wow, must be nice. I always thought I would end up here one day, but it never worked out." *Too much information, Emma.*

"That's too bad, it's a great place to live." I caught him trying to steal glances of me when I wasn't looking and I suddenly felt self-conscious.

We talked as we walked and I saw that my things were where I left them and untouched. I pulled my bag over my shoulder and we continued walking past the fishing pier. The pier was full of over-tanned fishermen trying to pull in dinner. Pelicans lined the roof waiting for someone to clean a fish or drop some bait. We walked past the pier and made it to a small concrete wall where we decided to sit and talk for awhile.

"So, how long are you vacationing here?" he asked.

"I'm not sure. I rented a place for the summer, so at least that long."

"What do you do for a living?" he asked while fidgeting with a piece of metal protruding from the concrete wall.

"Well, um . . ." I struggled to find an answer that didn't give too much away. "I sold my business, so I'm a professional vacationer until I find something."

"What kind of business?"

"I owned a CrossFit gym. My college roommate and I opened it together after we graduated. I sold her my half." I couldn't keep the sadness out of my voice thinking about not being a part of my business anymore.

"Wow, you owned a CrossFit gym? I've heard a few things about CrossFit."

"All good I'm sure, it's awesome." I smiled. "And what about you? What do you do?"

"I'm a real estate investor."

"A real estate investor," I repeated, trying to figure out what that meant exactly. Obviously he put money into real estate, but how did he make a profit? I thought I saw him smirk out of the corner of my eye before he explained the details of his work.

"I buy properties, turn them around, and sell them for a profit. I enjoy it and I've grown the business quite a bit over the years, but it's been stressful these last few weeks. I'm not usually out of the office much

during the week, but today I just needed the beach."
He paused to look out over the ocean. "So, where does
the beautiful Emma come from?"

"Tennessee. I was born and raised in a small town
close to Chattanooga. Where are you from,
originally?"

"Born and raised here on the island," he replied,
pride evident in his expression.

"What was that like? Did you hit the beach every
day after school? How did you concentrate on
homework, knowing that this was waiting for you?" I
waved my hand toward the water.

He answered all of my questions, and as he talked
I envisioned a little bronzed boy playing in the surf on
his boogie board.

"I would like to take you to dinner tonight,
Emma," he said, breaking my daydream.

My heart lurched and a knot formed in my
stomach. "Um, thank you but no. I . . . I can't go out
with a stranger," I said, trying to hide the
disappointment from my voice. My heart ached,
wishing I could just be free to do what I wanted. He
seemed like a really nice guy, but my history proved
that I had never been a good judge of character.

A crooked smile spread across Sheldon's face,
"I'm hardly a stranger—we've been talking for a
couple of hours at least. What else do you need to

know? How about a copy of my driver's license?" Sarcasm oozed out of him.

"Yes, and a set of fingerprints." I matched his sarcasm with my own.

"I promise to have a full background check with fingerprints right after dinner. It'll be a great way to end our evening."

I suddenly felt the need to flee. It was hard to debate with this man and I felt sure I would eventually lose the battle. I stood up and tried to look at him but ended up studying a pen shell on the ground as I ran my toe across the prickly top. "There's no point getting involved with me, I don't know how long I will be here. It really was nice talking to you though. Maybe I'll see you around sometime." I looked up at him, finding my last strand of courage, and I was sure his startling blue eyes and muscular body would forever be branded in my mind. Nevertheless, an islander and a tourist could only lead to heartbreak and I just couldn't handle that now. I came here for peace and healing, not a summer affair.

I could feel his eyes on me as I walked away and it took all of my concentration to walk—right foot, left foot, right foot . . . Sheldon caught up to me and handed me the shells I had left behind in my hasty exit.

"Hey, you forgot your treasures. Will you be coming back to this spot tomorrow?" His hand lingered on mine as he handed me the bag of shells, and I was surprised at my inability to move.

Torn between the inexpressible desire to see him again, and the need to protect myself from certain heartbreak, my heart and my brain battled. Eventually my brain won. "I'm not sure what tomorrow will hold or what I will do." I shrugged my shoulders and tried to be blasé. "Listen, I'm not the type of girl that plays games, when I said there was no point in getting involved with me, I meant it."

"Alright," he said as he raised his hands in defeat. "I thought you might like a friend to hang out with this weekend, but I get that you want to be alone." He smiled and I was surprised that his tone was kind and not brusque after my unyielding rejections.

I smiled back at him and then turned to walk back to my car, silently scolding myself for not being more uninhibited. I had always been outgoing and unguarded, but now I was full of fear and distrust.

Four

When I awoke the next morning early enough to watch the sun rise on the back porch with my tea, I observed two lizards speed across the ground and onto a ponytail palm, their throats occasionally expanding with a bright red disk. I wondered if this was a mating call or a warning. Goose bumps rose on my skin as the morning breeze blew through the yard, rustling the palm fronds and filling my nose with the sweet smells of the island. I tucked my knees up under my shirt and wrapped my arms around my legs as I took a sip of tea.

My only company was the two crazed red-throated lizards flirting on the side of a tree trunk. I found myself talking to my Nana, hoping for some sign of what I should do. *Stay here where I feel a deep pull in my soul or move forward and start a new life in a town that has no memories, no attachments?* The only reply was an osprey lighting on a tall Norfolk Island pine tree. *Nana's favorite bird.* I smiled and took another sip of tea. It wasn't an audible voice, but I heard my answer in my heart and decided to stay . . . at least for the summer.

After breakfast I dressed and decided to spend the day shopping and driving around Fort Myers. Periwinkle Place helped tick away the time until lunch. I picked up a new sundress, a cute pair of white shorts and dressy halter top, and a pair of sunglasses before heading to the Blue Giraffe for a quick lunch. I ordered the bistro salad which was mixed greens topped with fresh strawberries, mandarin oranges, walnuts, blue cheese, and blackened salmon. It was delicious, but I could only eat half of it. My thoughts were of Sheldon and wondering if I would ever bump into him again.

***

After two days of rain I was desperate to get on the beach and take in some natural Vitamin D. I walked onto the sand and headed toward Lighthouse Point. I looked around to see if Sheldon would magically appear in the same spot I had seen him before, hoping for some reason that he frequented this part of the beach for a daily bike ride. There wasn't a bicycle in sight—or a strikingly good-looking male, for that matter—only a few families building sand castles with their kids, a couple of college-aged girls running on the beach, and a portly man with thick, dark chest hair throwing a tennis ball into the water for his golden retriever. I sighed and let my thoughts scold me for being so foolish. *Even if he did come here every day, who are you to think he would talk to you again? There are tons of beautiful women on the beach—do you honestly think a guy as hot as he is would prefer a casual friendship to a noncommittal romance? Sheesh!* I couldn't help the slump of my shoulders as the disappointment set in.

I took a few shots of the lighthouse and got some close-ups of a coco plum and its fruit. I looked around one more time for Sheldon, but only saw a few people pointing toward the sea. I was sure they saw dolphins, so I fit my Nikon D90 with the zoom lens and walked to the shoreline. There was someone in a kayak while four dolphins played all around him. I put the camera to my eye and zoomed in to snap some shots. I focused on the man in the kayak as he got closer and gasped when I saw it was Sheldon! Just as I brought the camera back into focus, he jumped out of the kayak and started swimming with the dolphins. As Sheldon swam around, it seemed as if the dolphins were actually playing with him. He rubbed his hand down the back side of one of them as it swam by and then he climbed back into the kayak to make his way to shore.

I put the lens cap on the camera and stood there amazed and envious of his encounter with these beautiful creatures, and then realized he was close enough to see me watching him. A thrill ran up my spine and my heart started beating out of my chest. I looked around for a place to hide but there were no options in sight. I could lie down in the sand and pretend to be sunbathing. *Oh my, I didn't even see you—have you been here long?* I would say as he approached me, waking me from my sun-induced dozing. *Yeah, right—lying in the sand sunning with a huge camera around your neck? Really bright, Em.* Before I could think of another plan, his tan, wet, muscular body was coming right for me. *Okay then, just be cool, and for heaven's sake quit looking at his stomach!*

"Hi, I didn't expect to see you here—must be my lucky day," Sheldon said as he came toward me with his kayak over one shoulder. I knew my mouth was hanging open when I replied, "Oh my goodness, I can't believe you just did that! You actually swam with wild dolphins. I'm impressed and incredibly jealous!"

He smiled at me and my cheeks flushed when I caught him taking in my blue and green paisley bikini.

"You really aren't supposed to touch them in the wild, but I just couldn't resist a quick stroke down its back."

"Aren't you afraid of sharks when you're out that deep?"

"No, when dolphins are around, you don't have to worry about sharks. Sharks are actually afraid of dolphins."

"Sure, sure. Do I look like I came down the river on a log?" I smirked and rested my fists on my hips.

Sheldon threw his head back and laughed loudly. "That's a new one. Must be a Tennessee saying. And, no, you definitely don't look like you came down the river on a log." He looked me up and down with a cocky grin, and I stirred the sand around with my toe. When I finally looked back at him, his eyes were roaming over my face and I wondered if I was still flushed. "I'm serious about the sharks and dolphins," he said, breaking the uncomfortable silence.

"I came back to get some shots of the lighthouse." I couldn't think of anything else to say. I looked around and took in the scenes on the beach. Everyone was having a good time playing, relaxing, and talking. I tried to find my confidence and searched for something to say. *What kind of music do you like? No. What's your favorite restaurant on the island? No, that sounds too touristy. Are you planning on having a summer fling with me, because I can tell you right now that is not going to happen . . . Good grief, I'm a lunatic standing here talking to my subconscious.*

"Are you up for a bike ride? I would like to show you around the island a bit," he asked, saving me from the lunacy of talking to myself.

"I don't have a bike."

"I have two in the back of my truck, which is just up here in the parking lot."

"I don't think so."

"C'mon, it's just a bike ride. You'll have your own bike and can pedal away from me if I try anything. Which, by the way, would be difficult on a bicycle," he chuckled and I had to agree with his point.

I exhaled and looked up at him cautiously, knowing I was stepping into unchartered water—diving in with no life jacket actually summed it up more accurately. My heart was beating so forcefully I could feel it in my ears and I wondered if the thumping was visible through my skin. "Alright, a bike ride sounds nice." I followed him nervously, offering to carry the oar while he carried his kayak.

Before we got on the bikes I grabbed my sunscreen. Sheldon took it out of my hands and looked it over. "Whoa, SPF 8? This is south Florida—you need at least a twenty here." He took my sunscreen and grabbed his out of the truck. "But I want a tan, look at this pale skin!" I complained.

"Trust me, you'll tan. Let me put some of this on your back, and you make sure you get your arms and hands covered. You'll burn before you know it here."

"My hands?" I looked at him quizzically as I obeyed and rubbed the lotion in. I had never applied sunscreen to my hands before. Sheldon took the sunscreen and squirted some onto his palms. As soon as his hands touched my back I felt like I had been hit with electricity. His hands were large and rough as they gently and meticulously rubbed over my shoulders and back. I forced myself to think about the steps of making Pâté de Canard en Croûte to take my mind off of his touch and extinguish the burning in my cheeks and neck.

After I was completely covered in sunscreen, we rode the bikes away from the lighthouse toward the main road. Bicycle trails lined the entire island and the pavement was smooth and mostly flat which made for an easy ride. There was a gentle breeze that kept us cool as we pedaled along.

Sheldon turned to look at me when he talked, pointing at various trees. "This large palm with the smooth trunk is called a 'royal palm'—my favorite. I also like this date nut palm. Now these on the right with the crisscross trunks and fan-like leaves are 'cabbage palms,' probably my least favorite." He told me about the coconut palms, banyan trees, mangroves along the bayside and much more. I took it all in and enjoyed the ride and information.

"My parents live down that street there." He pointed down a street boasting beautiful homes on the bay. We biked down another road leading us to a marina where we stopped and parked our bikes. "Do you like manatees?" he asked.

"Yes, I love them."

"Have you ever seen one up close?"

"No, they have one here? Is it injured?" I asked, knowing they wouldn't have a captive manatee for any other reason.

"No, no. Sometimes you can see them in the wild. They like hanging around the marina. Let's see if we can spot one," Sheldon said as he took my hand and led me around to where the boats were. After the sudden shock of his touch, I relaxed and enjoyed how comfortable his hand felt in mine.

Sheldon took a water hose, turned it on, and held it over the water. With an excitement in his voice he said, "See those two round things in the water? Those are noses. Let's see if we can get them to come closer."

A thin man on the dock, probably in his late forties, threw his hand in the air to greet Sheldon, and Sheldon returned his wave. Their laid-back hello convinced me that they had known each other for a while. I wondered if this was where he brought all the girls he picked up on the beach as a way to impress them. I felt my body start to tense in humiliation and defensiveness until I saw the two round bumps in the water slowly come closer. I was too excited to worry about Sheldon's game. I could see short whiskers attached to their noses just above the surface of the water and I could barely see the outline of their huge gray bodies that followed behind their round noses. "Oh my goodness, look at that!" I squealed.

The pair of manatee was a mama and her baby. I got my camera ready and snapped a few shots as they swam up, lifted their noses out of the water, and took a quick drink from the hose. It only lasted a few seconds before they ducked back down into the water and swam off.

"Thank you! That was amazing to see!" I was still squealing with delight. I found a streak of cockiness and before I could filter my thoughts, they spilled out of my mouth. "Is this where you take all the girls to impress them?" I had to admit it was a good plan.

His eyes flickered up at me under long dark eyelashes and a smirk crossed his lips. "No, Emma. I think you're forming the wrong idea about me." He stopped walking and turned to face me in the parking lot. "Have dinner with me tonight. Let's get to know each other better so you can quit assuming the worst—I have no hidden agenda."

I didn't want this day to end, but I knew I should say no. I needed to end this now and quickly. My insides were fighting with my mind and I wasn't sure who was going to win. All it took was one look into those warm hypnotizing eyes and my insides won the battle. "Yes, I would like that."

Five

I tried on every outfit I owned and ended up wearing a turquoise halter dress with brown leather slides that had a small heel. I blow-dried my hair and tried to brush out the slight waves that the Florida air had added to my hair. I saw the sun had slightly bronzed by my face today, even with all of the sunscreen Sheldon insisted on, so I decided a little lipstick and mascara was the only makeup I needed to apply.

When I heard his car pulling up, my heart began to race. I grabbed my purse and keys and met him in the driveway. He wasn't in his truck, but a small, sleek charcoal-gray car. He stepped out and jogged over to the passenger side.

"You look amazing," he said as he opened the passenger door, holding it open for me until I slid in. I thanked him and watched him walk around the front of the car, studying his muscular frame. Butterflies were slamming against my stomach and I wondered if I would ever get used to looking at him. I had a feeling he had this effect on most women.

As we pulled into the Jacaranda restaurant, I watched him walk to the front door and hold it open for me. He was wearing tan pants that sat perfectly on his hips with a white oxford tucked in and the top two buttons casually unbuttoned. The Jacaranda had a casual but elegant feel to it. Guests were dressed in everything from evening wear to casual island shorts and collared shirts.

Our table was dressed with a starched white tablecloth and large charger plates in between silverware. A wine glass and water goblet were set and a candle was lit in the center of the table.

Our waiter brought us water and bread with an olive oil dipping station and asked for our drink orders.

"Do you like oysters and caviar?" Sheldon asked.

"I love oysters, I've never tried caviar."

"We'll have a bottle of Pinot Grigio and Oysters Romanoff to start, please," Sheldon told the waiter. The efficient server brought our appetizer and wine within minutes.

"I think you'll like this," Sheldon said as he put an oyster onto a small plate and handed it to me.

I slid the oyster into my mouth and tasted the saltiness of the caviar—it was the best thing I had ever tasted. The tender oyster was sitting in a pool of pepper vodka and topped with a dollop of sour cream, minced shallot, and three types of caviar. The shallot gave it a bite that was subdued by the sour cream, and the caviar was crisp, fresh, and salty. I let out a little moan as I ate another one.

"I knew you'd like these," he smiled.

I took a long sip of wine and watched Sheldon as he popped one into his mouth. I felt the little electric shocks to my heart as I looked at him. My cheeks started to warm and I picked up the menu to cover my blushing. "What do you recommend?" I asked with the menu still up to cover my crimson cheeks.

"Everything is good, but if you like seafood, this is a good place to get it." He raised his glass of wine for a toast. "To a great vacation, and to finding what you're looking for." We both took a long sip of wine and I felt the welcome relaxing effect.

For dinner I ordered the sea scallops. Sheldon chose the blackened mahi mahi with shrimp and island salsa. We dined on salads while waiting for our entrées and I finished my glass of wine as we talked.

"So, Emma . . . you never told me your last name."

"Peroni."

"Italian?"

"Yes, my father was Sicilian. That's where the mafia originated, you know." I lifted one eyebrow as a warning and then laughed.

"I'm sure you were the best little mafia princess too, weren't you?"

I lowered my eyes and said in a low, serious voice, "Actually, there is no such thing as the mafia." I put a finger to my lip insinuating this was a hushed matter.

We both laughed and took another sip of wine.

"Do you speak Italian?"

"No, I took a course in college and have tried to pick up a few sentences, but I'm not fluent."

"So, Emma Peroni," he finished off his wine and grabbed the bottle to fill our glasses again. "Who are you? What do you like to do for fun?"

"Hmm, let's see . . ." I took a swig of wine hoping to gain a little more confidence. "I was raised by my grandparents, I'm an only child. After college I opened a gym with my college roommate. I enjoy working out, running, most sports, being on the water, adventure . . ." I tried to think of something else I liked to do that didn't involve raising my heart rate. "I also like reading and photography." I let out a breath implying this was a long winded answer. "How about you?"

"Well . . . I was raised on the island by my parents. I have two brothers that moved up north after college.

They're both married. Sam has two sons ages five and seven, and Grant has a thirteen-year-old daughter and a nine-year-old son. My parents and I still live on the island. Of course I don't live *with* them anymore." He flashed a crooked smile as he told about his family. I could see the love and pride in his face.

My attraction for him escalated and I couldn't take my eyes off of him.

"For fun I love windsurfing. There is something about standing up on the water, controlling the direction and speed of the board. I get a little excited when a storm is approaching—the waves are high and I can actually get some good air." He sounded like a kid as he told me about his windsurfing adventures, and I smiled and hung on every word.

Our entrées arrived and the scallops, tender and mild, were cooked perfectly, lightly browned under the broiler. Sheldon offered me a bite of his mahi mahi which had been bronzed to perfection. It had a mild, buttery flavor and melted in my mouth.

After the waiter cleared our plates and we passed on dessert, we finished the bottle of wine as we talked. I learned that Sheldon was twenty-eight, four years older than I. His dream was to open a windsurfing hotel in Fiji, but ended up getting into real estate when looking for a home for his brother and wife.

We talked about life on the island, books we've read, and our common love for poetry. I finished my last sip of wine and realized his glass was empty too. I had no idea how long we had been sitting there, only that I had really enjoyed the conversation and didn't want the night to end—I should have sipped my wine more slowly.

"It's late and I think they want to start closing up." Sheldon nodded his head in the direction of our waiter standing against the wall waiting patiently with a vacuum. I looked around the restaurant and realized we were the only ones occupying a table.

"Oh dear." I giggled and started to get up out of my chair. The effects of the wine hit me hard and I had to hold onto the back of the chair until I got my balance.

"You okay?" Sheldon smirked and offered his arm.

I took it, glad for the support as I walked in my unstable slides. "Yes, thank you, I normally don't drink that much."

I held onto his arm until we reached the car and he opened the door for me, helping me in and gently shutting it behind me. I watched as he walked around the front of the car and slid into the driver's seat.

"I've really enjoyed getting to know you better, Emma."

"Me too, and thank you for dinner." I looked into his eyes and realized it was a mistake as I immediately blushed.

Good grief, will I ever be able to look at him without turning pink? I hate that he knows the effect he has on me.

Before starting the engine he gazed into my eyes for what seemed like an eternity and smiled with a playful crooked grin.

"What?" I said as I looked down at my hands, knowing that he was enjoying watching my cheeks flush.

"I don't want this night to end and I'm trying to think of something we can do at this late hour."

My body started to tense as I became defensive assuming he was thinking of inviting me to his place, but instead he threw out a completely different idea. "We could get an ice cream and walk the beach."

I was relieved and my body relaxed again. "That sounds nice."

"There's one catch, everything on the island is closed. We'll have to go to Fort Myers Beach."

"I'm okay with that as long as you let me buy the ice cream," I offered.

"Um, no. I asked you out, I pay," he said, grinning. "Now if you want to take me out sometime, you can pay."

"Can I at least pay the toll to get back on the island?"

"Because I live here, I have a barcode—I don't have to pay to get back on."

"Oh." I buckled my seat belt and searched the car for a clock to see how late it actually was. I watched Sheldon's hands as one held the steering wheel and the other one shifted the gears using the stick shift in between us.

We headed off of the island toward Fort Myers Beach and grabbed an ice cream cone from a small ice cream shop. I chose a mango sorbet, and Sheldon got mint chocolate chip.

We walked down the beach, eating our quickly melting ice cream cones, and Sheldon reached over and slipped his hand in mine.

My heart pounded in my chest and all I could concentrate on was his hand. It seemed like all of the heat from my body was focused on where our skin was touching. I let a sigh escape my lips and it was too late to take it back.

Sheldon smiled a mischievous grin without looking at me and kept licking his ice cream. He knew the effect he was having on me and he was enjoying every moment of it. The old me would have played the game right back, but I was too broken to play games now.

My mind was inundated with thoughts of the unknown. I didn't know what I wanted or even where I was going at this point. My plan was to stay for one month at a time and hopefully all summer on Sanibel to get some peace and healing—alone. After that . . .

well, there were no plans. I never considered for a minute that I would be walking down the beach with someone of the opposite sex that I really enjoyed spending time with. I realized a relationship with an islander was a big mistake. *What if I really started to like him and then had to pick up and move on? What if he only wanted a fun, no-strings-attached fling with a tourist that he knew would be gone in a month?* I said I wasn't going to worry on this trip, but as I walked along the beach eating ice cream and holding hands with the most gorgeous man I had ever laid eyes on, I was filled with just that—worry and fear.

I decided I would leave for a few days, maybe visit the Keys. This would give me time to shake off Sheldon and who knows—maybe he would find another tourist to show the island to.

My ice cream was fully melted now and I found a trash can to toss it into. Sheldon had already finished his. We looked each other over and laughed with the mess we had made. We both had ice cream streaks down one arm. He led me toward the ocean and we washed off the sticky ice cream in the water.

Music was playing in the distance at one of the restaurants, and it sounded like a live band. As we got closer to the restaurant the music got louder. The band was playing "No Woman, No Cry" by Bob Marley, and Sheldon grabbed me around the waist with one arm and held my hand with the other. We started to slow dance as I looked around to see that we were alone on the beach with only the moonlight reflecting on the water to light the night. I tried to wriggle free, suddenly aware that I was sending the wrong message and needing to set things straight as soon as possible. I felt like an idiot letting it go this far. He felt me trying to wriggle away and took it as embarrassment which made him laugh and hold me tighter. I gave in and enjoyed the feeling of his body against mine as we danced until the song ended.

Sheldon stopped moving, gently took my chin in his hand, and looked into my eyes. "You are so beautiful, Emma."

His eyes locked with mine and my body froze, my legs felt like Jell-O and I had to work hard not to crumble. *Oh good heavens, he is hot. What if he tries to kiss me? My mouth tastes like mango sorbet thankfully and there's no trace of the shallot from the oysters.* I ran my tongue across my teeth. *No! You can't kiss him on the first date. Good grief, Emma! Besides, this isn't just the first date, it is probably the only date. Once he finds out I am not into hooking up he is not going to be interested anymore. Just say something about the weather—how hot and humid it is out here. Okay, maybe I shouldn't mention the word "hot," my voice will surely crack and it will be way too obvious that I dig him. Hmm . . . a joke—I could tell a funny joke! But I can't think of a single funny joke except—a horse goes into a bar and the bartender says "Hey, why the long face?" Stupid! Just walk on your hands, he can't kiss you if you're upside down.*

My bewitchment was broken with the sound of laughter behind me as a group of college-aged girls were coming up the beach and they had obviously been drinking. Sheldon gave me a crooked smile and we started walking in the direction of the car.

As we drove back to the island, he got into the left lane of the tollbooth and only had to slow down for the scanner to read the barcode sticker on his window.

We pulled up the gravel driveway of my rental cottage, and he jogged around the car to open the door for me. There was a little more pep in his step and I didn't know how I was going to stay on this island without seeing him or thinking about him.

"I have to be in the office most of the day tomorrow, but how about dinner tomorrow night?" he asked as he leaned against the cottage as I searched for the key.

I felt like all of the air was being sucked out me when I told him I couldn't. "I planned on driving down to Key West to spend a few days. I might stay a week."

He frowned. "A week? Have you ever been to Key West? Do you have a place to stay?"

"I thought I would just drive down and land where I land," I said flatly.

"No, absolutely not." His eyes were dark and his voice was serious as he looked sternly at me.

Who does he think he is? He bought me dinner and now he can boss me around like this? It might be easier than I thought to get over this guy.

"It is too dangerous for a beautiful woman like you to travel to Key West alone." He put his hand on mine to stop me from opening my front door. "Listen to me, if you look like an innocent—tourist—and you do, you will be an easy target for a mugger or worse."

"I can handle myself, thank you," I said as I gripped the doorknob to open the door, anger taking hold of me quickly.

He grabbed me from behind and locked his arms around mine pulling them down to my sides. I couldn't move and he was too close for me to even try to kick his shins or step on his foot.

Panic rose in my chest and tears welled in my eyes. He let me go and rage consumed me. I turned around to face him and before I could think about what I was doing, I drew back my arm and punched him in the stomach as hard as I could.

"Oomph," he let out as he doubled over and held his stomach. "What the hell was that for?"

"How dare you . . ." I tried to speak but the tears started to flow and I knew I couldn't speak without squeaking out unintelligible sounds. I tried to get my hand on the doorknob again to get away from this crazy man.

"I was just trying to show you how easy it would be to mug you. You think you're so tough, but some of these jokers play a serious game, they have the experience to get what they want." He sighed and straightened his body back upright. "Do you think I would actually hurt you?"

Sheldon's last words were soft and low, almost a whisper. I could hear the confusion and hurt laced through each word. *Do I believe that he could hurt me? I don't know. I am a bad judge of character, but he has proven himself a gentleman on more than one occasion. I don't know if I will ever be able to trust him, or anyone for that matter. I do know that I am sick and tired of assuming everyone is plotting evil schemes against me.* I decided to give him another chance.

"I'm so sorry, I really am." I timidly looked up at him. "I got scared and I reacted. Are you okay?" I was really feeling like a jerk now and wished I could explain why I was so defensive, but I was trying to end this . . . *well, whatever this thing is that we have started. Spilling my guts wasn't an option.*

"Yes, I'm fine. You do have a great right hook, but I hold my ground on you not traveling there alone." He smiled, and I felt better but I was still riddled with guilt over punching him. "I have a friend in Key West that has a place. He and his wife are vacationing in Maine for the summer. I have permission to stay there any time, and I'm sure it would be okay for you to use it too."

"That is very generous, but I couldn't do that. You don't know me well enough to trust me with your friend's property."

"Emma, I do trust you. When I look into those big brown eyes, I see how sweet and kind and innocent you are. You don't trust me yet, I see that. I don't know if something happened or if that's just who you are, but I do hope to gain your trust."

My shoulders slumped as I wondered if I was that transparent. "Let me think about the place in Key West. I don't have to leave tomorrow."

"While you think about it, think about me going with you. I'm serious about not wanting you down there alone."

Oh I'll think about it, but it will never happen.

We exchanged cell phone numbers and he kissed me sweetly on the hand before heading to his car. I looked back before shutting the door and watched him back out of the driveway. There was no way I was spending a week in Key West with him, no matter how much of a gentleman he may be.

I picked up my phone to call my friend Julie Bristol, but saw how late it was and put it back down.

As I brushed my teeth and slipped into pajama shorts and a tank top to sleep in, I recalled my last conversation with Julie.

"Do you have to go?" Julie was crying as she helped me pack the last of my things. She was a beautiful spunky girl with brown hair, big brown eyes, and a stocky muscular build from years of gymnastics training. We had been friends since we were toddlers in the same Sunday school class at church. We argued like sisters through the years, fighting over boys and other friends, but our friendship was strong enough to overcome anything even rooming together in college and being business partners at the gym.

"I need to get away, you can understand why, right?"

"I know, but I need you here."

"Jules, I will probably come back. I just need to get away and find myself again. I feel like I have been robbed of the very matter that made me who I was."

I knew Nana would have been able to put me back together—she had done it more than once in my life. Once in middle school when I didn't make the cheerleading team and thought I would die from devastation. I didn't want to go back to school and show my face to a school that watched me fall on my butt during an attempted running back handspring. Another time Nana helped put me back together was high school. My boyfriend of two years spread a rumor around about how we had finally slept together after the prom. I was the last to hear the rumor when a surprised Julie came up to me and said, "Wow, I thought you were waiting. How was it?" I cried for hours wondering how I would straighten that mess out. Nana not only helped me with the most creative public breakup, but also helped me make the truth known to everyone after he apologized in an email and we "accidentally" forwarded it to the class gossip, Beth. But Nana was gone and there was no one like her to put me back together now. The next best thing was to go to a place that held so many memories and good times for us—Sanibel Island.

"I hope that you come back soon. You will be back for the wedding, right?"

"Of course, I'm your maid of honor. I wouldn't miss your wedding, Jules. Of course, I understand if you want to choose another maid of honor. I would be perfectly happy being a bridesmaid."

"No, you're my best friend. Your position stays and I am holding you to a bachelorette party too." She hugged me and helped carry some bags out to the car. "Be safe and call me every day."

"I will. I love you, Jules."

"I love you too, Emma."

I wiped away the tears that were blurring my vision as I pulled out of the driveway and drove toward the interstate access.

Six

The cool crisp sheets enveloped my body in the darkened room, but sleep would not come. My mind spun round and round, full of thoughts of Sheldon. I went over our conversations, holding hands on the beach under the moonlight and then that dance. I thought of how his body felt against mine and how romantic it had been to dance on the beach. I was sure it was in my top ten list of romantic things to do one day. I made a check mark into the air with my finger and then frowned when I remembered punching him.

My thoughts were interrupted with a *ding* from my phone. There was a text from Sheldon:

I had a great night with you, beautiful island girl. Sweet dreams.

Island girl. That's what Nana used to call me when I was little. I loved the island so much that I would get up before sunrise and have to be dragged back in for meals and bedtime. There was never a time that I didn't cry when it was time to leave. Going over the Causeway to go home was devastating every time—I would turn around in my seat and watch the lighthouse getting smaller and smaller with tears streaming down my cheeks. Only the promise of coming back soon would stop the tears.

I typed a quick text back:

I had a great time too. Sorry about the sucker punch. Forgive me?

I lay there and held my phone waiting for a response, until it finally dinged:

Yes, forgiven. Now close those beautiful brown eyes and dream of me.

He was so cocky sometimes, but I enjoyed his confidence. I read the last line of his text a few more times before drifting off to sleep, sure that I would obey his command and dream of him.

I woke up dripping with sweat and crying from the same nightmare. After splashing water on my face, I decided to go for a run. I kept a decent pace for four miles, leaving behind the nightmare for the enjoyment of the warm tropical air. After the run I took a quick shower and got dressed, letting my hair air-dry on the way to breakfast.

I tried a place called Lighthouse Café, a small, busy diner-type spot with framed pictures of lighthouses from all over the world covering the walls. I nearly licked my plate clean of a delicious spinach, crab, and asiago cheese omelet and finished my glass of freshly squeezed grapefruit juice while reading the island paper. I decided to spend the day at Lighthouse Point again and found a quiet spot that wasn't crowded. I put down my beach chair and covered it with a towel before sitting back and getting comfortable. I pulled out a book that I found in the rental, *Master of the Game,* and started to read but got distracted gazing at an egret and the feathery wisps standing out on its head and wings. I watched the snow-white bird stick his beak down into the sand and pull up little morsels for his breakfast until he flew off to hunt another spot down the shoreline.

Knowing I couldn't concentrate on it any longer, I put my book back in my bag. I looked out to sea watching the waves roll in and bring the sweet salty breeze my way. I knew I could live here and be a part of all this. I had always loved this island and always would. Nana used to call me her little island girl, and now Sheldon had returned the nickname after all these years. I had enough money to stay here for a while, but then what? Would a CrossFit gym work here on the island? I didn't see how. I would have to train the movements to guests continuously and I wasn't sure how many of the locals would be interested in membership. Maybe I could look into opening one in Fort Myers.

My phone dinged to alert me of an incoming text and my heart quickened when I saw it was from Sheldon:

Hi beautiful. Want to see a movie with me tonight?

I texted back: Yes, what time?

Movie starts @ 7:00, so I'll pick u up at 6:30.

ok, see u then. I texted back and hit *send*.

I lay back in my chair and smiled, soaking in the sun and ocean breeze. Heaven must feel similar to this.

After spending a few hours at the beach and snacking on almonds and water, I was famished so I gathered my things and drove home. As I grabbed ingredients to make a sandwich from the fridge, I remembered that I never called Julie. *Shoot!*

"Hey, are you busy?" I asked as I heard music blasting in the background, hoping she wasn't too angry with me. Surely she could understand my absentmindedness.

"Emma! Let me step into the office so I can hear you better."

The music faded as I heard her shut the door. I looked at the time and remembered that the four o'clock class was starting their workout.

"How are you? I was worried when I didn't hear from you."

"Sorry, I'm great. I was out late last night and it was too late to call you." I held my breath hoping she didn't have time to question me.

"Out late? With who?" I heard the curiosity and excitement in her voice. If the tables were turned, she wouldn't hesitate to go out with Sheldon, she had always been fearless and I remembered a time when I was too. The pair of us could have been dangerous if Jake hadn't come along to sweep her off her feet.

"I met someone on the beach. He took me to dinner." I tried to give away as little information as I could. I heard a knock and then the music blaring again.

"Hold on, Emma." Julie cuffed her hand over the phone, so all I heard was muffled voices.

"Emma, I have to go. Call me tonight. I want to hear every single detail."

"Yeah, yeah, I will."

We hung up and I wondered what was going on at the gym. Maybe an injury or visitors that had just come in?

After showering and blow-drying my hair straight, I raided the closet for something to wear. I finally decided on a pair of cuffed denim capri pants and a green polo shirt.

Sheldon was on time and we headed to the Island Theater next to Bailey's. The movie theater was like nothing I had ever seen before. As we walked in the door a few people were lined up at the concession stand, so we decided to get our seats first and come back for refreshments. The room was very small with only twenty rows of seats. Five large comfortable black leather chairs lined each row. Sheldon stood and asked, "What would you like from the concession stand?"

"Twizzlers, please."

"Would you share some popcorn with me if I get it?"

"Sure."

While Sheldon was getting the snacks I listened to a couple in front of me talk about their time on the island. They had two children with them, a son about sixteen and a daughter planning her eighth birthday party. The girl's brown curls bounced as she talked with her hands, harassing her brother with details of her upcoming princess party.

Sheldon sat down next to me and handed me the Twizzlers. He held the popcorn between us. When the movie started I offered him a Twizzler and he smiled and took it. The movie was good and we laughed out loud several times. When the popcorn was gone, he reached over and held my hand, setting our clasped hands on his leg for support. His jeans were soft and rugged and my hand felt like a ton of bricks resting in his. I gazed at the screen and the images playing in front of me, but I had no idea what was happening, I could only concentrate on the electricity surging through my hand.

When the movie ended we lingered to watch the credits roll, trying to find our first or last names on the screen. The cleanup crew waited patiently until we left before sweeping the aisles and picking up any trash left behind.

Once outside, Sheldon tugged gently on my hand. My curiosity flared as he led me around to the back of the movie theater. I could barely make out a little pond ahead under the sliver of moon that hung in the night sky.

"Where are we going?" I whispered.

He let out a low chuckle at my hushed tone. "It's not a secret, you don't have to lower your voice. It's an alligator pond."

"Um, there's no fence, why are we walking right up to a pond full of alligators?" I was apprehensive and slowed down.

"We won't get too close, and if one does come after you, just run in a zig-zag pattern—they can only run straight," he said while laughing, and I knew he was pulling my leg.

"Well, I will probably be on your back, so I hope you've got that zig-zag running trick down."

We inched closer and closer to the pond, not sure if we could see anything without stepping on it first.

Nervous but curious, I walked forward, holding onto to Sheldon's arm, pressing into him tighter and tighter.

Just as we reached the water's edge, Sheldon grabbed my arm and shouted "Stop!"

I was on the brink of passing out with fear. As Sheldon pulled me back, I looked around to see what he saw. There was a small alligator on the edge of the water, half of its head resting on the grassy ground. We walked backward until we got enough distance between ourselves and the alligator.

"That scared the tar out of me!" I said breathlessly.

Sheldon held me in his arms as I tried to inhale and slow my heart rate down.

"Are you okay?" he chuckled.

"Yes, I'm fine," I answered as I pulled away from his chest and arms. *I could stay in the embrace of these strong arms for hours actually*, I thought to myself.

"What are your plans for tomorrow?" Sheldon asked as we walked to the car.

"Most likely the beach, just not sure which one. I'd like to take my camera and get some scenery shots along with birds, flowers, and maybe those bright green sea grape bushes. Any recommendations?"

"Well, you really can't find a spot that isn't pretty, you can get pictures of those things all along the island. Have you been to Bowman's Beach yet? There are lots of shells there, and it's one of my favorite spots. I wish I could go with you but I have an important meeting tomorrow." Sheldon frowned.

"I'll check it out. Do you have to work all day tomorrow?" I knew he didn't want to spend every waking moment entertaining me, but I did like spending time with him.

"Yes, tomorrow is a busy day for me at the office." Sheldon's face revealed how disappointed he was and I was rewarded with the knowledge that he would rather spend time with me too. "How about dinner at my place tomorrow night?"

Dinner at his house? What to do? Is it safe? Is it too soon? My heart told me to go for it, he was the most handsome man I had ever laid eyes on, plus he was good company and made me relax a little. Hesitantly I formed my answer, but wanted to have a little fun with him first. "Tomorrow night? Hmm . . . I usually wash my shoelaces on Tuesday evenings, but I suppose I could make an exception." I grinned.

"You're a little smart-ass," he retorted.

"Maybe a little bit." I shrugged. I couldn't help it, it was in my blood. "Tomorrow night sounds good. What time?"

"Let's say six o'clock, we'll have time to eat and see the sunset. I'll text you directions tomorrow."

Sheldon drove me home and walked me to the door. I was surprised that he didn't try to get an invite in, but instead kissed me on the cheek and told me goodnight. It was a sweet gesture but I wanted so badly to feel his lips on mine. *Maybe he's afraid I'll punch him again if he tries to kiss me?* I giggled to myself as I shut the door.

Seven

The shrill whistle of the copper tea kettle let me know that my much-loved cup of tea would soon be ready. Once the honey slowly dissolved in my Earl Grey, I plopped into the overstuffed paisley chair, picked up my cell phone, and dialed Julie.

"Hey, everything okay at the gym?"

"Yes, just fine. How are you?"

"I'm great, I've been to the beach every day so far." I missed her and wished she could be here so we could hang out together.

"Sounds wonderful—I'm so jealous. It's been raining here for three days straight. Now tell me about this guy."

"Well . . ." I drug it out. "I met the most amazing, gorgeous, fun guy who is showing me around and making me laugh constantly. He's a local, owns a house here. I'm going to have dinner at his place tomorrow night," I said cautiously, knowing I was going to get the overprotective friend speech.

"Really?" She elongated the word for effect.

"Em, are you sure about that? How well do you know this guy? Maybe you should have more dates in public first."

Julie was always either trying to protect me or talk me into doing something I was uncomfortable with. She was bold and daring and always wanted to have a good time, but when Nana and Papa passed she seemed to take on the role of older sister.

"Jules, I've had several public dates already. You know I'm careful, but so far he seems like a really great guy—and did I mention he's smokin' hot?" I giggled.

"Seriously? Tell me details," Julie grilled.

"He's tall dark and handsome. You should see the abs on this guy!" My heart rate picked up as I talked about him. "His eyes are what really got me though. His eyes are a shade of blue . . . and so intense, they instantly take your breath. I know he sounds too good to be true, and he most likely is. I know I'm going to get my heart broken, but I just can't stay away from him. I tried to blow him off, but he pushed and I caved."

"What do you mean you tried to blow him off? Why? You deserve some happiness, Em, why not enjoy yourself a little? Just be safe and protect your heart."

"I'm trying but I'm scared. What if I do fall for this guy and then I have to leave? I'm not sure I can take it, my heart and my mind are so fragile right now," I complained.

"Emma Olivia Peroni, you listen to me!" She was shouting. "You are stronger than you give yourself credit for. You've been through some crap, but you have fought to stay alive and succeeded. Now, as your best friend I'm commanding you to reward yourself with a good time." She spouted off her orders like a drill sergeant and then calmed down and her voice was soft again, "How are you sleeping? Have the nightmares passed yet?"

"No, I'm still having bad dreams. I don't know how to make them stop. I guess as long as he's out there . . . Maybe if he's caught . . ."

"*When. When* he is caught," Julie corrected. "The police haven't quit searching. A guy from the gym up and told me something he wasn't supposed to after the morning workout a few days ago. He overheard a few of the officers on the case talking about how sloppy Marc . . . Sorry, I know you don't want to hear his name . . . about how sloppy your attacker was. They think he will strike again and leave enough clues for an easy catch."

"Oh God, I hope he doesn't attack someone else. You know not to lock up on your own, right? You promised you would always have someone at the gym with you," I said anxiously.

"Yes, Rob has agreed to stay and lock up each night since he coaches the evening classes, and you know how protective Jake has been since this all happened."

"I wish you were here with me, Jules. It would be so great to hang out together on the beach or by the pool," I said poignantly.

"Sounds heavenly. Maybe I can take a few days and come hang out soon."

"That would be great! Think about it and make it happen. I miss my best friend."

"I miss you too. Have fun and enjoy that hot guy. Bye, Em."

"Bye, Jules." We hung up and I wallowed in my pity for a moment.

I wasn't ready for sleep, although it was getting late. I picked up the book that I started and set it on the nightstand as I brushed my teeth and got ready for bed. I fell asleep after reading a horrific rape scene and was haunted by the scenario playing out in my dreams.

It was 3:00 a.m. when I woke up drenched with sweat. I walked into the bathroom to splash water on my face and dried it with a towel. I looked into the mirror and talked to the frail girl staring back at me, "When will this stop? I don't know how much more I can take." She didn't answer me so I went back to my bed.

I tried to fall back asleep, and eventually did . . . with the lamp on.

Eight

I woke up with swollen eyes and stood in the shower, allowing the stream of hot water to comfort me and stir me to life. After I dressed and tied my hair up in a ponytail, I drove to Bailey's. I grabbed eggs, sweetened condensed milk, Key lime juice, and a couple of limes to make a Key lime pie to take to Sheldon's tonight. I decided to save some time and energy with an already made graham cracker crust. *Thank you, Keebler elves,* I thought to myself as I tucked a strand of wind-blown hair behind my ear.

Before putting the remaining groceries away, I zested a little lime rind into the filling and poured it into the graham cracker crust. After it cooked for the proper amount of time I stuck it in the fridge to cool and decided to wait and make the Chantilly cream just before leaving so it would stay thick and fresh.

In the meantime, the sun shone brightly so I put on my dark sunglasses and headed to Bowman's Beach with my camera.

I approached the path to the beach and treaded through the thick white sand. The path was lined with a small gate made of wood and rope while sea oats filled in the space outside of the gate. I squatted down and snapped a low shot of the sea oats against the blue sky as I loved the contrasting colors.

The pristine shore had a different feel to it than Lighthouse Beach. The sea wasn't as calm on this side and several rows of waves crashed onto the sand. As I watched three young boys on boogie boards enjoying the waves I got lost in the thought of one day bringing my kids to Sanibel. I wondered if I would have all girls, all boys, or one of each.

I found a tall bush of sea grapes and zoomed in to get a close shot. In the next shot I captured the stark contrast of the green leaves against the blue sky. I shot pictures of shells, palm trees, snowy white egrets along the shoreline, a brown pelican flying low just above the water, and several tropical flowers. My last shot was a picture of the thick layer of shells running down the shoreline with a wave bringing the water up the shoreline just far enough to make it in the shot.

I spent the whole morning enjoying Bowman's Beach and the sun. My stomach abruptly alerted me that I was hungry by growling loudly so I gathered my things and headed out to grab a turkey sandwich with mustard and avocado from Island Cow and took it home. I whipped up the fresh Chantilly cream and spread it over the pie, allowing myself to remember a time when Nana and I would make Key lime pies for the neighbors when we stayed on Sanibel. We would make twelve at a time and pass them out. In exchange we would be invited for dinner, receive cards, or have different desserts brought over to our rental. I wiped a tear that had escaped down my cheek and placed the pie in the fridge.

I put on shorts I bought last week at Periwinkle Place and a pink polo shirt with my white slides. I smiled at the mirror noticing how the white shorts deepened the color of my new tan. I blew my hair dry and slipped it into a low ponytail that lay down the center of my back. I had enough color from the sun that I didn't have to worry about makeup.

Sheldon's directions were easy to follow and two royal palms greeted me at the entrance of the bricked driveway. Beautiful landscaping and thick green grass led the way to the house, which was much bigger than I expected. A light tan stucco with a brown clay shingled roof that looked like something straight out of the Mediterranean. I was sure I was in the wrong place and rechecked the address twice to confirm.

After five steps led to the large mahogany door, I rang the bell and looked around to see bright red bougainvilleas on each side surrounded by other tropical foliage.

Sheldon opened the door and stepped back, inviting me in. "Good evening, beautiful." His white T-shirt clung to his body and revealed every curve of the muscles in his chest and shoulders. "What have you got there?"

"It's Key lime, one of my favorites—I hope you like it," I said, suddenly feeling shy.

"Wow, beautiful *and* she can cook." Sheldon winked and took my hand to lead me toward the kitchen where he placed the pie in the fridge and handed me an already poured glass of Pinot Noir.

"You have a beautiful house. I love the royal palms out front." I sipped my wine.

"Let me give you a quick tour."

He led me back toward the foyer and pointed to the rooms on either side. "The dining room is on the left and my office on the right."

As we walked into the rooms I finally got a feel for Sheldon's personality and taste. Everything was clean and simply decorated yet warm and inviting with a large mahogany table in the middle of the dining room and brown leather furniture in the living room. I could tell a bachelor lived here with the large flat-screen television. The kitchen was large with stainless steel appliances and my mouth dropped open when I saw the six-burner gas stove with double ovens. *I would love to cook in this kitchen.* I smelled something delicious, but didn't see the stove or oven in use. Sheldon led me out of the kitchen toward a set of stairs leading up.

"The stairs are made of coral stone. This is what made me fall in love with the home. Well, that and the view." Sheldon took my hand and led me past his bedroom and onto a screened-in porch that covered the back of the house. The porch looked straight out to sea. There were more waves on the Captiva side and the sand was powdery white. A small path through sea oats led the way to the beach.

He opened the glass doors and we headed outside through the screened porch around to the side of the house where a large pool lay hidden amongst tropical foliage.

"It's beautiful." I paused at the pool and looked around at the manicured landscaping. It looked like the garden of Eden was crafted into his backyard.

"I try to swim every day." We stood there for a moment watching the stone fountain spill water into one side of the pool. Sheldon held my hand and rushed me back into the house and up the stairs.

"This is one of the guest rooms," he said.

I took a quick glance at a room decorated in whites and yellows before he led me to the next guest room, where a puffy white comforter trimmed in navy with monogrammed shams gave it a crisp, light look.

Sheldon drug me to the final room where two sets of bunk beds dressed in pale yellow and navy striped comforters completed its nautical theme. I wondered why he had a kid's room. Maybe he bought the place furnished and didn't change anything.

"Is this your room?" I teased.

"Yes, I always wanted bunk beds as a kid but my parents wouldn't get them for me, so I am living the dream." He matched my wit with his own and grinned. "Actually, I had this room done for my nephews and niece when they visit. Of course now that my niece is a teenager, she wants her own room." He rolled his eyes and smiled. "We usually do Christmas and Thanksgiving here at the house now that there are so many of us."

I could see in his expression that he had a great relationship with his family and I found myself instantaneously coveting his big family and their closeness.

"Wow, this is an amazing house—nice pool, and right on the beach. I have to admit I am seriously coveting right now," I said as we headed back downstairs. Sheldon didn't take me to his bedroom and I was glad although I wondered about the meaning behind it.

"Thanks, it's a lot of wasted space most of the time, but I really look forward to the whole family hanging out here on holidays."

I wondered if they played cards, watched movies—*the kids probably swim and play on the beach.* I thought about the sounds of a house filled with people and laughter and wondered what that would feel like.

"I grilled steaks and asparagus for dinner. I don't know how to use that fancy stove, but I can grill anything," he said with a cocky grin.

"Mmm, sounds good," I said realizing I was really hungry.

He pulled the already fixed plates out of the warming drawer of the oven and we carried them and our glasses of wine outside to the screened porch to eat.

I cut into my tender steak and chewed. "Mmm, the steak is delicious." I took another bite. "I like mine medium rare, you were spot-on."

"Tell me more about CrossFit, what makes it different from other gyms."

He had found a topic I loved. "We do pull-ups, push-ups, squats, box jumps, Olympic weight lifting, kettle bell swings, running, sprinting, gymnastics moves."

"Wow, sounds tough."

"All moves can be modified to accommodate each person's level of fitness. The results are dramatic. One of my members lost a little over one hundred pounds."

"That's incredible. I don't know if I could keep up with you in a CrossFit workout."

"Whatever—yes you could. It's obvious that you take care of yourself. Didn't you say that you swim every day? You probably have an incredible endurance built up." *Oh—my—word! Did I just say that?*

Sheldon grinned at me and I realized I had just inflated his ego. I tried to recover, "What time did you say the sun was setting tonight?"

"Eight thirty, we should go on out there. I'll pour us another glass of wine." He grabbed my empty glass to refill it and I took our plates to the sink.

"So when are we going to do this CrossFit workout together?" he asked with a crooked smile that lit me up inside.

"I can fix us up with a workout here. We could do an AMRAP—as many rounds as possible—in fifteen minutes of swimming the length of the pool, ten push-ups poolside, and twenty squats."

"Sounds fun." He rolled his eyes. "I'm sure I can kick your butt in that workout." A mischievous smile crossed his face.

I smiled back up at him. *I'll have to come up with a harder workout.*

Sheldon handed me a full glass of wine and took my hand. He led me through the back of the screened porch and onto the beach. There were a few others down the beach waiting for the show too.

"It's going to be a pretty one tonight with the few wispy clouds." Sheldon looked out across the sea with his hand still in mine.

He was absolutely stunning and cocky and intimidating when those blue eyes gazed at me, but I allowed myself the luxury of enjoying his company. I knew a relationship could not arrive out of this experience, but I decided to enjoy the ride while it lasted and my heart skipped a beat at the thought.

"The sky looks like it is on fire, it's beautiful!" I gasped as I took in the display of bold color across the sky. Flaming reds, oranges, purples, and grays were splashed across the sky as if someone took a large paintbrush and drug the bristles from side to side. "You have to see it to believe it, it's indescribable." I was truly in awe of the beautiful show God had just put on for us. I instinctively reached for my camera only to realize it wasn't there. "Ugh, I can't believe I forgot my camera! Again!"

"Don't worry, this happens every night at this same spot. You have plenty of time to capture it." Sheldon gave me a reassuring smile. My heart received a small jolt at his words, assuming that I would be back here to watch more sunsets with him.

The few people on the beach started clapping as the sun sunk down below the sea and disappeared out of sight, and I quickly joined in the clapping. We finished our wine and lingered outside a bit longer as it grew darker, nothing but the stars to barely light the night.

"I can't believe something so beautiful and inviting can look so scary when the sun goes down." I was in awe of the vast sea and understood its power now that it was dark. I would hate to be stranded in the middle of the ocean at night. I shivered at the thought of how lonely it would be.

Sheldon wrapped his arm around me and pulled me in close, rubbing my right arm up and down with his hand. "Are you cold?"

"No, I was just thinking about how terrifying and lonely it would be to be stuck out there in the middle of the night."

"You're right—it is intimidating and I wouldn't like to be stuck out there either, but I do love watching it at night," he said in a low serious voice.

"Mmm, yes, I could easily be hypnotized."

"Oh, really?" The mischievous smile returned to his face.

Sheldon gently cupped my face in his hands and whispered, "You are so beautiful, Emma."

I warmed instantly under his gaze, aware that my wish was about to come true—he was about to kiss me. My subconscious scolded and warned me but I argued back. *Just one kiss . . . that's all I want, just one kiss. I'll leave tomorrow if I have to, but surely I deserve one kiss from this beautiful man. I'm not going to sleep with him, I'm just going to kiss him. I can handle that. Besides, at this moment I am sure I have never wanted anything more and I know I cannot resist him.*

My heart was racing and I could feel the heat in my cheeks. I was thankful it was dark and he couldn't see me blushing.

He leaned in and it took forever for his lips to touch mine, each second seemingly trapped in time. His lips pressed ever so gently, causing me to close my eyes and savor this unbearably sensuous moment. It wasn't enough to satiate me, I wanted more, so I leaned into him and we kissed again. He held my arms and pulled me in closer and I instinctively wrapped my arms around his back. When we finally pulled away he looked into my eyes with a smoldering look, and my body felt so weak and dizzy I knew I would sway if he let me go.

With a deep husky voice he whispered, "I think you can see right into my soul with those big brown eyes."

I tried to think of something clever to say but shyness took over and I tried to put my hands in my pockets. I slid my hands over the place where pockets should be several times before looking down to see that these shorts didn't have pockets.

We looked at the stars for a moment longer and then walked hand in hand back inside to watch *The Great Outdoors* and eat a piece of Key lime pie.

"This is delicious, you really made it from scratch?"

I beamed. "Well, not the crust."

I declined another glass of wine and got up to leave.

"Won't you stay? I mean, I have guest rooms and it's pretty late."

"No, I really need to get back. You know, I don't have pajamas or a change of clothes. Oh and there's the whole 'I don't spend the night on the third date' rule." I giggled and tried to make it sound less rude than it was. I would have really liked to stay, but I knew it wasn't proper and I didn't want to send the wrong message.

"More than three if you count our time at Lighthouse Point." He lowered his eyes and the mischievous grin returned. I wondered how many women he had shared his bed with and I had to shake off the thought quickly.

I wasn't ready to debate the subject of how many dates was proper etiquette before jumping into bed with someone, so I changed the subject and said goodnight. "Dinner was great, thank you, and the movie was hilarious—I don't remember the last time I have laughed so hard!" I laughed again with him as he recalled the scene of the bat loose in the cabin.

When we reached my car in his driveway, I fumbled for my keys, trying to get my finger on the button that unlocked the door. *I need to get out of here before he kisses me again and I lose all sense of morality and do something I will regret. Don't look at him, just open the door and slide in. Shoot—too late. Those blue eyes have caught me. Good grief, I am in so much trouble.* I could feel the heat in my cheeks as I looked into his eyes that burned right into me.

He planted a soft kiss on my lips before holding the door open for me to climb in. "Lunch. Tomorrow. I'll pick you up at noon," he said in a low, breathless whisper.

Disarmed by his penetrating eyes, all I could do was nod my head, "Mmm hmm."

Nine

I awoke to a sliver of light breaching the window treatments and checked the clock. Nine o'clock—I hadn't slept that late in a long time. I stretched my arms over my head and realized I didn't awake to the nightmare but actually slept through the night. I snuggled under my covers and lay there a while longer thinking about the last two weeks. Sheldon had either taken me out or met me on the beach for a picnic lunch every day through the week. Nearly every night ended with texting flirty banter back and forth and occasionally the sharpening of wits on each other.

It was too late for a run when I got out of bed, so I grabbed the book I started reading off of the coffee table, and plopped down in my favorite paisley chair by the window. After a while, I checked the time and was surprised to find that I had been reading for two hours. I quickly put my hair up in a clip and showered. After dressing, I ran a brush through my hair—it was unruly so I slipped it into a ponytail just in time to hear the doorbell. I pinched my cheeks to add some color before walking to the door.

"Hi, come in." I held the door open while Sheldon stepped into the living room. He looked handsome as always and was wearing khaki cargo shorts and a rust-colored T-shirt with leather flip-flops.

"Hi, ready to go?" I caught him looking me over and I felt my cheeks turn crimson. *Enough with the blushing, Emma. Pull it together—he's going to think you have blood pressure issues!*

"You look nice. I love your hair pulled back—shows off that beautiful face."

"Thank you." I grabbed the key out of my bag to lock the door behind us.

We drove down Periwinkle and then took a left on North Yachtsman Drive into the Sanibel Marina.

After parking we walked up to a cute screened-in restaurant. Every seat in the crowded small restaurant had a view of the water. We chose our seats and were immediately served water with a lime wedge. "Hi, Sheldon." The waitress smiled quickly at me and lingered on Sheldon. "I'll give you two a minute to look over the menu."

"A lime wedge with water?" I asked.

"Try it, it's much better than lemon."

I squeezed some lime into the water and took a sip. "Mmm, you're right, I like it."

Gramma Dots was full of ambiance with a large wooden bar as the center of the restaurant. It felt like a beach bungalow with the wind blowing in through screens, but the décor made you feel like you were in an old ship. Framed photos of boaters lined the wall close to the ceiling.

We looked over the menu and I chose the curried lobster salad. Sheldon had the blackened grouper Caesar salad. Savoring each bite, we took our time and talked about the island. I learned that Sheldon loved boating and had plans to own his own boat one day.

"What's holding you back?" I asked as I took another bite of the creamy lobster salad.

"I don't know, time maybe. I have put so much time into my business, I guess I just forgot about it for a while. I'll show you one similar to the one I'd like to have."

A loud clap of thunder rumbled and we both looked outside. "Hmm, looks like a storm is coming in." The sky began to darken as the storm quickly rolled in and brought a cool breeze with it.

The storm held off long enough for us to walk to the docks and look at the boats. Sheldon took my hand in his and I could hear the excitement in his voice as he described the details of each boat and how fast each of them could go.

We came to the boat that he wanted to show me. "This is very similar to the one I want to buy one day. It would look just like this one but with a stronger engine, and I'd like the white leather to be trimmed in navy rather than tan."

I looked over the outside of the boat. It truly was regal. "Would it have to be made or do they already have what you want?"

Before he could answer me it started raining. We had to run to the car as the rain pelted against our skin. He opened my door to let me in and said, "I'll be right back, I want to check on something." Then he disappeared across the parking lot.

When he came back to the car, drenched with rain, I could see the excitement in his eyes. "Guess what we're doing tomorrow?"

"What?"

"I'm taking you boating."

"Really?" I couldn't hide the excitement in my voice. I had always loved a good adventure.

During the rain shower we drove to Bailey's to get supplies for the boat.

"Don't you have to get back to work? I can get the supplies if you give me a list."

"Friday's are usually pretty slow, I'll just need to wrap some things up before the weekend. It should only take a few minutes—I'll go in later."

We got way too much food and snacks for a day trip on a boat so I assumed Sheldon was stocking up his fridge at home too. He also grabbed another bottle of sun block before we got in the checkout line.

"Would you like to come back to the house and watch another movie?"

As long as you kiss me the way you did last night I wanted to tell him. "I thought you had to go to the office?"

"Would you mind coming with me? I really shouldn't be long at all."

"Sure, I can do that."

We walked up to the kiosk and viewed the movie selections. We decided on an old movie about a man and a wolf. I didn't care what we watched I just wanted to be with him.

Sheldon's office was tidy and simple. A large mahogany desk sat in the room with faux date nut palms in each corner behind it. He sat in his large leather chair and typed away at his computer while I sat in one of the chairs across from him watching his serious eyes focus. Occasionally he would look up from the computer and grin at me with a youthful expression. When he was finished he turned off the computer and led me out of his office. He introduced me to a couple of ladies in the main part of the building who greeted me with smiles and handshakes.

"Okay, sorry about that, but now I can relax and enjoy the weekend," he said as we reached his car.

"No problem." I smiled and let my mind wander to the weekend. I knew we were boating tomorrow, but I wondered how he would spend the rest of his weekend and how much of it would be with me.

After the movie, Sheldon drove me back to my place and walked me to the door. He kissed me and said goodnight—nothing compared to last night and I was disappointed.

It was too early to go to sleep so I got ready for bed, slipped into the comfy king-sized bed with my book and read until I couldn't keep my eyes open any longer and switched off the light after setting the book down on the nightstand.

I fell asleep quickly and slept hard until I woke sometime in the middle of the night to pull my covers back over me. I had gotten too cold and was shivering. I tried to reach down for my comforter but my arms didn't move—couldn't move. I felt the panic rising in my chest as I tried to free my arms. *What's happening?* Then it hit me—the smell of liquor and body odor. Bile rose in my throat and burned. I tried to scream but nothing came out of my mouth. A dark figure was holding me down, laughing and mocking someone . . . me? I realized what was happening and tried to kick and scream but nothing moved and the only sound I heard was the deep throaty laughter. Tears streamed out of my eyes and into my hair, suddenly jerking me awake as I sat straight up in bed and screamed.

I looked around dazed and confused until I got my bearings. I was in the rental on Sanibel. I was alone. I said the words aloud to calm myself, "It was just a dream . . . it was just a dream."

I couldn't go back to sleep, so I got a glass of water and the book off of the nightstand and took them both back to bed with me. I read until I fell asleep again, leaving the bedside lamp on for the rest of the night.

My alarm woke me up a couple of hours later and I went to the bathroom mirror to see that my eyes were puffy from the bad night. I splashed cold water on my face and held a washcloth full of ice cubes under my eyes trying to bring the swelling down. I was thankful for the sunshine that came through the windows knowing that I could keep my sunglasses on. I slipped on my black two-piece swimsuit and cover-up and tied my hair up on top of my head. The doorbell rang and I realized I hadn't eaten breakfast, so I grabbed a couple of bananas before opening the door.

Sheldon looked ridiculously handsome with his freshly showered and combed hair. His blue eyes were rested and appeared even bluer against his clean shaven skin. He was wearing his navy blue swim trunks with a white polo shirt and brown leather flip-flops. My breath caught just looking at him.

"Good morning," he whispered.

"Good morning." I smiled.

"Ready to go?"

"Yes, I'm excited! Would you like a banana? I didn't have time to eat."

"Thank you, I didn't either." He took the banana and peeled it from the bottom instead of the top.

"Why do you peel it backwards?"

"If you peel it from the bottom, it never smashes the tip of the banana and you have a handle to hold. Try it."

I did try it and he was right. I always smashed the first bite of the banana when I peeled it, but this worked. Two things I had learned from him that I was sure I would adopt—lime in my water and peeling bananas backwards.

We drove to the marina, and people were on the boat working when we arrived.

"Hey, Sheldon, boat's all ready to go and it is perfect boating weather today. You two should have a great time."

"Thanks, Bob, for letting us take her out. This is Emma, the girl I was telling you about."

"She just might be out of your league, Sheldon!" Bob teased and winked at me. "You two have fun."

We walked up to the beautiful white and navy boat.

"Clever . . . I like it," I said, pointing to the name across the back. *To Sea Oar Knot to Sea.*

"Bob's wife came up with the name."

Sheldon climbed aboard first and I handed him the cooler and bags we brought. He set the bags down and then held his hand out for me as I climbed on board. The floor of the boat was a light wood, possibly teak, and was magnificent against the navy and white boat.

"I love this boat. It's a 395 Trawler with a 380 horse power engine." I was lost listening to his boat lingo, but nodded my head encouraging him to go on. "You can steer from the living area or the deck."

He was thrilled to show me every detail of the boat, opening every cabinet, including one that revealed a small flat-screen television.

"There's more." He took my hand and we stepped down two carpeted steps into a bedroom. The queen-sized bed was elegantly dressed in a muted tan plaid and sat on top of a wooden base. "Look, here's another television." He pointed to another flat screen, slightly larger than the one in the kitchen. Eight steps led to the top deck. "Check this out," Sheldon said as he opened the doors to a white storage cabinet. "A small grill and mini fridge . . . this boat has everything."

I stifled a giggle as I watched him.

He caught me smiling at him and held my gaze. "What? I'm acting like a kid, huh?"

"I like it—I like the way your eyes light up when you're excited."

"Yeah?" He grabbed me and pulled me in to his chest. I had to lift my head up to look at him. "Well, I have a feeling you're going to see these eyes light up a lot more." He leaned down and kissed me hard on the lips.

"Ready to head out?" Sheldon's voice was filled with excitement as he turned the key and the motor came to life.

We drove slowly along the no-wake zone to avoid hitting any manatee that might be grazing in the shallow waters, and when we finally passed the no-wake zone, Sheldon sped up and we were sailing along the coastal channel. I stood up next to him as he drove the boat, the salty sea air blowing hard against our faces and through Sheldon's hair making it whip all around. He looked so good driving the boat—he was meant to be on the sea.

Ten

Our first stop was Picnic Island, a primitive island with no lodging, only ten campers. There, we walked along a skinny peninsula laced with familiar-looking shells.

"These shells look just like oysters, don't they?"

"They are oysters. One day we'll have to collect some for eating, but it's not worth fooling with today."

My thoughts got carried away with thinking about "one day" and I wondered how long I would be able to stay on Sanibel. I had so many memories on the island and I could already feel the healing beginning. Sheldon picked up a live conch shell to show me and it reminded me of the time Nana and I walked the beach after a monstrous storm. There were conch shells washed up all over the beach and we were trying to save as many as we could, filling our arms with the live shells. I giggled to myself recalling one of the live conch muscles coming out of the shell and climbing up her top. She screamed and flung them, barely missing a man behind her. Once we gathered our arms full of shells, we walked out into the water and threw them as far as we could into the sea. We later learned that we probably killed them on impact. It was like throwing a human off of a thirty-story building. We had been so proud to save so many conchs, and then devastated to learn what we had done.

"It's a beautiful one," I said as I looked over the bright orange conch shell in Sheldon's hand. He gently placed it back in the water and we watched it hesitantly peek out of its shell and scoot across the ocean floor. After walking around Picnic Island for a bit and not finding anything interesting to shoot photographs of or any shells to collect, we got back in the boat.

I was sitting in the captain's chair again, next to Sheldon on the upper deck as he drove the boat across the water. There were numbered signs in the water, and we were staying in between them. The signs on our right side had green squares and the ones on the left had red triangles. I wondered what they meant and what they were used for.

As if reading my mind, Sheldon interjected, "Those are channel markers. They serve a couple of purposes: one is to keep you in the channel of deep water—there are shallow areas all over that we need to avoid, and the numbers tell you where you are. For example, if you want to go to Cayo Costa, you go to marker 48, I believe."

"I see."

Sheldon suddenly slowed the boat down and came to a stop which made my heart jump into my throat thinking something was wrong.

"Look! Over there, two o'clock—a family of dolphins!" he shouted.

"Oh, I see them!" Five dolphins came up for air and then sank back into the sea.

"Let me see if I can get a bit closer." Sheldon pulled the boat foward in front of their path.

"*Pfft . . . Pfft . . .*" I heard as they came up for air and blew the water out of the blowholes on top of their sleek heads.

We both leaned over the side of the boat and watched them lazily make their way along the sea. One of them was a baby and he jumped into the air as he spun around and showed his belly before diving back into the water.

"Ahh! That was amazing! Aren't they the sweetest things you have ever seen?" I asked, every part of me wanting to jump in and swim with them. I had to contain the urge to jump up and down. *Now who's acting like a kid on Christmas?* I asked myself.

"Yes, my favorite. We should see a lot more too. Keep your eyes peeled. I can stop the boat anytime."

We did see many more dolphins along the way, probably thirty total, and stopped the boat to watch them. I put my camera on sports mode and captured several great shots of them coming out of the water.

Sheldon slowed down the boat as we approached another island. As we dropped anchor off the front of the boat, I wondered how we were going to get on the island, as it looked like quite a ways to swim from here. The current pulled the back of the boat around until it was facing the island, and Sheldon heaved another anchor off of the back of the boat.

"Brilliant!" I exclaimed and he flashed me a cocky smile.

When Sheldon jumped in, I saw that the water was much shallower than it looked, only waist high. I chose to use the ladder to climb off of the boat, and the water felt amazing as it splashed up around my stomach. We both dipped down to our shoulders letting the water cool off our bodies before going to shore.

"This island is called Cayo Costa. You can only get here by boat," Sheldon informed me as we walked on a sandy path through massive pieces of driftwood laced with mounds of bleached white shells. The island looked deserted except for two couples and a family of three walking in the distance. He continued to tell me that the other end of the island had primitive cabins you could rent overnight.

Sheldon held my hand as we walked across the white powdery sand beside the turquoise water. I could feel the heat traveling through my hand and making its way into my chest. I realized I was walking down the beach with the most gorgeous man I had ever met and I secretly wished there were more people around to witness.

I squatted down to find an orange conch shell amongst a pile of bleached shells. While I was picking it up I saw several lettered olives and realized I was in shelling heaven. Sheldon was patient while I found all kinds of treasures and slipped them into the net bag that I brought with me.

"I usually find some pretty great shells just off the shoreline, and I brought two sets of snorkel gear. Would you like to join me?" he asked as he held up the masks and breathing tubes.

"Yeah, sounds like fun. Do I need to worry about sharks?" Suddenly I was nervous at the thought.

"No, this area isn't known for sharks. Too many dolphins around. Remember, I told you—"

I rolled my eyes and interrupted him, "Yes, I remember . . . if dolphins are around, you can be sure sharks are not. I'm still not sure I buy it, I might have to look that up when I get home." I laughed and bumped my hip into his side. I grabbed the snorkel and tightened the mask over my eyes and nose. "I'll just follow you." My words came out muffled like I was plugging my nose and I wondered if I looked as funny as he did in the gear. I tried to smile but my mask was smashing down on my top lip. Sheldon looked at me and laughed so hard he had to remove his mask, and eventually I was removing mine too as we were rendered breathless with laughter.

We snorkeled for about an hour and found some really great shells. I found an alphabet cone, two lettered olives, a fighting conch, and one whelk that was still alive, so I gently placed it back after showing it to Sheldon. Sheldon had found four fighting conchs, a few small lettered olives, two shark eyes, and three turkey wings. He also showed me a live crab that he just picked up, and I screamed and tried to walk on water to get away from it.

He laughed hard and let the crab go in the opposite direction with the current. I loved to see him laugh and joined in when I knew he didn't have the crab any longer.

He swam up close to me and took me in his arms. The electric waves began in my chest again and I looked down in embarrassment but he pulled my chin up to face him. He kissed me for a long moment and then I realized my bikini top was no longer on my body. My eyes were wide in shock as I threw my arms across my chest even though I was covered by the deep blue water. Sheldon guffawed as he swam away with my bikini top. Stunned and unsure of what to do, I stood there in the water waiting, my anger and frustration building.

"Come and get it!" he teased, a wide grin spread across his face.

"Give it back, Sheldon," I managed to whisper. "I—am—serious. Give it back!"

He swam back over to me and tied my top back on and I swam to shore, furious and embarrassed.

"Are you angry?" He was still laughing at the fun he'd just had at my expense.

"You think? You left me out there topless. How did I know you were going to give it back? And, just for the record . . . do not touch me without asking!" I was sure steam was coming out of my ears I was so angry.

"I'm sorry, I thought it was a fun gag." His eyes were suddenly shrewd. "How about if I let you steal my swim trunks for a while? Will we be even?" He grinned.

"Uh, no, because you would no doubt enjoy it and I imagine you would chase me down the beach to retrieve them in all your glory."

Sheldon laughed out loud at the thought and I came down from my hissy fit to join him, cackling at the thought of the people on the beach and the look on the face of the older lady that had just walked by us in a skirted bathing suit.

I put the newfound shells in the net bag inside my beach bag and grabbed two waters. After taking a long drink, we lay on the sand together and soaked up some sun.

I saw a little mole crab bury into the wet sand and sat up to dig him out, finding a few more. As I dug deeper, I found tons of these little crabs in all sizes and decided they were fun to watch.

Sheldon sat up on his elbows to watch me. "I'd like to know more about you."

"What do you want to know?" I glanced up at him, letting the tiny crabs dig back down into the sand.

"What's your favorite color?"

I rolled my eyes playfully. "Green."

"What's your favorite flower?"

"Birds of Paradise and orange roses, oh and gardenias." I could actually go on and on, but those were my top three.

"Favorite movie?"

"Now that's a hard one because it varies with my mood."

He raised an eyebrow and nudged me with his eyes to give him an answer.

"*Gone with the Wind, Pride and Prejudice, Sleeping with the Enemy,* and *Raising Arizona.*" I rambled off my top choices.

"That is quite an eclectic mix. *Sleeping with the Enemy*, really?"

"Yes, I love how clean everything is in the beginning, how all the cans are facing in the same direction and organized and then I love the end when . . ." I fell short not wanting to spoil the end for him if he hadn't seen it. "Have you seen it?" He nodded so I continued. "I love it when she gets her revenge in the end."

"You are something, Emma. Too innocent to enjoy a playful gag, yet your favorite movie is *Sleeping with the Enemy.* You crack me up." He shook his head and then pushed me over into the sand and laughed.

"I'm starving, want to grab some lunch?" Sheldon asked as we washed the sand off of our bodies in the ocean.

"Yes, I am too. I'll fix us some sandwiches on the boat."

"No, I have a place that I'd like to take you for lunch." Sheldon took my hand in his, and I could feel the heat converge between our hands. I wondered if he felt it too.

We walked back to the boat, reeled in the anchors, and took off. Sheldon taught me how to steer and to follow the signs, keeping the boat in between the red and green arrows.

We slowed the boat down to idle speed as we approached the "no wake" zone and he took over the steering again.

"This is Cabbage Key. It, too, is only accessible by boat. The staff either lives on the island or has to boat here. They have the best hamburgers."

The dock master helped guide us into a slip and tied the boat. He was a thin man with white blond hair and a deep tan. He and Sheldon talked while I slipped my plaid cover-up over my bathing suit and found my flip-flops.

Cabbage Key Restaurant was at the top of a small hill. Tropical trees and flowers surrounded the screened-in white building. The inside of the restaurant was completely covered in dollar bills that people from all over the world had signed and taped to the walls and ceilings. We ordered cheeseburgers and sipped on Bay Breezes while signing a dollar bill with our names and the date and looked for a spot to hang it. We decided on a spot above the ceiling fan next to our table and Sheldon stood on a chair to tape it up.

After lunch we climbed to the top of the water tower to see the most beautiful view of the island surrounded by the deep blue sea. We sat on the bench at the top of the tower and enjoyed more conversation.

"My turn." I smiled.

"Your turn?" He angled his head to the side quizzically. "Your turn for what?"

"What's your favorite color?"

Sheldon gave me a crooked smile. "Blue."

"Favorite flower?" I tried to keep the laughter out of my eyes, but couldn't stifle the giggle that played at my lips. "Just kidding—what's your favorite movie?"

"Hmm, can I name more than one?" I nodded my head. "*Braveheart, The Godfather, The Matrix*, and *The Princess Bride*."

"*The Princess Bride?*" I smiled and raised one eyebrow.

Sheldon jumped up, pretended to swing a sword, and quoted a line from the movie using his best Spanish accent, "Hello. My name is Inigo Montoya. You killed my father. Prepare to die."

I laughed, enjoying his skit. "I've never seen that movie, but I loved *The Godfather*."

"You've never seen *The Princess Bride*? You *did* come down the river on a log!" he teased. I was impressed that he remembered my Southern colloquialism.

We walked back down the water tower toward the boat. Sheldon handed the dock master a tip and backed the boat out of the dock so we could head back out to open water.

"Let's go toward Boca Grande, there are usually quite a few dolphins that way."

"Oh yes, more dolphins!" I clapped my hands together in excitement.

Sheldon came up behind me and wrapped his arms around my waist as we watched the dolphins play and swim. I decided that I would rather enjoy the enchantment of his arms while watching the dolphins play, than trying to capture more photos.

"This is the best day I've had in . . . well as far back as I can remember. Thank you," I whispered with my back resting against his bare chest. The day was coming to an end and I started to feel melancholy.

"It doesn't have to end yet," Sheldon said cautiously and turned me around to face him. "We can have the boat overnight and go back to Cayo Costa in the morning if you'd like." His eyes were pleading.

"You know I can't do that." *As tempting as it sounds*. I truly didn't want this day to end and my heart suffered a pang knowing that I was taking him away from the boat that he had been so excited about.

"The couch pulls out to a full-size bed—I'll sleep there and you can have the bedroom." His face was serious as he looked into my eyes. "Of course I would like to share a bed with you, Emma, but I understand if you need to take things slow. I promise to be a gentleman and you can even lock the bedroom door."

My heart thudded against my chest and I wondered if he could hear it. I wanted to take some time to think long and hard about the offer, not wanting to make a foolish decision, but those mysterious blue eyes disarmed me as they pierced right through to my soul.

Eleven

"I'd love to stay," I said shyly. "But I *am* locking the door!" I gave him a light shove and smiled up at him.

"Thatta girl! Good choice. Now, what would you like for dinner? Grilled chicken or cheese crackers?" He laughed.

"Grilled chicken for sure," I answered and asked what I could do to help.

"Pour us a glass of wine and join me up top at the grill, gorgeous," he said in that cocky voice that I was starting to enjoy. I slipped my cover-up on over my swimsuit before pouring the wine and walked up the stairs to the top deck. We were anchored in the ocean, away from the channel and close to a small deserted island. I handed Sheldon a glass of chilled

Chardonnay as he flipped the chicken over on the grill.

"Should be another stunning sunset tonight. I think we have a pretty good view, don't you?" He held up his glass for a toast. "Here's to our first overnight together."

My eyes widened when he slapped me on the butt and winked. "You tease me constantly." I gave him a scolding glare. "Here's to wishful thinking on your behalf." I winked and *clinked* my glass against his. We both took a sip of wine and I held the plates out for him to put the cooked chicken on.

"We don't have any fancy sides, how about some grapes?" He plopped a cluster of grapes onto each plate and we sat down at the table on the top deck to eat.

"Mmm, this is so much better than cheese crackers." I chewed a piece of tender chicken still hot off the grill. Twilight was approaching and the sea became tranquil as we enjoyed dinner. I found myself talking about my Nana and shared a funny story. "We had just finished watching Verdi's *Rigoletto* at the Bijou Theater in downtown Chattanooga. I had curled my hair and probably emptied a can of hairspray into it." I rolled my eyes. "Anyway, we went to the bathroom and while I was in the stall, Nana unrolled a bunch of toilet paper and wet it in the sink. Would you believe she climbed up, reached over the stall, and dropped that huge ball of wet toilet paper on my head? *Splat*! It all separated and stuck in my curled and heavily sprayed hair." Sheldon and I both laughed. "We used to talk about that and laugh until we couldn't breathe."

After dinner we took our plates down to the kitchen sink. I washed and he dried them off before putting them back in the cabinet. I refilled our wine glasses before we climbed the steps to watch the sunset from the top deck. The sky flaunted muted colors of red, orange, and purple as the sun hid behind a few clouds, giving the effect of a watercolor painting. When the sun presented itself below the clouds, it looked like a massive peach melting into the water. It was just the two of us on the boat floating in the water, but we both clapped in unison for the show we had just witnessed.

"Breathtaking. Do you ever tire of it?" I asked, wondering if watching the sun melt into the sea every night for the rest of your life could ever get monotonous.

"No, it's never the same and it always amazes me. I have seen gorgeous sunsets in my travels, but nothing compares to the ones over the sea." Sheldon hugged me closer to him and rubbed my arm as if to warm me. I wasn't cold but the movement of his hand on my arm quickly raised goose bumps. He grabbed a blanket to wrap around my shoulders in reaction to the goose bumps making their appearance.

"I'm not cold, but thanks anyway."

"You have goose bumps all over." He lowered his eyes curiously at me and then the reality of my statement registered in his eyes and in the smile displayed across his face.

"Hmm . . ." He cocked one eyebrow up and smiled mischievously. "Let's see what happens when I do this . . ." Sheldon traced a finger across my arm and the goose bumps were back.

I quickly rubbed my hands up and down over my arms to make them disappear. "You must be very pleased with your goose bump raising powers. That takes pure talent—your parents must be so proud," I grinned.

"Yes, they are, and I finished the program two months earlier than the other kids."

Sheldon laid the blanket on the floor of the upper deck and we lay on our backs watching the stars. We both witnessed a star shoot across the sky and it looked like sparklers were going off in a trail behind it.

"Holy cow, did you see that? I have never seen a shooting star that big and dazzling!" I propped up on my elbows hoping another one would follow behind it. "Incredible."

"Close your eyes and make a wish," Sheldon instructed.

I immediately shut my eyes and made an extravagant wish.

"What did you wish for?"

"I'll never tell!" I grinned.

Sheldon rolled onto his side and looked at me. He traced his finger across the top of my thigh and watched the goose bumps rise in reaction to his touch, laughing silently as he made his way to the other leg.

"I'm glad I can bring you such amusement," I smiled, embarrassed.

Sheldon's mood sobered as he looked soulfully into my eyes. Was he trying to see if he could make goose bumps rise all over just by looking at me? He leaned in and traced my bottom lip with his thumb. Shivers ran through my body and I closed my eyes in response, willing him to kiss me. He read my body language and granted my wish with a soft kiss, his lips barely grazing mine. I had to restrain my desire to pull him closer, my willpower suddenly weak. My patience was soon rewarded with another kiss so full of hunger and passion that I began to feel dizzy. I knotted my fingers in his hair and let a soft moan escape my lips. He responded by pulling our bodies closer together, one arm supporting my back. Our passion for each other grew out of control and I felt his hand slide across my thigh and travel up my backside. I was engrossed in his kiss and my desire for him superseded my ability to ask him to stop. His hand eagerly moved across my stomach up to my breast. I exhaled sharply, mostly from pleasure but partly from disappointment in myself for letting things go this far. Everything in me wanted to let go, let it happen, but the screams of my subconscious were deafening and I suddenly snapped back to reality.

"You have to stop," I managed, barely audible and breathless.

"Are you sure?" He moaned against my lips. His hands were still exploring as he kissed me again.

"Yes . . . please stop." My words were pleading yet still full of desire and I couldn't blame him for the confusion that I was sure filled him. I was confused too. I wanted to trust him, and this was definitely a very romantic setting, but I knew deep down that it wasn't right. I put my hands on his chest and gently pushed him off of me.

Sheldon took his hand away, his eyes seeking mine. "What's wrong?"

"I'm so sorry. I really am . . . but . . ." I fell silent, suddenly feeling self-conscious and shy.

"You're not ready." Sheldon exhaled in a huff and rolled over onto his back. I could see the frustration on his face and in his body language. His hands were laced behind his head as he looked up as if counting the stars to take his mind off of the rejection that had just taken place. *He's probably never been turned down in his life and here I am alone on the boat with him . . . who wouldn't expect something in return. But did you have to huff? What's next, kicking your feet and throwing a tantrum because you didn't get what you wanted? Well, too bad for you, dude. I'm not that kind of girl and I am not selling myself for a ride on a boat.* My anger was rising by the second and I had every intention of telling this arrogant man what I was thinking. *Ooh, what's the word I'm looking for? Pompous . . . self-centered . . . egotistical . . . I can't believe that he thinks I owe him something and is going to get mad when I say no. I can't even think straight I am so livid!*

I stood up and stormed down the stairs into the living room. Sheldon was right behind me and I felt trapped. There was nowhere to go—no escape from him except for locking the bedroom door. "Please take me home." I folded my arms and held his gaze. *Ha! Those blue eyes aren't so disarming right now, are they?* They actually portrayed confusion and I could tell the tantrum I had envisioned wouldn't happen now.

"What just happened? Why are you so furious?"

"Just take me home, please."

"Okay, but first tell me why you're so angry. You at least owe me that."

"Do I? And what else do you think I owe you? You think just because you took me out on this boat that I should sleep with you? Because you're a man and I'm a woman we should 'hook up'?" I exaggerated the air quote marks over my head for effect. "I mean, that's what people do—whatever makes you happy in the moment, never mind the consequences." I was fuming and knew that I was losing control of my rationale letting the anger take over.

"Whoa, settle down. I never said that you owed me anything. I took you on the boat because I enjoy your company. You seemed to be just as into me as I was you up there and then you threw a fit. What gives?" Sheldon looked to me for clarity.

How could I explain that I was twenty-four years old and had never been with a man before? I was so tired of the looks, stifled laughter, and having to explain my desire to save something so precious for marriage. I thought about the times that Andrew begged me to sleep with him. "We're engaged for shit's sake!" he would say angrily. I took a deep breath, feeling the anger receding and my pulse calming before I looked back up at Sheldon. I searched for the words to explain my position but couldn't get them to come out of my mouth. Instead I said, "Yes, I was caught up in the moment too, but when I asked you to stop, you huffed and seemed perturbed."

"I wasn't mad, I was frustrated. You're a very desirable woman and of course I want you, surely you don't expect me to come out of a situation so heated and go straight into singing a happy camp song." Sheldon grinned, trying to end the argument and I was grateful. "Listen, I know you want to take things slow, I just got caught up in the moment. I wasn't mad at you—I was just a little surprised and needed a moment to cool down. I've never cared for swimming in the ocean when it's dark or I would have cannonballed right off the side of the boat."

I giggled at the thought of him jumping off the side of the boat with his knees hugged to his chest and then thought of how terrifying it would be to swim at night. The same creatures that swim in the ocean during the day swim at night, but it was just frightening after the sun went down.

"So do you still want me to take you home, or are we good?"

"We're good," I smiled, mollified, and let him pull me in for a makeup hug.

"Good. Let's flip through the channels. Do you want a glass of wine or a water bottle?"

"Water, please. Do you happen to have a T-shirt I can sleep in? I only brought my swimsuit and cover up." I hoped he did, sleeping in my swimsuit was going to be miserable.

"Nope, you'll have to sleep in the nude." He shrugged his shoulders and smirked before flashing me a wink.

I was glad to see that he was back to his tantalizing self and wasn't afraid to flirt with me after all of this. "No problem, I've already checked the lock on that door and it's a good one," I replied flippantly and flashed a wink right back.

"Well, look at you . . . you're not as naïve as you seem," he replied, smiling. "I have a T-shirt you can sleep in."

"Thank you. You're a big jerk, you know." I teased and pecked him on the cheek when he handed me the shirt.

His plain black T-shirt was soft and much more comfortable than my cover-up, but it didn't cover as much. I climbed the two steps up to the living room area where Sheldon sat pushing the buttons on the remote to the television. "Do you think there's a blanket that I could cover my legs with?" I asked, tugging on the shirt. I felt exposed even though I had my swimsuit bottoms still on underneath.

"Oh. Heaven. Help. Me." Every word was spoken staccato. "You look damn fine in that shirt." Sheldon's eyes were humorless and I wondered if I needed to run back and lock the bedroom door, forfeiting any channel surfing with him in the living room.

I flushed and looked down at my toes as I walked over to the couch. Sheldon handed me a thin navy blanket and continued flipping through the channels on the small flat screen. "Tell me if you see something you're interested in."

We landed on a show about traveling to Tuscany and Rome, Italy, hosted by a petite blonde with cropped hair and a British accent. She gave advice on the best hotels, restaurants, and must-see attractions.

"I have always wanted to go to Italy," I swooned.

"You've never been?"

"No, have you?"

"Once when I was younger my parents took us to Rome. I was too young to really appreciate it." He put an arm around my waist and scooted me closer to him in one effortless motion. I looked up at him, worried that things would become intense again being so close to him.

Sheldon held up three fingers mimicking the Boy Scout hand signal. "Trust me." His smile was reassuring and I began to relax, pulling my legs up to curl beside me.

It felt good to be so close to him like this, contented and secure, and I let my thoughts wander to a future with him. I barely knew him and yet I was drawn to him like a strong magnetic field was pulling me in. I didn't want this day to end, and I was sure I wouldn't be satisfied with letting it end tomorrow or the next day for that matter.

I was exhausted from the full day of activities in the sun, and I let my head rest on his shoulder, gauging his reaction to make sure I wasn't sending mixed signals—I certainly didn't want to be a tease. He wrapped an arm around me assuring me that it felt good to him as well and stroked my hair with his hand.

Sheldon gently shook my shoulder waking me from sleep. "Emma, let's get you to bed."

"Hmm?" I murmured groggily and wished he would just continue to hold me like this all night. I was comfortable and too tired to move.

"Come on, get up."

Sheldon led me to the bedroom and pulled back the covers. I slid into the cool sheets and enjoyed being tucked in.

"Thank you," I whispered. He kissed me on the forehead and gently shut the door behind him.

***

Walking along the beach, I watched a group of Ibis fish for their breakfast along the shore. Their long orange beaks pecked into the water several times before taking pause to swallow. I heard someone walk up behind me and turned to greet them with the usual

"Good morning." Dark eyes penetrated my own, causing me to take a step backward. The smell of alcohol radiating off of his breath and skin—the kind that sits deep within your pores as if you've marinated in it—caused my lungs to burn in protest. As the evil smile crossed his face, he reached for my arm. I took another step back, but the birds were behind me. I tried to avoid them as I was falling to the ground, but I could feel their bodies being broken underneath my back. Survivors pecked and clawed at my arms and face, while the human predator hovered over me. My cries were a mixture of fear, pain, and heartbreak. The nefarious man called my name over and over trying to make me stop screaming.

"Emma. Emma!" His voice grew louder and louder. Finally it was thunderous in my ear, causing me to sit up in bed. My face was damp with tears as I looked around the room trying to get my bearings. Sheldon was sitting on the edge of the bed, his eyes troubled as he looked down at me. I sat up and wiped the tears off of my face with the back of my hand, searching his eyes for answers.

"You were having a nightmare, but you're alright now, I've got you." Sheldon had his arms wrapped around me and was holding me tightly against his chest. I wrapped my arms around him in response, wetting his bare chest with the tears that continued to flow down my cheeks.

"I'm getting you all wet." I pulled back.

"Don't worry about that." He gently wiped my tear-stained cheeks with his thumb.

"Did I wake you?"

"You were screaming. It scared the crap out of me—I thought someone was in your room."

"Jeez, I really am sorry." I looked around the room for a clock but didn't find anything offering the time.

"Don't apologize, it's okay. Do you want a glass of water or something?"

"No, I'm alright now, thank you." Another sniffle escaped. "You can go back to sleep."

Sheldon cupped my face gently in his hands and looked into my eyes. "Okay, but I'm right outside the door if you need me."

As he started to get up I grabbed his hand and he turned back to look at me. My voice was shaky and small when I tried to speak, "could you just stay in here with me?" I was still shaking from the nightmare and didn't want to be alone, but was surprised that I had just asked him to sleep in the bed with me. Before I could take it back, he responded.

Without saying a word, he slipped in under the covers next to me and guided my head onto his chest. He wrapped both arms around me and kissed the top of my head. Neither of us said a word as we lay there, my body calming from the intense shivering, and eventually we both drifted off to sleep.

When I woke up the next morning, the sun had breached the blinds on the small windows so I closed my eyes to blot out the invading light. My body was radiating heat on one side and I remembered that I was in Sheldon's arms. I had never felt so warm and safe and comfortable. My head fit perfectly into the dip of his chest and I didn't want to move for fear of waking him up, I just wanted to lay there and savor this feeling. My arm was draped over the upper part of his stomach and I wanted to run my hand along his abs and chest, feeling the contour of every muscle. Instead I concentrated on his breathing and the rise and fall of my head on his chest.

This incredible man was reeling me in faster than I thought possible and I just couldn't fight it anymore. My heart might be shattered into a million pieces at the end of the summer, but I had traveled too far down this road to turn around now and I was suddenly aware that I was starting to fall in love with him.

Twelve

Sheldon stirred next to me, nudging my somnolence back to reality. I tried not to move a muscle as I thought about the previous night. I felt his hand stroke my hair as he inhaled deeply and I closed my eyes enjoying the feel of his loving touch.

"Good morning," he whispered, his voice husky with sleep. "Did you sleep okay?"

"Mmm hmm." I nodded against my pillow, suddenly feeling shy. "Thank you for staying," I said appreciatively and turned to face him.

Sheldon sat up and looked at me, his eyes inquiring. "Emma, what was your nightmare about?"

I was so not ready to talk about the reasons behind my bad dreams and wondered if I had said anything aloud during the nightmare. I tried to change the subject. "It was nothing." I waved it off. "I'm starving, want some breakfast? Do we have anything for breakfast or shall I grab the cheese crackers?"

"We have eggs. Now answer me. You have just spent the night in my arms and I didn't touch you. Surely I've gained your trust by now."

It was true—he had been a gentleman last night and let me fall asleep in his arms. I couldn't imagine how tired I would have been this morning after a night of hugging my knees to my chest while shaking and trying to calm down. I could see by the expression on his face that he was not going to relent so I tried to give him as little information as I could. "I was being attacked—must have consumed too much wine last night."

This answer seemed to satisfy him for now and his eyes lit up as he started tickling me. "Attacked by a shark?" He laughed, and continued tickling until I was a giggling heap on the bed.

Sheldon left the room to start breakfast while I made up the bed and washed my face. I was still in his T-shirt when I came out of the room to the mouth-watering smell of bacon. I looked over to the couch and noticed that it had not been pulled out into a bed. The pillow was propped up against the arm rest and the thin navy blanket was piled at the other end. I couldn't imagine how uncomfortable it had been for his long frame to sleep on that small sofa and was glad he was able to sleep at least half of the night in the bed.

"Mmm, bacon." I moaned and my stomach growled.

"The only thing I know how to cook on the stove. I tried to make eggs . . ." Sheldon looked over at me and stopped short. "Seriously, woman, you are hotter than hell in my shirt. I think I might have to keep you." He teased but all humor left his face as he took me in with his eyes.

I discovered that I loved to be ogled by him, he made me feel alive and beautiful. "Here, let me make the eggs. Do we have butter?" I found a bowl to crack the eggs into and a pan for cooking them. We were side by side in the tiny kitchen but it didn't feel crowded. My skin heated up and prickled every time we accidentally brushed against the other.

We feasted on the eggs and bacon at the dinette table and then took our glasses of juice onto the upper deck. The sun was still rising and the sky was lit up with beautiful pastels and bright rays of sun shining down from behind the clouds. The sea was serene and quiet with a few dolphins in the far distance fishing for their breakfast.

"It's so peaceful out here right now," Sheldon remarked, and I nodded my head as I exhaled, overcome by all of the beauty surrounding us.

We sat up on the top deck for at least a couple of hours watching the dolphins dip in and out of the water, pelicans dive into the sea to catch breakfast, an osprey devour a small fish while perched on a branch, and a couple of fishermen casting and reeling in their fishing lines as a trolling motor carried them along the banks.

When the sun had risen high enough to burn through the thin clouds and warm the air, I started to feel sweat beads forming on my forehead.

"I'm going to change back into my swimsuit, it's getting hot." I stood and picked up our juice glasses, stopping to look back at him. "Oh, and I think I'll keep this shirt." I winked and flashed him a smile before turning to go down the stairs.

"Hell yes." I heard him say in a low husky voice as he followed me down the stairs.

"Do you want to use the bedroom first?" I offered.

"No, I'm not that modest." A mischievous grin spread across his face as he started to strip off his boxers in the living room. "I'll just change here."

"Sheesh!" I turned quickly and headed for the bedroom. I could hear Sheldon's laughter through the closed door.

After we changed, he led me to the back of the boat where the swimming platform was.

"I'm going to take a quick dip."

"Okay, I just want to dangle my feet in the water for now." I started to lower myself down on the edge of the platform, but before I could sit down I was being scooped up in his arms and he was jumping off the boat. The water was cool and chilled my skin. After I was over the shock I splashed him with both hands.

"You are constantly tormenting me, Mr. Barringer!"

"You are so fun to torment, Miss Peroni." He swam after me and I was too weak with laughter to put in much effort to get away from him. We continued to laugh together as he held me in his arms, grinning from his easy capture.

"I thought you were the competitive type." He raised one eyebrow.

"You made me weak." I laughed. "Giggling makes me weak." I corrected my statement, even though it was true, he did make me weak.

We splashed and had a great time in the water together. Sheldon pulled out two floats for us to lie on while we relaxed on the water. We kept one foot on the back of the boat so we didn't drift away and held hands to keep our floats close while we talked and soaked up the early sun. I was in a blissful state out there on the water, being gently rocked on the float and coming close to a sun-and-sea induced nap. *Mmm, this is the life.* I kept my eyes closed and tried to think of something to say.

"What kind of music do you like?"

"I like a variety of music. My favorite playlist right now though would probably be the Waterboys, Mumford and Sons . . . hmm . . . I also like reggae and classic rock. What about you?"

"I like most everything except country. Classical is my favorite, but I like Creed, Foo Fighters, Dave Matthews, and I also love reggae and anything with steel pans." *I'm also a diehard opera fan and have every CD of Andrea Bocelli's, but you don't need to know how big of a nerd I am just yet.*

"Let me see what I can find, there's an awesome stereo system on the boat." Sheldon rolled over off of the float and into the water. "Ooh, that feels nice." Sheldon shook the water out of his hair spraying a mist across my hot skin and grinned, "The sun is out in full force, we need to get some sunscreen on you."

I rolled off of my float and let the silky water cool my skin for a moment before climbing onto the boat. We put the floats on the platform and dried off. Sheldon squirted some of the white lotion into his hands, "I'll get your back and you get mine."

I savored the feeling of his hands on my skin. He moved his hands methodically across my shoulders and back and a current coursed through my body. I knew my goose bumps were visible and that he was aware of what his touch was doing to me. Reading my body language, he turned me around for a kiss. Wrapping my arms around his neck, our bodies came together, returning to the passion that filled us so deeply last night.

"I think another dip in the ocean is needed," Sheldon said as he did a cannonball into the water sending a splash straight up.

I giggled and held up seven fingers. "I'll give that a seven for the splash, but I had to take off points for form."

"A seven? You're killing me. That was a nine and a half at least."

You'll probably have time to improve your scores if you keep kissing me like that. I thought to myself. "Where's the stereo?"

"Right up there." Sheldon pointed in the direction of the stereo and I found it easily. I scanned through the channels and lucked upon a station playing reggae. "Promise Land" by Dennis Brown was finishing up and then Bob Marley's "One Love" came on. I squirted some more sunscreen into my hand and covered my chest and face.

"You didn't let me get your back," I shouted to Sheldon as he treaded water.

"The sun can't possibly do as much damage as you, babe." He grinned. "I'll get some later. Come back in the water."

We lay on the floats and swam in the sea as reggae played in the background. Sheldon eventually got out of the water for sunscreen and brought back two delicious cocktails for us to sip on while we talked.

"This is delicious, what is it?"

"I think it's called a Vodka Volcano. It has pineapple juice, orange juice, grapefruit juice, a splash of grenadine, and of course, vodka."

We talked about where we attended college, what we studied, and favorite foods . . . the basic topics to get to know each other better, and then the more personal questions came.

"Tell me about your parents, Emma. Are they still in Tennessee?"

"Actually, my parents were killed in a car accident when I was two. My father's parents raised me."

"Oh, I'm sorry." Sheldon frowned apologetically.

"Thanks. I had a fantastic childhood. Nana and Papa were the best parents—they raised me in a loving home and encouraged me to do anything I dreamed. Nana absolutely marinated me in love and I loved them both so much. Papa retired early and Nana was a homemaker, so we used to come to Sanibel every summer and holiday break—except Christmas. Papa liked to be somewhere that had snow for Christmas."

"Are they still living?"

"No, they've both passed."

"I am so sorry."

I could see the rueful look on his face and wanted to erase it. "Really, it's okay. They lived life to the fullest and are together again in heaven now. I know I'll see them again one day. Tell me about your parents."

"My parents are great. They're older—I was a surprise," he smirked. "My dad is almost sixty— he plays golf and loves to fly fish. Mom has a bridge group that meets weekly. My parents head to Europe for two weeks every summer and make the rounds to see the grandkids up north fairly often, so they stay pretty busy." Sheldon took a drink of his cocktail before continuing. "My dad and I are good friends, he's easy to talk to. Mom is great too, but she can be a little protective and she's still trying to plan my life. I know she means well, but she makes me feel like a child sometimes." He shook his head and smiled, obviously thinking of a recent encounter with her.

"Have you ever been married?" I asked, silently praying that he hadn't.

"No, have you?"

"No. I was engaged once, but realized we were too different, it never would have worked." I lingered for a moment on the thought of Andrew. I thought of how different my life would have been if I had married him, and then I wondered how many mistresses I would have had to compete with. Thank God Nana helped open my eyes about him in time.

"Do you regret the split?"

"Oh no, best decision I have ever made. Nana helped me see that he wasn't a one-woman-man. I can't believe I never saw it, but she did. She just knew things. For a long time I thought she was psychic, but later learned that she was just protective. She hired a private investigator to follow him a few times and snap some photos for me. I would've eventually caught him, but not before we were married. It was humiliating and I was devastated, but thank the Lord we never . . ." *Crap. Just spill everything, Emma. You have never been able to just keep your mouth shut.*

"Never what?" Sheldon lifted my chin to make me look at him and my brain searched for a way to get out of answering his question. "You were never intimate with him?" His eyes explored mine for an answer and my silence was answer enough. A satisfied smile spread across his face and he changed the subject.

"Sounds like your Nana was quite a lady."

"Yes, she is . . . was. She was hilarious too. You would have loved being around her, but she would have sharpened her wits on you and she didn't take crap from anyone. I dated this guy once in college that was so full of himself. His family had just come into some money and they spent it at will. Anyway, Nana commented that she liked his shirt and he said

"France—two hundred dollars." A few days later he repaid the compliment and told her he liked her sweater. My smart-mouthed Nana didn't miss a beat and said, "Kmart—twelve dollars." She was the funniest and sharpest lady . . ." I smiled and drifted off into thoughts of her smile and the way she smelled. She wore the same Halston perfume my entire life and no one else smelled like her. I still have her half-full bottle and hold it to my nose when I'm feeling lonely and missing her.

"So now I know where you got your smart mouth from, and all this time I thought it was because you watched too many episodes of *Gilmore Girls*." He shot me a crooked smile and rolled off the float into the water again.

I looked around for him to pop back up in the water but he didn't appear. I started to sit up on the float to get a better look and see where he had gone when I felt something under my float.

"Agh!" The next thing I knew my float was being flipped over, tossing me into the water. I heard Sheldon's roaring laughter as I came up for air.

"Oh, if I wasn't a lady, what I would say to you!" I giggled.

The water felt so refreshing on my sun-baked skin so I treaded water for a bit instead of climbing back on my float.

"I'm starving, want to grab some lunch?" Sheldon asked, still laughing.

"Yes, please, I'm getting hungry too."

We tossed the floats onto the platform and climbed into the boat. I realized we had had a few cocktails on empty stomachs as I fought to maintain my balance.

"Whoa, you're a lightweight." He flashed me a teasing smile and helped steady me.

After we ate salads topped with leftover chicken and fresh fruit, we drove the boat back to Cayo Costa and spent the rest of the day shelling and snorkeling.

We were the only couple on the beach and it felt like we were stranded on a deserted island. I was sure that being stranded wasn't as luxurious as the movies portrayed it, but so far this was heaven on earth. A fishing boat motored by and I wondered how we would catch fish if we were stranded. I could imagine Sheldon making a spear out of a stick and pen shell while I fastened palm fronds together to cover our shelter. *Of course there wouldn't be any no-see-ums or mosquitoes in my fantasy.* I rolled my eyes at my silly daydream.

Sheldon wrapped his arms around me, "What are you thinking about?"

"Oh, um, I was just enjoying my surroundings and thinking that this must be what heaven is like." *Great, I just lied and mentioned heaven in the same sentence—good grief. But what was I supposed to say? "I was just daydreaming of being stranded on an island with you. You were fishing while I was making our house out of palm fronds." Yup, the little white lie was absolutely necessary.*

"Well I hate to be the one to remove you from heaven, but we need to head back, island girl. I've had the best two days with you, I'm so glad you agreed to this trip." He pressed his warm lips to my forehead and exhaled a slow, deep breath.

I knew I needed to tread carefully with my words so I didn't scare him off, these two days had been the best in my memory and I wanted more. "It has been great, hasn't it? Swimming, floating, shelling, and that boat—it's an amazing boat. I hope I get a chance to thank Bob again, it was really too kind of him to let you rent his boat."

"I didn't rent it. He's an old friend of the family. He was happy to let us use it."

"Oh my. So he knows your family and now he thinks we have spent the weekend together?" I suddenly felt humiliated.

"I'm sure he'll figure out that we didn't sleep together when he sees the pillow and blanket I purposely left out on the couch. Don't worry, your reputation is safe." He smirked and I sighed a breath of relief.

Thirteen

The sun gradually rose over the palm trees, spreading a cheerful display of muted pastels across the sky as I jogged along the deserted bike path early Wednesday morning. My pace was faster than normal as I thought back to the many dates with Sheldon over the last week since our boating adventure. Time spent with him was magical and the nightmares seemed to be diminishing, or was that wishful thinking? As the rhythm of my breathing settled in I thought about what I was going to do for a living. Thoughts of personal training and the possibility of opening a CrossFit box on the island filled my mind and I wondered if there was enough clientele to make it work. I waved as a couple on bicycles passed me going in the opposite direction and it reminded me to look at my watch that tracked my mileage. I had run two and a half miles and decided to turn back. Sheldon had invited me over to enjoy the beach behind his house while he was at work, and I didn't want to be late. When I arrived at his house I took in a deep breath before ringing the doorbell, not sure why I was so nervous. We had been on several dates, but a shiver traveled up my spine each time I saw him.

Sheldon answered the door with a white towel around his waist and still dripping wet. "Hi, beautiful." He kissed me on the cheek and then looked down at his towel, "Sorry, I just got out of the shower, went for a quick run this morning."

"Me too, how far did you go?" I said, taunting him.

"Six miles. How about you?"

"Five." My shoulders slumped in defeat.

"Competitive streak, huh?" He lifted one eyebrow.

"Oh yes." I returned a confident smile.

"I'll have to remember that, I've got a few challenges in mind for you already." He pulled me into him with one arm, holding onto his towel with the other.

"You're on," I challenged. "What's first?"

"Let's see . . . I think we should start with . . ." He lowered his head toward mine and kissed me. As the kiss became more passionate, his lips tugged against mine. Instinctively, I wrapped my arms around his neck and drew him closer. I was lost in his kiss until I realized he had dropped his towel and I suddenly pulled away. Everything in me wanted to look at his naked body, but I turned around quickly to face away from him only to receive his ragging on cue. When he came back out of the bedroom he was dressed in navy slacks and a crisp white shirt that transformed his demeanor from fun surfer to serious businessman—I decided I liked them both.

"Please make yourself at home and enjoy the beach. I'll try to get back around lunch time."

"Thank you. Want me to have lunch ready when you get back?"

"No, enjoy yourself and we'll go out. Besides, I don't have anything in the fridge."

It was a gorgeous day on Captiva. The sky was blue and there were only a few wispy clouds that reminded me of cotton candy. I walked along the beach taking in the surroundings and looking for shells which were scarce on this side of the island. Massive homes lined the beach and I tried to guess what they did for a living. *Bank owner—famous artist—an actor definitely lives in that one.* I made my way back to Sheldon's house and took a seat on the powdery sand, closing my eyes as I reveled in the splendor of the perfect day. I pulled my legs up, wrapping my arms around the knees and gazed out to the mesmerizing sea. It would be good to have some time alone to wrap my mind around how fast this relationship was growing.

As the warm water washed over my feet and receded, tiny pastel-colored coquina shells washed up and I watched as they swiftly dug back down into the sand around and under my feet. It was fascinating to observe, and their quick movements tickled the bottoms of my feet. I wondered how the birds managed to crack the shells open with their beaks to feast on the tiny morsel inside.

I had one arm curled around my legs while the other hand dug in the sand trying to find more coquinas before the water rushed up. I was totally relaxed and in my element when I felt a warm hand gently touch the top of my left shoulder and the words *hello, love* pour softly into my ear.

I had been sitting there on the beach longer than I realized and Sheldon was already home before I had even given one thought to our relationship. *I guess I'll just have to find time to think about it later. Right now all I want to think about is those piercing blue eyes,* I thought to myself as I stood up and wrapped my arms around him. I felt so warm and safe in his arms and I seemed to fit just perfectly in his embrace. I wanted so badly to feel his lips on mine so I stood on my tiptoes and leaned in for a kiss. He pulled me in closer and we lingered there for a moment before pulling away.

"Are you hungry?" Sheldon asked in a low husky voice.

I didn't want to leave his embrace, but knew he must have been starving, so I resigned my dream of spending the rest of the day kissing him. "You must be starved."

The Island Cow was crowded but we were seated inside the airy restaurant after only a short wait.

"Would you like a drink?" Sheldon asked as I took in the sights of the restaurant. It was colorful, casual and splashed with cow décor.

"I need to cut back on the drinking. I definitely felt it during my run this morning."

"Yeah, me too. It just feels like vacation when I'm with you, and I usually indulge a bit on vacation."

My heart leapt in my chest at his words—*I felt like vacation to him.*

After lunch Sheldon took my hand as we walked back to the car. "Do you have room for ice cream?" he asked.

"Always."

We drove down Periwinkle toward the lighthouse. Pinocchio's was on the left. There was a small line which gave me time to view my choices. I chose the Sanibel Crunch and Sheldon chose the Dirty Sand Dollar. The ice cream was served in a waffle cone and topped with an animal cracker.

"Mmm, this is amazing—have a bite," I suggested. Sheldon took a bite of mine and offered me a bite of his.

I knew I wasn't going to make it halfway through the mound of ice cream they had served me, so I offered the rest to Sheldon when he finished his. He took a few bites and tossed the rest before we left.

Sheldon turned the car down Anchor Drive and I looked at him curiously.

"I'm taking you to meet my parents, they should be home."

"What?!" My eyes widened in protest. "Sheldon, I'm not dressed to meet your parents. I look like a beach bum." I begged him to wait until I was more presentable.

"You look great, and you *are* a beach bum." He looked at me teasingly and then took my hand in his. His fingers gave my hand a gentle squeeze of reassurance. "My parents are going to love you. Just be you and how could they not?" He tried to make me feel better, but I was nervous. Meeting his parents was a big deal and I shouldn't be meeting them in a swimsuit and cover-up.

"Ugh." I sighed as he led me out of the car and up the driveway.

"Hey, Dad," Sheldon called out to the man washing his car in the driveway. His dad was a handsome older man with a warm smile that resembled Sheldon's, and the same blue eyes.

"Hi, son." He looked at Sheldon and then at me. I was still apprehensive, but there was something welcoming about his dad that made me relax a bit in his presence.

"Dad, I'd like to introduce you to Emma. Emma, this is my father Bill."

Mr. Barringer wiped his wet hands off on a towel and then held one out to shake mine. He smiled with his whole face and I instantly felt comfortable with him and was grateful for his realness.

"Very nice to meet you, Emma."

"It's a pleasure to meet you also," I smiled and shook his hand, happy that my confidence had returned and allowed me to speak.

"Can I offer you a drink?" The offer was meant for both of us, but his eyes remained on me so I answered first.

"No, I'm okay, thank you."

"So what have you two been doing today?" Mr. Barringer asked.

Sheldon put his arm around my waist and I waited for his dad to give me a look, but he didn't. "We ate lunch at Island Cow, Pinocchio's for ice cream, and now we're going to work it off with a swimming competition." I felt Sheldon give me a playful squeeze into my side but I was too tense to respond.

"Sounds fun. Did you try the Dirty Sand Dollar?" Mr. Barringer waited for my answer.

"I tried a bite of it but ordered the Sanibel Crunch. They were both amazing. They give you a lot of ice cream, I couldn't finish it all."

"So you brought it back to me?" He smiled teasingly and I knew now where Sheldon got it from.

"She tried, Dad, but it all melted on the way here. I hate to make such a beautiful girl clean my car, but it's a sticky mess now—can she borrow your cleaning supplies?"

Mr. Barringer shook his head at his son and then looked at me. "You've got to watch this one, Emma." He winked at me and I blushed. "You should take Emma inside. Your mother is finishing up some laundry."

"You sure you don't want me to leave her here to help you wash the car?" Sheldon laughed.

"Son, you better keep a tight hold on her, you know I'm quite the ladies' man." He grinned at his son before dipping his sponge into the soapy bucket and washing the hood of the car.

I was surprised at how quickly I felt a connection to him. Maybe it was because he reminded me of Sheldon, or maybe because he was so laid-back and kind to me. It didn't feel like a first meeting, I felt comfortable around him.

Sheldon shook his head at his dad as we walked toward the front door. The home was surrounded by lush landscaping that had been well groomed, and I could see a glimpse of the bay lined with boats behind the house.

Mrs. Barringer was in the living room folding laundry entranced by a cooking show when we approached her. She was a lovely lady, petite and well groomed. Short, dark hair laced with gray framed her dark brown eyes and I took a quick moment to remember learning gene dominance in Science. Usually brown eyes were dominant, but Sheldon had his dad's blue eyes. She looked like she was dressed for an outing in pink plaid shorts, a crisp white polo shirt tucked in, and a pink sweater. I was immediately self-conscious when she looked at me.

"Well hello, son." She hugged him and smiled at me. Her smile was warm and inviting as she took me in and studied me with her eyes.

Sheldon must have been able to hear the stuttering pattern of my heart as he reached for my hand and gave my fingers a gentle squeeze. My apprehension subdued slightly, but I still hadn't found the confidence to speak.

"Hi, Mom," he replied sweetly. I could immediately tell the difference between his relationship with his mom and dad. He was much more relaxed with his dad and he treated his mom with a certain delicateness. "Mom, I would like you to meet Emma. Emma, this is my mother Helen Barringer."

"Emma," she paused as if rolling the sound around on her tongue. "It's so nice to meet you. Are you hungry?" She looked at both of us and started walking toward the kitchen before either of us could answer.

"No thanks, we've already eaten."

"How about a drink, then?"

"No, we need to get going. I just wanted to stop in and introduce you to Emma."

Mrs. Barringer stopped and turned around to face us again, "Well, how did you meet? Where are you from, dear? Are you visiting or do you live here?"

The interrogation began and I steeled myself, still trying to find the confidence to speak. Just before I could answer her questions, Mr. Barringer walked in and joined us. He grabbed a beer from the refrigerator and asked why we didn't have drinks.

"They can't stay, dear, I offered. I was just trying to get to know Emma a bit before they take off." She looked at me expectantly and I knew I needed to answer her questions now. I did feel a bit more at ease now that Mr. Barringer was in the room.

"Um, I was born and raised in Tennessee and now I'm here," I answered and hoped she was satisfied.

"Oh, Tennessee is beautiful. We've been through there a few times. So what house did you buy? I saw that the house on Donax just sold, is that you?"

No ma'am, I'm actually a gypsy just going wherever the wind blows me. I have no plans past this summer, no job, no family. I had no intention of falling for your son, I just wanted to come to Sanibel for some peace and healing, but he was persistent and—have you seen this man's eyes? I rambled on in my head before trying to give her an answer that might satisfy her and make me sound less like a wanderer. "No ma'am, actually I'm just renting a place for now, I'm not really sure where I will settle in permanently." This answer was vague enough for her to assume a few possibilities. One, she would think I was a drifter with no ambitions. Two, she would be satisfied that I might not be a permanent fixture in her son's life and would soon be moving on, or three, she thought I was renting the place until I found the home that fit my needs. I hoped she would choose to believe the latter and didn't form a negative opinion about me, and I was thankful we wouldn't find out now as Sheldon stood up and took my hand.

"Well, we need to get going. I just wanted to stop by, see if you guys were home and introduce you to Emma." Sheldon hugged his mom and we all exchanged another round of polite goodbyes.

"Why don't you come by for dinner one night this week?" Mr. Barringer asked. "Mother, what night is good for you?" He searched his wife's face for an answer and I smiled at the thought of him calling his wife *mother*, evidence of years with their kids.

"Oh, any night except Tuesday, that's my bridge night."

"I'll give you a call and we'll plan on a night then," Mr. Barringer said as we all walked down the driveway toward the car.

As we were pulling away, Van Morrison's "Brown-Eyed Girl" was playing loudly in someone's backyard. Sheldon looked over at me and sang a few verses while grinning. "So I was right, my parents liked you."

"I'm not so sure about your mom." I was suddenly shy and disappointed.

"She's a hard one, but she liked you. Believe me, you would know if she didn't like you. She's never been afraid to speak her mind. I brought a girl home from college one time and . . . well, let me just say that my mom made it very clear that the girl wasn't right for me."

"I can see how protective she is of you. That's a good thing, you know. Some little vixen with blond hair in a black cover-up might swoop in and purloin her son." I chuckled.

"I'm not fighting your attempts, babe. Take off with the goods."

I was caught off guard by his mischievous smile and my neck and cheeks instantly flushed.

Fourteen

We never made it to the pool for our competition and I didn't care because I was sure he would beat me. Instead we spent the rest of the day playing and swimming on the beach.

After drying off and coming in for a cold drink of water, Sheldon took a quick shower. I looked around his house and studied the paintings on the wall. My favorite was an oil painting of a brown pelican. I made my way to the stereo cabinet and browsed his music collection. CSNY, the Sundays, Waterboys, Bob Marley, Pearl Jam . . . and then I found Bach. I smiled and slid the disc into the player, quickly finding the volume control to turn it down a bit. The lonely sounds of the bow gliding across strings filled the room and I sat on the couch, closing my eyes to savor each melody. When Sheldon emerged from his bedroom I opened my eyes to look at him. He was freshly showered and dressed, wearing a pair of stone-colored slacks with a black shirt tucked in. I couldn't take my eyes off of him as the black shirt made his eyes look intimidating and intensely hot.

"You found something you like, I see." He grinned.

"Mmm hmm," I agreed and wondered if he was asking about the music or himself.

He smiled confidently and grabbed his keys. "Let's go."

I followed him to the car, wondering where he was taking me, what he would show me next. I suddenly remembered that I was still in my swimsuit and cover-up, greatly underdressed compared to him and started to panic. If he was bold enough to have me meet his parents for the first time in a cover-up, who knew where he would take me next. Sheldon turned the car in the direction of my rental cottage and my heart took a nose dive.

I was surprised that the date was coming to an end so quickly and I couldn't contain the expression of disappointment over the day ending. I looked down at my hands and said in a voice too low, "I had a nice time today." I wondered if he had a change of heart after introducing me to his parents. Had they given him a disapproving sign? He said I would know if his mother didn't like me, but maybe they had a code that I wasn't privy to.

Sheldon squeezed my hand bidding me to look at him and I obeyed. "I'm not ready for it to end, I just thought you might like to shower and change for dinner." He grinned and looked hopeful. "I'd like to feed you after a day in the sun and making you meet my parents."

My heart was suddenly resuscitated and filled with happiness again. "Especially since you introduced me looking like this." I took the hem of my cover-up in my hands. "Are you sure you want me to change for dinner? You seem to enjoy having a sloppy beach bum on your arm."

"You look great to me. Ready to go, then?" He started to put the car in reverse.

Good grief, he plays the game well. I can't pull anything over on him. "Absolutely not! Come on in, I won't take long to get ready."

Sheldon followed me into the cottage and took a seat on the couch. I could hear him flipping through the channels when I turned the shower off. I quickly ran the dryer through my hair and left it slightly damp to dry in soft waves.

"Ready."

"That was fast. You look lovely as usual." I watched his eyes take in the fitted navy dress I chose and my stomach received the familiar jolt that usually took place when his eyes roamed over my body.

We dined at Sweet Melissa's and enjoyed the music of a solo guitarist while sipping wine and waiting for our entrées.

"I thought after dinner maybe you could come back to my place and watch a movie?" Sheldon looked enticingly at me before taking another sip of his wine.

"It will be late, don't you have to work in the morning?"

"It won't be that late, Emma. I can have you home before midnight."

"Well, I'm on island time, so I'm in." I lifted my glass in mock cheer before taking a sip.

"We can stop by and pick up a movie on the way."

I studied him as he watched the guitarist play and wondered why no one had snatched him up yet. He was a gentleman, always opening doors for me, he was gorgeous, had a great job. My only conclusion was that he was a happy bachelor that didn't need or want to settle down. He probably had women falling over themselves to have a one night stand with him and that was enough for him at this stage in his life.

"Penny for your thoughts," he said, interrupting my ponderings.

It'll take more than a penny for my thoughts. Think, Emma! You could tell him you were thinking of which movie to rent . . . No . . . I've got it! "I was wondering if you played an instrument."

"I took piano lessons through high school. I still like to play sometimes now that no one is forcing me to practice. What about you?"

Sheldon on the piano—the thought made my skin tingle. I could imagine him sitting at the piano late at night with nothing but a pair of faded blue jeans on playing something classical—maybe a lonely tune by Philip Glass or Bach. However, I didn't see a piano anywhere at his house and wondered where he played.

"I took piano for a few years, and then switched over to the cello. I never went far with either, just enough to dabble."

"The cello, huh? I have to admit the image going through my mind right now is sexy as hell."

I smiled and met his gaze until the waiter interrupted and set down our plates. Sheldon ordered the beef tenderloin with truffle mashed potatoes and offered me the first bite. "Mmm, that is amazing—so tender and buttery. Here, try a bite of mine." I handed him the large spoon that was served with my bowl of seafood stew.

"Mmm, that's really good too."

"It has shrimp, scallops, clams, mussels, fish and chorizo," I said as I scooped my spoon down for a bite.

"You're such a foodie, Emma." Sheldon smirked. He had almost finished his dinner and I was slowly savoring each bite of mine. I had always loved food cooked properly and creatively. With each bite I tried to single out each ingredient and planned on making the dish at home.

After picking a classic old movie, we drove to Sheldon's house and sat on the couch. I was incredibly uncomfortable in my dress and wished that I had chosen to wear something different.

Sheldon looked over at me while I tried to get adjusted on the couch. "You're not comfortable, I can tell. Would you like a pair of boxers and a T-shirt? I'm sure they will be huge on you, but much more comfortable."

I could not imagine how I would look in his boxers, but I was seriously miserable. "If you don't mind, I would really appreciate it."

Sheldon came back from his bedroom in a T-shirt and pair of long pajama pants to tell me that he had laid the clothes out on his bed for me.

"Do you need help getting out of that dress?" The cocky smile I now knew well spread over his face again.

"Why, do you want to wear it?" I feigned innocence and batted my eyelashes.

"You have a sassy mouth, Miss Peroni." He laughed and I could feel him watch me walk away but

I didn't dare look back. I slipped into his bedroom and shut the door, locking it just in case.

His bedroom was enormous but magnificent. It was very masculine with a large mahogany bed dressed in a tan and black comforter. A fan with palm-shaped wooden blades hung over his bed and was blowing a slight breeze over my shoulders. A leather wingback chair sat in one corner with a side table and lamp. I quickly glanced at the book sitting there to see what he was reading, *Desperation* by Stephen King. The opposite wall was all glass overlooking the ocean and sliding doors led to a separate porch with two cushioned chairs divided by a round table. I could just imagine sitting out there every morning with my cup of hot tea watching the day begin over the sea.

I quickly dressed in the boxer shorts and T-shirt Sheldon had laid out for me and returned to the living room.

"Only you could look hot in those baggy clothes." Sheldon pulled me onto the couch next to him before starting the movie. He had his arm around me and I eventually rested my head on his shoulder. The white T-shirt he had changed into clung to him and smelled like laundry soap and Sheldon—it was fantastic and addicting. I wanted to put my hand on his chest, but had to will myself to behave. I was so comfortable snuggled up next to him and let my thoughts wander instead of watching the movie.

I had known him for such a short time and I already knew my heart was going to be broken when our time together ended. I glanced up at him wondering if he felt the same way. I thought of scenarios that would allow us to stay together and grow our relationship. If I couldn't stay on Sanibel, maybe I could buy a place in Fort Myers and look into buying a small building to start another gym. I snuggled deeper into his arms and concentrated on how good he felt against my body, inhaling his delicious scent. Every part of my body that was touching his tingled and it was all I could focus on until I fell asleep.

I lazily opened my eyes to find that everything was foggy and moving in slow motion. I was being carried off by someone and I didn't know where I was or where they were taking me. Panic quickly took over and I was jolted out of my sleepy state. I struggled to get loose from his arms but he cradled me closer to his body and spoke in a soft, comforting voice that reminded me of my Papa carrying me when I was a child.

"Shh, Emma, I've got you. You fell asleep, I'm just putting you to bed."

I looked up, my eyes coming back into focus and saw that it was Sheldon carrying me. I was confused and groggy and it took a minute for reality to set in. "I fell asleep during the movie?" I asked and then rested my head back on his chest.

"Yes. You must be exhausted—you were out."

"I should head home." I tried to let myself down out of his arms but he didn't loosen his hold.

"No, it's late. You can stay here tonight and I'll take you home in the morning."

"Sheldon, you know I can't—"

He cut me off. "Em, surely you know you can trust me by now. I'm not going to do anything that you don't want me to."

That's the problem . . . I want you to. Just keep your mouth shut, Emma, and sleep on your hands if you have to in order to keep them to yourself.

"Okay." I relented, too tired to argue. I did trust him—I just hoped I could trust myself. I had to remind myself that I was waiting and would have to fight hard to stay strong.

Sheldon carried me toward his bedroom and paused, "Would you rather have the guest room upstairs?"

I shook my head against his chest, hoping that this wasn't going to be as hard for him as it was for me.

He tucked me in on one side of the bed and cracked open one of the sliding glass doors that led out to the porch. The room was filled with the sound of the waves crashing on the sand.

"Oh, that sounds wonderful. You may not ever get me out of your bed." *Did I just say that out loud? That couldn't have sounded any less inviting.* My subconscious shook her head at me disapprovingly.

"My plan has worked, then," Sheldon said before climbing into bed and although it was too dark to see his face clearly, I was sure he was grinning.

We both lay there awkwardly, trying not to touch each other and unable to move. I quickly realized that this was a mistake, *I should have taken the guest room upstairs. Hell, I shouldn't have fallen asleep at all. Now I am going to be the reason for an uncomfortable night's sleep and we will both be exhausted tomorrow.*

"Scoot over here and let me at least hold you," Sheldon suddenly said, opening his arms for me to lay my head on his chest like the night on the boat.

I was frozen and didn't know how to respond or what to do. *What if he makes the moves again? I am in his bed after all, but I really don't want another fight.*

"C'mon, I promise I won't touch you. Even if you beg me, as hard as it would be, I would turn you down." A chuckle made its way up his throat.

I hesitantly slid over to his side of the bed and he pulled me in close. I had my head on his chest in the dip above his pectoral muscle that I believed was made just for me. My head fit perfectly and my whole body was alive just laying there against him. Each nerve ending felt like a livewire where it was touching his skin. I wasn't sure what to do with my left arm and it was left hovering in the air until I decided where to put it.

"Here." Sheldon took my arm and placed it over his chest. My breath hitched and I knew it was audible. I was sure I wouldn't sleep a wink.

Fifteen

Muted light filled the room as I woke up feeling too warm. I remembered that I was in Sheldon's room and lay there listening to the waves as I watched him sleep. I propped up on one elbow so I could see the view of the ocean. Sheldon stirred and I tried to remain still so I didn't wake him.

"Good morning, beautiful," he whispered. "Did you sleep well?"

"Good morning to you, and yes I did. The sound of the ocean lulled me to sleep. I can't tell you how envious I am that you get to listen to that every night."

Sheldon pulled me in to him and kissed the top of my head. "I would invite you to stay here every night, but it drove me wild not to touch you last night."

I inhaled sharply at his last statement and wondered what he would think if I told him it had been hard for me too.

"Are you hungry?" Sheldon pulled back the covers to get out of bed and then stretched his arms over his head.

"Can we eat out there?" I pointed to the two chairs on the porch facing the sea.

"Sure, I just stocked the fridge. I have cereal, fruit, eggs . . ."

"I'll fix some eggs. Do you have bacon?"

"Of course, I *am* a man," he smiled.

I cooked bacon and eggs on the stove of my dreams and I am sure pure joy was radiating over my face. Sheldon poured orange juice and cut up some pineapple, grapefruit, and melon. We took our plates to the porch off of the bedroom and watched the day begin just as I had envisioned in my daydream.

"I wish you had brought your swimsuit over, we could go for a swim."

"Yeah, that would have been nice."

Sheldon impulsively scooped me up out of my chair and threw me over his shoulder. "What are you doing? Put me down!" I shouted through giggles and demanded him to put me down. I was dangling off the back of him, bouncing as he took long quick steps. I found the courage to smack him on the butt, but he didn't flinch, he just kept walking around to the side of the house, cackling loudly. My eyes widened at the site of the swimming pool and I realized he was going to throw me in.

"Sheldon, don't you dare!" I shrieked as we both went into the pool with a splash.

I was still in his boxer shorts and T-shirt and I could barely keep them on my body in the water.

"You big jerk!" I teased and splashed him with one hand as I held onto the shorts with the other. "These clothes are too big and I'm having trouble keeping them on." I held my shirt down as it tried to float up to my shoulders. I swam to the side of the pool and pulled the boxers back up to my waist, cinching them with the hem of the shirt so they would stay on.

"That's not something I'm worried about," he beamed. "Take them off. Your bra and panties probably cover more than your bikinis do." He laughed and looked at me with daring eyes.

He was right, my bikinis were probably skimpier than my underclothes, but it just seemed too intimate. However I had never been the kind to fear adventure or pass up a dare, so I looked him dead in the eyes as I stripped off the shirt and shorts and pulled them out of the water, tossing them onto the concrete floor that surrounded the pool. I was rewarded with a stunned look that quickly turned molten and watched his body tense in reaction.

Without skipping a beat I dove under the water and swam to the edge of the pool next to him. "Ready for that race?" I enticed. "Ready . . . set . . . go!" I swam the length of the pool as fast as I could and found myself alone in my win. Sheldon hadn't moved and his eyes were still on me. "You are a cheater," he whispered.

"What? I didn't cheat." I couldn't control the laughter that suddenly erupted from me. He cheated the other day by dropping his towel, and I had just played his game and beat him at it.

"You knew exactly what you were doing. I never thought you would actually take the clothes off. What happened to Miss Modesty?" He folded his arms in front of his chest feigning disappointment. "You think you can do something like that to me and then expect me to be able to swim?" His cheeks were flushed and his eyes had changed to a deeper blue. I suddenly felt horrible for doing that to him, but at the same time my inner goddess was cheering.

"Sorry. Let me know when you are ready and we'll race again on your go." I couldn't stop the mischievous smile from crossing my face.

"Come back over here. I am so ready to kick your butt now."

I knew he was going to beat me, but I was prepared to give it all I had and readied myself.

Sheldon called out, "Ready . . . set . . . go!" and we both swam as hard and fast as we could to the end of the pool. He had beaten me by at least one body length.

I laughed breathlessly, "Tie! Wanna go again?"

"Tie? You call that a tie?" He grabbed me and pulled me into him, kissing me hard on the lips. We were in the deep end and I was glad he was holding onto me as my body had turned to putty.

When we finally pulled away, he looked at me with evocative eyes and seemed to exhale each word, "What are you doing to me?"

My breath caught at his words and the way he said them with such surrender. I could feel the heat that already coursed through my body rise and send chills all the way down to my toes. I tried to think of a quick-witted retort in my reflection as I stared into his eyes but it didn't offer any help at all and I came up short.

"I have to go into work before they wonder what has happened to me."

I climbed out of the pool, suddenly aware that I was in my bra and panties and felt exposed. Sheldon wrapped a towel around me and then got one for himself.

"You know your white bra and panties are transparent when wet." A mischievous grin spread across his face and I was sure he was finding it entertaining to watch my face turn scarlet. "Do you have plans for the weekend?"

"Um, let's see . . ." I looked up pretending to go over my schedule in my head. "Nope, no plans."

"Good, plan on spending it with me."

"Okay." I smiled, wondering what the weekend would hold.

"So what beach are you going to go to today?" he asked and I could see that his mood had dropped too at the thought of going into work instead of the beach.

"I don't think I will go to the beach today. I thought I would check out the outlet stores in Fort Myers . . ." My voice trailed off as I didn't really have a plan.

"Take my car when you go off island. You have to pay six dollars to get back on the island. I have the barcode on my window so you don't have to pay."

"No, I can't take your car. It's only six dollars. Thanks anyway though."

He tried to insist but I didn't back down. He had been so giving this past week and I was starting to feel uncomfortable not giving much back in return. I had always been independent and paid my own way, but Sheldon wouldn't hear of me paying for anything when we were together.

After getting my navy dress back on I cleaned our breakfast dishes while he showered and got ready for work. He drove me back to my place and walked me to the door.

"Thank you for . . . well, thank you for everything. I had a really nice time with you." I sounded way too formal as I struggled for the right words. What I really wanted to tell him was *I think I am falling in love with you. Yeah, I know we have only known each other for a few weeks, but it's true and I need to know exactly how you feel about me so I know whether or not to let this go any further.* But I didn't have the courage so I dug in my purse for the door key.

"Me too." Sheldon held both of my hands in his and looked into my eyes. "Um, would you . . . Can I— I'll just call or text you later, okay?" he stuttered.

"Okay. Talk to you later. Have a good day today." I shut the door, leaning against it after it shut and let the thoughts run rampant through my head. *What that was all about? I knew I shouldn't have spent the night. Maybe he is used to sleeping with women and feels rejected by me. But he was so fun in the pool this morning and we seemed to have gotten along great. The kiss we shared earlier gave me the impression that he really liked me. So why was it so awkward just then at the door?* I went over to my favorite paisley chair and slumped down into it as my thoughts rambled on.

***

Sheldon walked through the door of the company that he had put his heart and soul into and was greeted by a few stares.

"Hey dude, where have you been?" Charlie slapped him on the back of the shoulder as they walked toward Sheldon's office.

"I've been around—bringing work home a lot lately."

"So tell me more about this hottie you met on the beach—what does she look like?"

"She's beautiful. Long blond hair, big brown eyes, and the tightest, curviest body . . ." Sheldon stopped short and fell silent.

"Shit, why did *you* have to be on the beach that day? Should've been me."

Charlie's statement rubbed Sheldon the wrong way and he was surprised by how irritated he had become. He glared at his friend and accepted a handful of paperwork from Hannah, nodding a thank-you as she stood there like she had something else to say.

"Is there anything else, Hannah?"

"No, sir, that's all."

Charlie paused long enough for Hannah to walk away. "Have you seen her again?"

"Yes, I've been seeing a lot of her."

"Is she good in the sack? Details, man."

"She's more than a body, Charlie," Sheldon snapped.

"Whoa, who are you and what have you done with my friend?"

Sheldon lowered his eyes and gave Charlie a look that implied he should choose his words carefully from this point on.

"Sorry, dude. You okay, man?" Charlie put a hand on Sheldon's forehead pretending to check for a fever.

"Back off, Charlie," Sheldon warned, not sure why he was so offended by him all of a sudden. They had always shared details about the girls they hooked up with, but this was different and he didn't want to participate in Charlie's ribbing today.

"Seriously, dude." Charlie walked with Sheldon into his office and shut the door. "Talk to me, buddy, do you have feelings for this girl or something?"

Sheldon calmed down at the serious tone in Charlie's voice. They had been friends forever and he knew he could trust him when the joking was set aside. "Her name is Emma, and I don't know, man, I find myself thinking about her all the time. She's smart, gorgeous, and hilarious—she has me in stitches all the time. We always have a great time together, you wouldn't believe what she did this morning." Sheldon grimaced realizing he should have left that last part out.

"This morning? So you have slept with her. I knew it. Be careful, dude, you know how women are, if she's sleeping in your bed, she's looking for a relationship."

"It's not like that. Yes, she slept over, but nothing has happened between us."

"I don't understand. She slept in your bed, but nothing happened? Who are you?" Charlie looked concerned.

"I know, right? Believe me, I barely slept last night—all I could think about was how badly I wanted her, but I respect her and don't want to push her."

"Crap, you've got it bad, my friend. I've never seen this side of you. You're not going to quit windsurfing again, are you?" Charlie asked.

"No. She's nothing like Victoria—she's very athletic and loves the fact that I'm passionate about windsurfing. Victoria . . . can you even imagine what my life would have been like married to that woman?" Sheldon simulated a shiver and shook his head.

"So when can I meet this girl Emma? I seem to have great instincts about your women, maybe I can use my Spidey senses on her for you."

"Spidey senses, huh?" Sheldon laughed. "I'm glad to know my best friend hasn't reached adulthood yet." Sheldon punched him lightly on the arm. "Why don't we have dinner Friday night? Surely you can find a date in your arsenal," Sheldon teased and braced himself for a return punch.

"Sounds good. I'll ask Annie and let you know." Charlie started for the door. He shook his head as he walked out of Sheldon's office. "My best friend is in love. Another one bites the dust."

Sixteen

I found myself in a daze as I stood in the shower and let the hot water wash over my body, hoping last night's nightmare would slip down the drain with the water. I had an ominous feeling that my heart would soon be broken and I couldn't seem to find the energy to get a good lather as I shampooed my hair. His words *I'll call or text you later* played over and over in my head. I usually looked forward to the weekend—the island was full of life and good music, but as reality set in that a weekend with Sheldon wasn't promising, I became disenchanted. Somehow being on Sanibel this weekend wasn't as appealing as it usually was. *I'll go away for the weekend—maybe Orlando, or the Keys?* I hated the thought of leaving the island, but I couldn't stay here in misery, trying to avoid running into Sheldon if things didn't work out between us.

The water suddenly turned cold before I got the conditioner rinsed out of my hair so I stuck my head in trying to quickly rinse it out, arching my back to avoid the cold water. I wrapped my hair in a towel, put on a robe, and made some tea to warm myself up from the chill of the water. After a few sips of tea, I dialed Julie.

"Hi, Jules, it's me. Got a minute?"

"Hi, Em. Yeah, I was just eating lunch. What's up? Are you okay?"

"I'm great. I just wanted to talk. I miss having you to talk to daily." I frowned.

"Me too. Hey, I looked at my calendar and I think I can come up next week. Jake has agreed to watch the place and post the workouts."

"That's awesome! I can't wait. We can hang out on the beach and sip cocktails by the pool." I was excited and couldn't wait for some girl time. She and I could enjoy one great week on Sanibel before I possibly had to leave my beloved island and the man I had let too close to my heart.

"I can't wait either! So how are things going with your stud muffin?" Julie giggled.

"I'm not sure," I sighed. We've spent a lot of time together and have had the best time. He is so fun to be around, Jules. I think I'm really falling for him, but

I'm not sure he feels the same way. I thought he did until this morning—I might have made a mistake, Jules."

"What did you do? Please tell me you didn't sleep with him, you barely know him."

"No, well, not like that anyway. I fell asleep on the couch and ended up sleeping over . . . in his bed. But I was fully clothed and nothing happened."

"So what's the problem? Are you concerned that he doesn't like you because nothing happened? Did he at least try to make something happen?"

"Oh, he would have been all about it if I had given the least little sign, but he was a gentleman and respected my wishes." The image of us in bed together sent a surge of electricity through my veins. "After breakfast we went for a swim. I had slept in his boxers and T-shirt which were way too big and didn't want to stay on my body in the pool. I decided to strip them off and swim in my underclothes. I mean, it's the same as a bikini, right?"

"Well, except it is your bra and panties—a little more intimate. So what happened? What did he do?" Julie encouraged me to continue.

"I had his full attention after that and felt like a tease—I shouldn't have done it. We shared a kiss that led me to believe he was into me, but then when he took me home he didn't say much. He said he would call or text me later. Sounds like he's blowing me off, huh?"

"I don't know, Em, I guess you'll just have to wait and see if he calls. I can't imagine he would just snap out of it that quickly when you two have shared so much, what about your time on the boat? I think he's into you and maybe he just doesn't know how to take you yet. Don't jump to conclusions, just wait and see what happens. Call me as soon as you hear from him, alright?"

"I will. I think I'm going to go shopping to get my mind off of it. I wish you were here already!"

"Me too. Soon though, I'm counting the days. Bye, Em."

"Bye, Jules." I hung up and got dressed quickly, I needed to get off island and into some shops before I had time to think too much.

The outlet shops helped the time pass quickly and I grabbed a light lunch before driving back over the Causeway. I decided to drive to Bailey's to pick up a movie and some ice cream to spend the evening with. I found a cheesy romantic comedy and pulled out a pint of vanilla bean ice cream from the freezer section before checking out and heading home.

My cell phone rang and I could see Sheldon's name appear on the caller ID. My heart sank in my chest and I decided to let it go to voicemail while I was driving.

I took a deep breath and braced myself for the inevitable. I had felt that something was wrong and had tried to prepare myself for this phone call but it didn't lessen the heartache that was threatening in my chest. I shut the engine off and pressed the button on my phone to listen to his voicemail, tears prematurely welling up in my eyes.

"Hey, it's me. Are you free for dinner Friday? Call me."

My spirits were suddenly lifted as I heard the excitement in his voice. If he was going to end things he would have done it over the phone, not dinner. Besides, the sound of his voice didn't imply that he didn't want to see me again. I walked into the cottage to call him back, forgetting the ice cream in the hot car. I had half of his number dialed when I realized I had left the ice cream and sprinted back to get it and put it in the freezer. I tossed the movie onto the coffee table and dialed his number.

He answered on the second ring. "Hi, beautiful." His mood had changed since I saw him this morning and I felt like I was on a rollercoaster ride.

"How's your day going?" I asked, trying to be casual.

"Very busy, I enjoyed some waves early this morning on the board and now I'm paying for it with a stack of papers to catch up on—but it does make the time pass faster. So how about dinner Friday night? It will be a double date."

"Double date? Who with?" I asked, not sure I was ready for dinner with his parents as I had suddenly lost my confidence.

"A good buddy of mine and his girlfriend."

"Sounds like fun."

"Good. I'll pick you up at six o'clock tomorrow night. We'll eat first so we can catch the sunset."

***

I quickly ran an iron over the new pale yellow sundress I picked up at the Ann Taylor outlet and slipped it on. The color enhanced my new tan making me look more bronzed than I probably was. I had a few minutes to spare, so I typed a text to Julie:

Dinner with the stud muffin—all is good :)

Sheldon showed up with flowers again, this time a smaller bouquet of celery green hydrangeas laced with a few white roses and gardenias.

"These are just beautiful, thank you." I held them to my nose and took in the sweet smell of the roses and gardenias. I was at a loss wondering what all of this meant, just this morning I had gotten the feeling that he was blowing me off.

"I'll put them in water for you while you pack a bag—and don't forget a swimsuit." He grinned as we both recalled my daring escapade that morning.

I looked at him curiously and handed him the flowers. "Why do I need to pack a bag?"

"You agreed to spend the weekend with me. It's Friday night, and I plan on keeping you hostage until Monday morning, so pack accordingly." The infamous cocky smile spread across his face and I knew I was in trouble.

My heart began to race as I contemplated my conundrum. *I can't spend the weekend with him. I barely slept a wink the last time, worrying that something would happen. Pull yourself together, Emma, you are a strong-willed, intelligent woman. You can do this—just insist on taking one of the guest rooms. If he doesn't like that idea, he can drive you home.* "I better warn you, I don't make a great hostage. I can get out of any restraint and I have seen way too many James Bond films," I smirked.

"Hmm," he said in a low husky voice. "You are putting some pretty steamy images in my head." His eyes were so intense they sent heat to my cheeks immediately. I drew in a quick breath as he leaned in to kiss me softly but with such passion that I could feel his body melting with mine. When he pulled away I was left breathless, dizzy, and without a chance for arguing my side, so I slipped off into my room and packed a few things in a bag, wondering why I had wasted so much of my day worrying that he was going to end things.

"Okay, I'm ready." I feigned concern as I looked up at him.

"I get the feeling I won't have to restrain you after all," he taunted. "This might be easier than I thought."

"Let the games begin." I grinned and held up my arm as I snapped my finger, finding my own cockiness again and turned to walk out to the car.

"I'll lock the door for you." Sheldon chuckled to himself and shook his head. "Don't get too cocky, little lady. You've got quite a match on your hands." He smiled and didn't take his eyes off of me as he fastened his seat belt.

***

Charlie and Annie were waiting outside of Charlie's condo when we pulled up. Charlie was cute in that typical surfer way. His hair was blond and had a mind of its own. Annie Graham was adorable with her chocolate brown hair falling in soft curls just past her shoulders. She was shorter than me, maybe 5′2″, and she smiled with her whole face. I instantly knew I would like her. She was wearing a pale blue dress with spaghetti straps. Charlie had his hand on her low back and helped her climb into the backseat.

I unbuckled my seat belt so I could turn around to face her. "Hi, I'm Emma." I smiled and noticed her navy blue eyes.

"Nice to meet you, I'm Annie." She smiled warmly and her dimples sank deep into her cheeks.

Sheldon waited for Charlie to slide in, ". . . and this is Charlie Cooper."

"Hi, Emma, nice to meet you." Charlie had crystal blue eyes and a great smile too, but he seemed to be studying me and I felt uneasy.

The Mucky Duck was already crowded with people outside listening to the live music by the bar. Sheldon put his name on the waiting list and we found a table outside. Sheldon and Charlie excused themselves to order drinks while Annie and I sat facing the ocean and chatted.

"So Emma, what did you do today?" Her voice was sweet and soft.

"I went to the Tanger Outlets. I didn't plan on spending so much of the day there, but time passed so quickly."

"Oh, I can totally relate. I love the swimsuit shop there. . . I can't remember the name of it." She looked up and to the right trying to find the answer.

"Swim Mart?"

"Yes, that's it. They have a huge selection."

"What about you? Do you work on the island?"

"No, I work in Fort Myers at Lee Memorial."

"What do you do?"

"I'm an R.N. I was off today. If we had met earlier I would have joined you shopping."

"I would have loved that. We'll have to exchange numbers and go soon." I would love to have a girlfriend to hang out with on occasion.

The guys returned with small plastic cups filled with crisp white wine and handed them to us. Before the guys could sit down the host called over the intercom, letting us know our table was available.

We were seated by the window overlooking the crowd outside and a picturesque view of the Gulf. The restaurant was filled with wooden tables, and the dark wood walls were adorned with funny signs and buttons from all over the world. There was a steady hum throughout the restaurant of families and friends enjoying the food and atmosphere. We ordered another round of drinks and looked over the menu as we talked.

Charlie asked me questions about my hometown and job before I came to the island. Feeling like I was in the hot seat being questioned by a prosecuting attorney, I did my best to keep my voice level and look him in the eye. He was beginning to irk me and I wondered what on earth Annie saw in him. To avoid any more questions, I scooted my chair back. "Excuse me, I'm going to find the ladies room." Annie didn't try to follow me, so I was confident I had maintained unflustered facial expressions. I needed a moment alone to take a deep breath and regroup.

Sheldon stood when I returned to the table. I took my seat and waited for the uncomfortable looks of concern, but they didn't come. Instead, Sheldon retold a story about Charlie showing off his windsurfing skills for Annie and crashing. "He ran right up onto the sandbar . . . threw him off his board . . ." His sentences were choppy as we all laughed at the hilarity. "You should have seen him, Emma. I swear it all happened in slow motion once he was in the air. First, he's grinning like the Cheshire cat, and then—"

All four of us erupted in laughter that would have been too loud for any other restaurant.

Charlie was the first to break up the guffawing. "Alright, sure, it was hilarious. Should've gotten it on video." He put his arm around Sheldon and looked straight at me. "What do you think of my friend, Emma?" I didn't know who had the greater look of shock, me or Sheldon.

The waiter interrupted the awkward moment just in time and asked for our order. I chose Snapper Almandine, Sheldon ordered roasted duck with orange sauce, Charlie decided on the bacon-wrapped barbeque shrimp, and Annie was torn between the seafood platter and snapper.

"Get the seafood platter, babe, I'll help you eat it." Charlie squeezed her knee and I saw a sweeter side to him which made me rethink judging him so quickly.

We all ate our entrées while getting to know each other and laughed out loud at some of the stories Sheldon and Charlie shared about their youth together. Between the wine and the company I was totally relaxed and felt like I had known these people for years.

Charlie's shoulders shook with laughter as he recounted a past memory with Sheldon. "Remember the time we rode our bikes across the Causeway trying to hold a surfboard between us?"

"God, that was so dangerous. I didn't think my mom would ever let me out of the house again after that. How long were we grounded?"

"I don't know, but as soon as we were released we were off getting into more trouble. Remember the time we boarded that boat pretending like we were driving it? The dude that caught us was mean."

I watched and listened to them reminisce about their past, laughing and enjoying themselves. Annie nudged me with her elbow and rolled her eyes causing us both to laugh. The sound of our laughter brought the guys back to reality again.

"Sorry, ladies, got carried away." Sheldon apologized and tried to stop laughing.

"No apologies necessary—I enjoyed hearing about your escapades. The bad boy is still in there though, you haven't grown up yet, have you?" I smiled playfully and he shot me a youthful but captivating smile.

After dinner we passed on dessert and walked outside. The sun hadn't started to set yet so Sheldon and Charlie went over to the bar to get us another glass of wine and refill their beer. We sipped on our drinks while listening to the musician play the steel pans and sing songs by request. Sheldon asked me to dance as the musician began another slow song and I realized it was "Can't Help Falling in Love with You" by Elvis. Sheldon didn't miss a beat as he led me around, never letting his eyes lose contact with mine. Time stood still and it seemed as if we were the only two people on the sand. The music played in the distance, and I thought to myself how appropriate these lyrics were for me right now. "Wise men say, only fools rush in, but I can't help falling in love with you . . ." *Yeah, I know I'm rushing in, but I don't think I can help falling in love with this gorgeous man with the most startling blue eyes. I am completely under his spell and I don't want it to ever be lifted.* I felt tears sting my eyes and I looked away pretending to pick out an eyelash.

"Are you okay?"

"Oh yeah, just an eyelash." I lied, but I could tell by the way he was looking at me that he wasn't buying it. He pulled me in close and stroked my hair, not pressing the subject any further.

Charlie and Annie were wrapped in each other's arms dancing too, sneaking kisses every now and then. She looked so happy with him and I hoped he was a stand-up guy. I gathered myself together and looked back up at Sheldon, "Is Charlie a good guy?"

"Yeah, he is." Sheldon looked over at them and smiled. "We've been friends for years—windsurfing all over the country together."

"How long have they been together?"

"They've been off and on for a couple of years now. Charlie likes to think he is a player, but I have no doubt that they will end up together. He's not ready to settle down yet, but when he does it will be her. I just hope she waits for him."

The two of them walked over to us as if on cue. "The sun is setting, let's head down to the beach."

We witnessed an amazing sunset. The sky was boldly streaked with shades of reds, oranges, and purples that seemed to intensify as the sun sank lower and lower, finally mellowing out into a shade of orange that resembled sherbet. The beach was crowded with people watching the brilliant show and we all clapped in unison when it took its final bow into the sea.

"Breathtaking," I whispered.

"Yes, I agree." Sheldon was looking at me, and I warmed instantly.

Charlie and Annie came back to Sheldon's house after picking up his car and we all hung out on the screened porch. Sheldon turned the stereo on and the lyrics to "Higher" by Creed flowed out of the speakers.

Annie and I were deep in conversation when Charlie walked over holding a bottle of wine.

"More wine?"

"Just half a glass, please." We both held out our glasses as he poured.

"I'd love to know what you two are talking about."

"Oh, Charlie, just girl talk. Go on and leave us alone." Annie smiled up at him and smacked him lightly on the leg. Her love for him was so transparent that I had to look away, feeling that I was intruding on their intimacy.

"Okay, blue eyes. I'll leave you to it, then." He winked at her making her dimples appear again.

"How did you two meet?" I asked as I took a sip of the cold dry wine.

"At a bar, I'm ashamed to admit. I was with some girls having a drink after work and I succumbed to his charms." She giggled. "He really is a sweet guy once you get past that exterior. He wants everyone to believe he's tough as nails. He is all man, don't get me wrong, but he's kind and caring and gentle too."

Annie was sweet but didn't lack confidence. She was probably one of those girls who knew she was beautiful but didn't let it go to her head. I wondered what she liked to do for fun, if she had a group of girls from work that she hung out with or friends that she had grown up with.

"Did you grow up here?" I asked.

"No, I moved here after college. I am from Texas originally, but went to the University of Florida to be with my boyfriend . . . who broke up with me after our sophomore year."

I grimaced and then gave her a look of apology for her misfortune. *But you did end up here and are now living the life that I have always dreamed of, so I don't feel too sorry for you.*

"So, how about you and Sheldon? Charlie tells me that he's crazy about you . . ." Annie fell short and blushed. "Oh I shouldn't have said that. Too much wine and I run my mouth without a filter."

My stomach was filled with butterflies and it felt like my heart had stopped for a moment at her words. I wanted to hear more but could tell she was uncomfortable and embarrassed that she let that information slip out.

"Let me try again." She paused to think of a way to change the subject but failed at her attempt.

I tried to help her out, not comfortable seeing her squirm. "Do you know Sheldon very well?"

"Yeah, he and Charlie are best friends. I watch them windsurf sometimes and have gotten to know

Sheldon pretty well." She seemed to read my mind that was full of questions and uncertainty. "He's a good guy, Emma. Hot as hell and I'm sure he knows it, but he's not a player if that's what you are asking."

"Thanks. I haven't known him very long, but I really like him." I was suddenly shy and looked down at my feet.

"And now because of my big mouth, you know that he feels the same about you."

Seventeen

I watched Sheldon step out of the house onto the screened-in porch, carrying a couple of beers. He sauntered over and kissed me on the forehead before taking a beer to Charlie.

Charlie got up from his seat and opened the door leading out toward the beach. "Let's take a walk."

Sheldon nodded letting me know they would be back soon and I smiled in approval. Trying to pay attention to Annie, I couldn't help wonder what the guys wanted to talk about in private. I nodded my head randomly, hoping to deflect my lack of attention to our conversation.

". . . and then I picked up the snake and laid it right on the operating table." Annie's voice raised an octave, causing me to pay attention.

"Uh huh, that's incredible. Then what?"

"Emma, you didn't hear a word I said."

"Sure I did." I lowered my head in shame.

"So you really believe that I put a snake on the operating table?"

I shrugged my shoulders and chuckled at the thought. "Sorry, I was distracted. I can't help wondering why Charlie needed to take Sheldon away to talk to him. I don't think he likes me."

"I'm sure you're wrong, Emma. Neither of us have seen Sheldon happier. They're probably just talking smack and didn't want us to see their juvenile side." She laughed, and my breathing resumed at a less chaotic rate.

When the guys returned, the tension that had built up in my shoulders began to dissipate. Charlie wore a wide grin upon entering the gate, and to my surprise it didn't leave when his eyes landed on me. If my assumption had been correct and he was warning Sheldon, he surely wouldn't have been able to look me in the eyes. Sheldon seemed unaffected by their talk, except maybe a little more intoxicated.

***

Charlie came back over and kissed Annie on the top of her head. "Time to go, babe, it's late," he said and then looked at me. "Emma, I enjoyed hanging out with you. You've got my man on his toes—keep it up, it's fun to watch him squirm." He laughed and gave my shoulders a friendly squeeze.

After they decided to leave, I was suddenly nervous being alone with Sheldon, knowing that I had agreed to spend the entire weekend with him. We walked them to the door and waved goodbye. "That was a lot of fun—we should do it again sometime."

"I'm glad you liked them. You and Annie seemed to hit it off."

"Yeah, she's really sweet. We made plans to go shopping next week." I tried to keep up the small talk to avoid looking into his eyes.

"Are you tired?"

"Not really." I was so wide awake and terrified to get in his bed again. I felt strongly about not being intimate with him, but my body desperately wanted to betray me. My muscles tensed at the thought and I looked away from his gaze.

"C'mon, let's take a walk on the beach then." He took my hand and led me through the screened porch onto the beach.

We walked along the beach that was illuminated by the full moon reflecting off the ocean. "It's amazing how much the moon lights up the beach," I avowed, looking out to sea. We stopped and looked out toward the water for a while. The waves rolled in loudly and made the sea seem mysterious and frightening. Sheldon turned back around to face me.

"Emma, I . . ." He fell silent and I waited as he probed his mind for the right words.

I watched him as he looked away from me and back out to sea. The air was starting to cool off now that the sun had abandoned us from its warmth and I suddenly wished I had a light jacket. I waited patiently for him to find his thoughts while swirling the sand with my toes and drifted off into my own thoughts, wondering what he was trying to say. *Maybe I should break the ice and just tell him how I feel. I wish we didn't have to play these games and we could just be honest with our feelings, but I suppose we are both afraid of getting hurt.* I exhaled, suddenly aware that I had been holding my breath and it caused Sheldon to look back at me.

He took both of my hands in his and faced me, searching my eyes for something. We stood there for a moment before he spoke again. "I don't want you to be nervous."

I tried to intervene, "I'm not—" but he closed his eyes and shook his head, requesting that I let him finish. "Back at the house, your body language screamed apprehension. I get that you're not ready, and I want you to know that I'm okay with that." He sighed and I could tell he wasn't *really* okay with it. "I just want to hold you in my arms tonight, nothing more." Sheldon smirked and rolled his eyes. "That's not true. I want you more than I've ever wanted anyone and I don't understand why you don't feel the same."

"I—" I started to speak but he cut me off.

"Let me finish. I don't understand, but I'll respect your wishes. You don't have to be concerned about my motives this weekend, we'll just have a good time. I promise, when we do make love, I'll have your full, unwavering consent."

I was overcome by his words and stood on the sides of my feet, watching the sand give way underneath them. I took a moment to collect myself and find my voice before looking back into the eyes that had a way of disarming me.

"I do want you, Sheldon—"

"Well then, what's the problem? Are you worried about protection? I have plenty."

I bit my lower lip in frustration and sucked in a deep breath. I needed to get this out before I lost my nerve. "Let me finish. I've never wanted anything so much, and that's what makes me so nervous. I don't trust myself in your arms, but I feel very strongly about waiting. I don't want to put myself in a position that I can't get out of without one or both of us getting hurt."

Sheldon looked at me intently, his lips forming a thin line. "I'll never hurt you. Don't you know that by now?"

"I do. I know you wouldn't purposely hurt me. I just . . ." Suddenly I felt like a child and had to look down at my hands before continuing. "I'm saving that for my husband." My cheeks were on fire and I didn't know why I suddenly felt ashamed of my choices.

"What do you mean?" he whispered.

I was floored by his question. *Are you kidding me right now? What do I mean? What else would I be saving for my husband—seashells? How can I explain it more clearly to you?* I was shouting to myself and becoming frustrated. I suddenly felt drained of all confidence but tried again. "I was raised by a very old-fashioned grandmother who taught me . . ." I sighed and fell silent, not able to find the courage to finish my sentence.

Sheldon gave my fingers a light squeeze and smirked. "Emma, I knew what you meant, I just—"

I stood there awkwardly for what seemed like an eternity, feeling his intense gaze burning into the top of my head and all I could focus on was my hands in his. They suddenly felt too heavy and weird. I was chilled from the cool night air, but my hands felt sweaty and hot, and oh—so—heavy.

Sheldon didn't speak for a long time—he just stood there holding my hands while I stared at the odd appendages at the end of my arms. I finally found my confidence and glanced up at him. He was staring at me with his lips slightly parted, breathing in and out but not saying a word. I silently begged him to speak, not caring what he said at this point, just wanting him to utter something.

"I'm sorry—I don't know what to say. I've never. . . I had no idea. How has someone that looks like you do go this long . . . I don't mean to sound crude . . . I just . . ." He was rambling on and on and I tried to listen, but his stuttering and lack of complete sentences had me lost and confused. I began to focus on the voice of my subconscious telling me that things were not going well and I instantly braced myself for the impending heartbreak. *Of course he doesn't want me anymore, I'm an inexperienced prude.* In order to protect my heart I debated on whether or not to just dive in and let go of this foolish desire to wait. None of my friends had waited. I thought of Julie and Jake's happiness together, Charlie and Annie were most likely intimate . . . *just do it, you don't want to lose him, do you?* I argued with myself, *No, but I also know that I won't be satisfied with a summer fling.*

I scarcely heard Sheldon taper off in his ramblings and felt myself unexpectedly being swept up in his arms. I hung onto him with both arms, squeezing tighter when he started swinging me around in circles. I was dizzy and confused at his reaction and tried to search his face for answers, realizing I should have been listening to him.

"So you have never been with a man?" He set me down and waited for my answer.

"No."

"How have you kept greedy hands off of this amazing body?" Sheldon put his hands on my waist. I raised my shoulders in response and thought to myself, *if you only knew . . .*

"God, you blow me away, Emma." He kissed me hard and quick on the lips. As we walked hand in hand back to the house, I stole glances of him while trying to figure out what had just happened. He smiled when he looked at me and squeezed my hand every now and then which told me things were going to be okay after all.

We paused at the back door as he faced me to speak. "You can trust me, Emma." He held one hand up as if he was swearing to tell the truth in a court of law. "It is now my rightful duty to protect your virtue."

I should have been grateful, but instead I feared that he would treat me like I had the plague and not want to risk touching or kissing me again. The words came out of my mouth before I was aware of it and I was immediately filled with regret for not thinking before speaking, "Great, you're not ever going to touch me again, are you?"

Instead of answering me, he pulled me close and kissed me until I was left woozy and spinning out of control with desire for more.

We lay in his bed holding each other, listening to the waves roll in and crash onto the sand. I was drifting off to sleep, my body fully relaxed and my breathing becoming slow and rhythmic when I heard him whisper into the top of my head . . . "I love you."

Eighteen

Marcus

Six Months Earlier

When he couldn't back squat as much as his friend Jeff, Marcus Santos was instantly filled with rage. He did his best to not let his anger show when Jeff had to spot him, helping him stand with the heavy weight digging into the back of his shoulders. "Damn it. My feet were spread apart too wide, I can do better than that."

They were both buff and had huge muscular arms. Jeff Forsythe was shorter than Marcus by a few inches, but they had similar builds and it was obvious they spent a lot of time with weights. Marcus had black hair and black eyes and looked like someone who had spent time in prison at some point in his life. Jeff was cleaner cut with russet hair and gold-flecked brown eyes.

"Sure. Lift that weight, buttercup." Jeff loved harassing Marcus and watching him come unglued. The guy had no sense of humor and was easy to razz.

Marcus lifted the weight off the rack and back onto his shoulders, squatting all the way down and then letting out a grunt as he gave it all he had and tried to stand. His legs were shaking and threatening to defy him until he surrendered and threw the weight off of his back. "Damn it!"

"C'mon, let's go. I'm wiped and starving. Want to grab some breakfast before work?" Jeff asked as he wiped the sweat off of his head with a small towel.

"Sure. You buying?" Marcus slapped him on the back. "I got drinks the other night."

"Yeah, I'll buy your breakfast, sugar."

They drove to the little diner with the cute young waitress and asked to sit in her section. They both ordered eggs, bacon, and toast for breakfast and turned away coffee, still too hot from the workout.

"They have a free trial at that CrossFit gym across town. I'd like to check it out, see what all the rage is about. You in?" Jeff asked.

"Hell no. I don't want anyone coaching me like a damn aerobics class." Marcus took a swig of orange juice and eyed the young brunette while she took an order at the next table.

"From what I hear it's nothing like that. Andy went with his brother to one in Dallas and said he got an amazing workout. There's a workout that you have to follow, but you do it on your own. He said they did some heavy weightlifting, rowing, and pull-ups—said it was full of hot babes too."

"In that case, count me in, dude." Marcus grinned and then winked at the waitress when she brought their food and laid the check on the edge of the table. When they finished eating, Jeff picked up the check and got in line to pay the bill while Marcus pulled away in his truck.

***

Marcus awoke the next day regretting that he agreed to meet Jeff at the CrossFit gym.. He liked his routine and hated walking into a place full of strangers. He checked again to make sure his bedroom door was locked and filled a syringe with the steroid medication. He tried to take quiet careful steps so his mother wouldn't hear him—he couldn't wait for that old hag to bite the dust. She was always nagging him and ordering him around like a child. He heard the floor beneath him creak and then the grating sound of his mother's voice shouting from the living room. "Where are you going now?" Her voice was raspy from years of smoking, drinking, and emphysema. "Get me a carton of cigarettes on your way home, would ya?"

Marcus clenched his fists and gritted his teeth, "Sure, Ma."

He started the engine on his truck and flipped through the stations on the newly installed stereo system and landed on a station playing Ozzy, turning it up loud enough to block out his mother's infuriating voice stuck in his head. *Stupid CrossFit gym . . . their music probably sucks too.*

He pulled into a parking spot and saw Jeff standing outside his car waiting. "Dude, this better not suck as bad as I think it's going to," Marcus growled.

Jeff just waved him off as they walked inside. They were greeted by a blonde wearing a tight black tank top and running shorts. She welcomed them, introduced herself as Emma, and asked them to fill out a waiver. Marcus started filling out the paper using his real first name before realizing it would be best to enter false information. "The last thing I need is someone calling the house and mailing me flyers," he said under his breath.

Emma returned to the counter as Jeff and Marcus were signing the bottom of the form. "Okay, let me show you around."

Marcus looked the blonde over as she walked in front of him. She had a rocking body and neither he nor Jeff could keep their eyes off of her.

"We'll warm up as a group since we have quite a few guests and then your coach, Jake, will go over the workout with everyone. Today's workout is an AMRAP which stands for as many rounds as possible. You'll have fifteen minutes to get as many rounds of fifteen box jumps, ten pull-ups, five burpees, and three dead lifts as you can. Jake will give you more details during the warm-up and demo all the moves."

"What's a burpee?" Jeff asked.

"A burpee is a four-step movement that starts out with a squat, goes straight into push-up position, back to squat, and finishes with jumping up as high as you can. Like I said, your coach will go over each movement in detail before the workout."

Marcus and Jeff followed Emma around the gym as she showed them where the weights, barbells, and boxes were. "Be thinking of what weight you want to use for dead lifts, and welcome to CrossFit." Emma smiled before she turned to walk back to the front.

"Damn, she was hot." Marcus whistled through his teeth.

"No kidding. I have a feeling I'm going to like this gym," Jeff agreed.

The workout was intense and Marcus let his competitive streak take over.

"That might have been the hardest workout I have ever done," Jeff managed to get out between breaths. They were both sitting on the floor panting and taking long pulls of water from their bottles.

After the cool-down and mobility exercises, Jeff gathered his keys and waited for Marcus. "Dude, you coming?"

"Nah, you go on without me. I got a vibe from that blonde that I'd like to pursue."

"Like you have a shot with her," Jeff retorted.

"Man, I've got a good streak going, you remember the redhead from the bar last weekend."

"This girl doesn't seem like the easy bar pickup, but I'll tell you what—I'll bet you a round of beers that she shoots you down." Jeff laughed and threw out his hand to seal the bet. "I just hope she lets you down easy."

"You're on, bro." He shook Jeff's hand but didn't take his eyes off Emma. "I can't wait to get my hands on that ass."

Jeff shook his head as he walked out of the gym to his car.

Marcus had always been cocky and never lacked confidence when it came to women. He thought of them as the weaker sex and treated them as playthings meant for men like him. He decided to wait in his truck until the gym was empty and approach Emma in the parking lot. As she neared her car, the door to the

196

black Ford parked next to her swung open, startling her. Marcus stepped out arrogantly and said, "After that workout I think we earned the right to have a drink tonight." Marcus looked into her eyes—most girls melted when they looked into his dark eyes.

"I can't, but thanks." She fished for her keys and unlocked the door to her car.

"You don't drink? A movie, then," Marcus tried again.

"Really, I can't, sorry." Emma got into her car without looking at him again and drove off.

What a bitch. Marcus said to himself. *She thinks she can shake that tight ass around the gym all day and play innocent afterwards. Little tease—someone needs to teach her a lesson.* Marcus got into his truck and slammed his fist on the steering wheel.

As the day ticked by slowly, all Marcus could think about was how he was rejected by the blonde at the gym. His rage was building as he thought about how the night could have gone so much differently. He could have been having drinks with her tonight instead of the guys that were getting on his nerves rather quickly. The thought of losing the bet and having to buy Jeff drinks again had his fists tightening at his sides. His increasing rage was interrupted by the sounds of quitting time around the garage so he clocked out and walked to his truck.

He was happy to see that his mother was passed out drunk on the sofa when he got home. He set the carton of cigarettes on the coffee table and showered, washing the grime and grease from the garage off. He sat in his truck, not pushing his luck with his passed-out mother and dialed his buddy. "George, it's Marcus. Where are the guys hanging tonight? Calvin's bar? Yeah, I'll meet you there. Yeah, I'm in for some pool. See you in a few."

Most of the guys he worked with at the garage were already there. Adam Flynn was short and stocky with a blond buzz cut. He sat next to Rick Henley at the bar who had longer dishwater blond hair that fell just over his shirt collar. Tim Luther was skinny and had wavy auburn hair with a large nose.

"Adam, Rick, what's up? Hey, Tim." Marcus bumped his fist against each of theirs and waited for the bartender to look his way. "I'll have whatever's on tap." Jeff walked in and Marcus's mood instantly dropped. "I can see by the look on your face that my drinks are on you?" He slapped Marcus on the back. "Sorry, dude."

Marcus played a few games of pool with his friends and finished off his sixth beer.

"Loser buys a round of shots when this game is over," Marcus slurred.

Rick bought them all a round of snakebites, and then it was Tim's turn to buy a round.

They were all feeling a little wasted now, and Marcus started bragging about his latest conquests. "Yeah, Mia was a tiger—something about redheads." His tongue felt thick in his mouth, but it was Friday night and the evening was just getting started.

"You're full of it, Marcus. She didn't leave here with you." Tim glared at him.

"You don't know shit, Tim." Marcus wanted to punch him in the mouth as he felt the rage building. He flexed his arm muscles as a warning. He was the biggest guy in the group and they all knew he could take them down easily.

"You should see this tight piece of ass that Jeff and I met today." He looked over at Jeff and nodded. "Blond hair and curves that make it hard for a guy to walk straight."

"I'm calling it a night," Adam said as he stood to leave.

"Right behind you, dude." Rick grabbed his keys out of his pocket and offered Tim a ride home.

"I'm outta here too. Thanks for the drinks, buddy." Jeff slapped Marcus on the shoulder and encouraged him to call a cab.

"Whatever, you're all losers anyway," Marcus said as his beer sloshed out of his glass mug. "Another beer," he commanded the bartender.

"Last one and you're cut off." She set his beer on the bar and handed him his tab.

"Slut," Marcus said under his breath. "They're all sluts."

Marcus fished for his keys after he drank the last of his beer and walked out of the bar toward his truck. He stumbled around, dropped his keys in the gravel, and hit his head on the door as he bent down to retrieve them. "Damn it." He gave his tire a kick and had to hold the side of the truck for a minute to steady himself.

He looked up to see Emma's silver Volvo stopped at the red light adjacent to where he was standing. "What are you doing out so late, sweet thing?" he mumbled to himself, a smile spreading across his lips.

He quickly hopped in the truck, started the engine, and waited for her to go through the green light before peeling out of the gravel parking lot in the direction of her car. His heart was racing with desire at the thought of all the things he was going to do to her. *Once she lets go, she'll see. She'll be begging for more.*

Marcus followed far enough behind her to go unnoticed and passed by as she pulled into her driveway. He shut off his headlights, turned the truck around, and parked at the neighbor's house that was obviously abandoned. The grass hadn't been mowed in weeks and the house was dark. A stack of old newspapers were piled at the end of the driveway signifying that no one had been there in weeks at least.

He walked around to the back of Emma's house and watched her struggle trying to get the key in the door while juggling a couple of bags of groceries. He watched her until she was just inside the door before he stepped out of the darkness and appeared at her door.

The startled look on her face made his body stir and he was quickly aroused.

"What are you doing here?" Her eyes were wide with shock. "You're drunk—do you need me to call someone? Do you need me to call you a ride home?" She was stuttering, and he had never been more turned on.

"Aren't you going to invite me in, doll?" He grinned as he pushed his way in. "The way you walk around in those shorts, I got the message . . . loud and clear." He lunged toward her and stopped short just to watch her face light up with fear. Her eyes were filled with panic and her screams drove him wild.

"I know you have to act like you don't want it, cuz you're a girl and all, but I know you do. Lucky for you there's no one home next door so you can scream all you want, no one can hear you."

Emma turned to run but Marcus grabbed her and slammed her into the wall. She was punching and kicking him which ticked him off so he grabbed her by the hair and dragged her backwards down the hall and into the first bedroom he came to. She was kicking and screaming which only excited him more. He threw her onto the bed and moved quickly to get on top of her, pinning her arms down and spreading her legs with his knees.

Emma was putting up a real fight, thrashing and trying to roll from side to side to get out from underneath him. "I like 'em feisty." He leaned down close to her face and laughed as he looked into her fear-filled eyes.

Emma stopped fighting him all of a sudden and whispered, "Okay, but kiss me first."

"What?" He pulled back in surprise and looked at her face which had become serious and unusually calm.

As he leaned down to kiss her, Emma leaned up and bit him hard on the chin, stunning him by the sudden shooting pain long enough to escape his grip and run for the door.

"You little whore!" he yelled, rage filling him and threatening to spill over into hysteria. "So you like it rough, huh? I'm good with that." His blood was boiling but he was still turned on. He would show that stupid little tease what pain was.

He caught up to her and grabbed her by the hair again, underneath her pony tail and close to the roots, not caring that he was hurting her. She was grabbing at his hands and trying to keep her hair from ripping out. Her screams were muffled by the sound of his blood pumping in his head. She hit him with something hard that didn't hurt enough to stop him, but made him angry that a weak little woman would try to strike him so he slapped her hard across the cheek before continuing down the hall back to the bedroom.

Suddenly pain shot through his head and he felt dizzy. Vomit threatened to erupt and burned his throat. His eyesight was blurry and he wondered if he was having a stroke or aneurysm from the rush of blood pumping too fast through his head. He let Emma go for a moment to balance himself against the wall and pressed his hand over the spot that was radiating with so much pain. There was something wet and slippery there and when he pulled it down to look at it, bright red blood was spilling through his fingers.

"What the hell?" he managed to get out before the blood dripped down into his eyes and began a burning, singeing pain that radiated through his temples. "What the hell did you do to me?" Marcus saw a blurry vision of Emma and lunged for her, grabbing hold of her shirt. He heard the sound of fabric tearing and he was left with just the weight of the shirt in his hand to let him know she was gone.

Marcus used the shirt to rub the blood out of his eyes and then squeezed it in his fist. His blurred vision began to clear, the walls coming into focus. He squinted to view the items on the floor around him, a few framed pictures, a cell phone, and what appeared to be the weapon she used to hit him on the head. He crawled toward it to analyze it and picked up the heavy object in his hand. It was hard and long and felt like it was made of concrete. Candle wax drippings had hardened down the sides—it was some type of candle holder.

"Oh no!" The blow to the head had sobered him up and reality had quickly set in. "I've got to get out of here." Marcus stood up slowly, each move bringing vomit up into his throat. As he made his way out of her house and into his truck, he remembered her whisper "kiss me" before biting him. The rage quickly built in him again and he mumbled to himself under the roar of the engine, "I'm not finished with you, whore. You'll get that kiss. You'll get a lot more too."

Nineteen

"Please . . . help . . . call police," I sobbed as I stood only in my bra and shorts at the doorstep of an unknown neighbor. A heavyset man with a large beer belly bursting through his white undershirt had answered the door. His hair was long, gray, and tied back in a ponytail.

"What the . . .?" His face changed from anger to worry when he saw me standing there in my bra, pleading for help. "Are you okay, Miss?" He invited me in and I shut the door and locked it behind me. For all I knew this man could be just as evil as Marcus, but I took my chances, instantly feeling safer locking myself in the house away from him.

"Here, you must be cold." The man with the gray ponytail offered me a plaid blanket after calling the police and I wrapped it around my shoulders, hugging it tightly to cover my bra and comfort me.

"Thank you." My sobs had turned into hiccups. "Thank you for helping me, Mr. . ."

"Myers. Tony Myers." He moved into the chair across from me. "What happened?" he asked, but the sound of sirens in the distance left us both silent.

Mr. Myers opened the door and led the police officers to me. "I don't know what happened, she ran to my door and cried for help. "

"Thank you for calling us. Is that the victim?"

"Yes," Mr. Myers answered. "I offered her a blanket, but she's still shaking."

Two men in navy blue uniforms walked toward me. "Hello, I'm Officer Andrews and this is Officer Kraig." The officer with brown eyes spoke to me with a gentle voice. His face was kind beneath his bald head and he looked to be in his fifties. His partner had a strawberry blond buzz cut and short mustache and was probably fifteen years younger.

Can you tell me your full name?" He pulled out a notepad and pen.

"Emma Olivia Peroni."

"Okay, Miss Peroni, tell me what happened," he said.

"I—I was attacked. In m—my house. He tried to rape me but I got away. He might still be there. I hit him pretty hard on the head." I was having a hard time putting sentences together, but tried to relay the important details including my house number.

Andrews looked over at his partner and they seemed to communicate without speaking.

Officer Kraig spoke into a small radio attached to his shoulder. "We need a detective on route to one-zero-six Red Maple Road due to an attempted rape." He looked up and asked, "Did you happen to see his vehicle, ma'am?"

"This morning he was in a black truck—not the small kind but a regular size pickup truck."

"Can you tell me what he looked like? Eye color, height, any markings, what he was wearing . . ." Officer Andrews asked and got his pen and notepad ready.

"He had black hair, dark brown eyes—almost black." The shaking started again and I had a hard time getting words to come out through my chattering teeth.

Mr. Myers came back into the living room with a cup of hot chocolate and handed it to me. After a few careful sips, the shivering began to subside and only came in intermittent waves. "He had on a black T-shirt with some kind of writing on it—the sleeves were cut off. He had a scar above his eye—I'm not sure which side. Oh, and a huge tattoo on his arm. It's some kind of snake and it wraps around his forearm."

"Kraig, call in a BOLO and set up a perimeter in the surrounding counties and call the paramedics."

I interjected before Officer Kraig spoke into his radio. "But I'm okay—I'm not hurt." I instinctively held a hand to my throbbing cheek.

"It's standard procedure, ma'am."

I heard several sirens getting closer and must have had a look of panic on my face as Officer Andrews explained what would happen next.

"A detective will be coming in to ask you the details about the attack and another will have you describe the suspect again for a composite drawing. The paramedics will then transfer you to the hospital where you will be checked over. I will accompany you and stay until you are released." He gave me a reassuring smile and stood up to talk to the detective. "Miss Peroni, I'm Detective Penrod."

I looked at the detective as he sat down. He was a stocky man with short brown hair and gray eyes and I guessed he was in his early fifties.

"Can I get you anything before we start?"

"No thank you." I just wanted to wake up from this horrible nightmare.

"I understand you were attacked in your home, correct?"

"Yes."

"I need you to tell me what happened and be as specific as you can with the details. I know this is hard, but we need all the information we can get in order to be successful in catching the suspect."

"Have you ever seen this man before tonight?"

"Yes, this morning. He and his friend came into my gym. Marcus something . . . Rigsby, I think. He filled out a waiver and should have listed his address."

"We'll need access to that information. Is the key at your home?"

"No, it's a code lock. The box is to the right of the front door. The number is three-two-four-two-one-two-zero. Once you're inside, the stack of signed waivers is on my desk. The door to my office is straight back and on the left."

Detective Penrod wrote the key code down in his notepad.

I continued telling Detective Penrod everything I could remember about what had happened when he interrupted and asked if he had broken in or I had let him in. "I didn't let him in, the door was still open. I had just come in with my groceries and he was just standing there. I—how did he find out where I live?" The shaking started again so I took a deep breath to calm down. I twisted my fingers together, trying to hold on to my voice. "I knew something was wrong before I got through the door, you know—that feeling you get when someone is behind you." The tears began to flow again. "He was so drunk and reeked of alcohol. I offered to call someone for him and that's when he grabbed me by the back of the hair and dragged me down the hall to my bedroom. I fought as hard as I could, but he was too strong. He held me down and I couldn't move. I managed to bite him and get loose, but he caught me again in the hallway and hit me." I instinctively rubbed my hand over my stinging cheek and jaw. "He started dragging me down the hall by my hair again and I couldn't seem to reach him to get loose from his grip. I finally grabbed a heavy candle holder on a side table and hit him as hard as I could on the head. He lunged and caught me by the shirt, but it tore and I managed to get out of the house and make it here." I wiped the tears with my hand and suddenly remembered that Julie should be coming home soon. "Oh no!—Jules! My roommate will be coming home soon." Panic filled my chest at the thought of her driving up to witness police cars everywhere and our house roped off.

"Don't worry, there are detectives at your place now. What's her name?"

"Julie Bristol. She has brown hair and brown eyes, about 5′6″—her fiancé will bring her home in a black Denali, his name is Jake Greene. He has short brown hair and greenish-brown eyes."

Detective Penrod picked up his cell phone and relayed the information I gave him about Julie and Jake.

"Miss Peroni, did the suspect remove his pants at any time during the attack?"

"Yes—oh God." I could feel vomit threatening and held my hand over my mouth. "I need the bathroom."

Detective Penrod looked to Mr. Myers who led me to the small bathroom in the hallway and I immediately leaned over the toilet to vomit. When I returned, the detective handed me a glass of water and I took a sip after wrapping the blanket tighter around my shoulders.

"Are you okay?" Detective Penrod asked.

I nodded my head and tried to pull it together.

"I have another difficult question for you, Miss Peroni, was there any type of penetration—either from the suspect or with any kind of object?"

I shook my head. "No."

"Just a few more questions, Miss Peroni, are these the clothes you were wearing at the time of the attack?"

"Yes. I was wearing a shirt but he ripped it off."

"Okay, someone will collect your clothes for DNA testing once you get to the hospital. I'm finished with my questions. Detective Swift will gather a detailed description of the suspect from you for a composite drawing."

Detective Swift was a young Asian man in his thirties with black silky hair and dark, tired eyes. I gave him a detailed description as he sketched a rough image of Marcus.

"No, his hair was spiked up with gel." I looked at the picture and pointed to his eye. "The scar was there, that would be his right eye."

"Miss Peroni, the paramedics are ready and I'm finished with my questions. I'll let your roommate know where to find you. You were lucky tonight, you know."

I nodded my head and wrapped the blanket tighter around my shoulders as a female paramedic with a short blond ponytail approached and led me outside. I looked down the street at my house. Several police cars lined the street out front and detectives were blocking off the entrance and exits with yellow police tape. I worried about what Julie would think and hoped she made it to the hospital soon. I needed someone by my side before I lost all sanity. I needed my Nana now more than ever to hold me in her arms and rock me. My body was overwhelmed with shaking and my sobs had turned to hiccups. I didn't have time to run back inside to the bathroom, so I leaned over the grass thinking I would vomit again. My body was racked with dry heaves until exhaustion took over and my surroundings became blurry. There were bright flashing red and blue lights everywhere that seemed to be fading into the distance. Blackness enveloped me like a fog and I realized I was about to pass out as the numbness climbed up my legs to my knees and my body slumped to the ground. I woke to the female paramedic leaning over me in the ambulance as she held a small white stick under my nose that smelled horrible like ammonia.

"Smelling salts. You passed out. You're in shock but you're okay now." She wrapped a blood pressure cuff around my arm and took my vitals as we drove toward the hospital, hot tears streaming down my face.

Twenty

Present Day

"Good morning, beautiful, sleep good?" Sheldon whispered.

"Mmm hmm." I stretched my arms over my head and felt my well-rested muscles pull and stretch in gratification.

I took a moment to feel the silky sheets on my body and take in my surroundings. I was in Sheldon's massive bedroom with the sounds of the ocean coming through the door and warm buttery sunlight streaking the walls. I imagined what it would be like to wake up in his arms every morning and suddenly remembered the words he whispered last night when he thought I was asleep. I wondered if he really meant it and if he would say it again. My body began to stir with little explosions threatening my stomach and chest when Sheldon ran a finger down my arm that was still overhead. It felt so good to be touched by him, but I faked a giggle and dropped my arms before things could go further. *I am so not in the mood to be tossed into the pool this early!*

"I'll make us some breakfast," I said as I pulled the covers off and slipped out of the bed.

"It's the weekend, I'm taking you out for breakfast," he said and slid out of bed.

Sheldon showed me the bathroom and laid out a towel for me. I locked the bathroom door and looked around to make sure I had privacy. I stepped into the massive tiled shower and looked at all of the handles and jets. *Good grief, how many people does he shower with? At least six could fit in here.* There was a rain shower above my head and jets surrounding me. After turning every knob on and off, I finally got a single shower head to come on by itself and stepped into the strong stream of hot water. I showered quickly and dried off, fingering my damp hair so it would air-dry in the hot sun.

I sat on the screened porch overlooking the ocean while Sheldon showered. It was another stunning day on Sanibel—the blue sky was filled with stark white puffy clouds that brought a breeze through the screened porch. A sweet smell filled my nose and I ventured off the porch to find its source. Large gardenia bushes hugged the side of the screened porch and they were in full bloom. I picked one of the soft elegant blooms and held it under my nose to draw in the scent. My eyes were closed and my mind was flooded with the memory of my aunt Grace putting one on my nightstand every morning when I used to visit her on Sanibel years ago. I could see her sweet smile light up her bronzed face as I approached her in the kitchen. She always had on her favorite red robe and her hair was wrapped up in a white cloth to protect her hair that she recently had styled. Nana was at the table with her as they laughed over a cup of coffee. They looked so similar with dark hair and hazel eyes. Nana's eyes were greener than Aunt Grace's, but you knew by looking that they were sisters. They both had a great sense of humor and were always laughing and making me laugh. Papa and Uncle Rob were more serious characters. They would do anything for their wives and loved them very much, but couldn't compete with their livelihood and would always end up retreating to another room to read the newspaper in peace.

Warm muscular arms wrapped around me and held me sweetly from behind. I kept my eyes closed knowing the way Sheldon's chest and arms felt and breathed in the familiar smell of his clean masculine scent.

"You seem to be lost in thought out here."

"Mmm hmm," I exhaled. "My aunt Grace, Nana's sister, used to put a gardenia bloom on my nightstand early in the morning when I visited her here on the island years ago. I woke up to this glorious smell every morning."

"That was sweet of her." He picked off another bloom and tucked it behind my ear. "Ready to go?"

We ate breakfast at the Sanibel Café, a quaint but busy restaurant in the Tahitian Gardens Plaza. Sheldon ordered the French toast trio which looked delicious. Each piece was coated in a different topping—coconut, almonds, or crushed cornflakes. I took a bite of the almond-encrusted piece and closed my eyes as I chewed. "Mmm, the French toast is cooked perfectly and the crunchy almonds with the syrup . . . Mmm." I groaned.

"Emma, I don't know whether to be turned on or laugh out loud at you describing French toast."

I giggled. "Sorry, I love food." I got a forkful of my eggs Benedict that was served over a thick, tender crab cake. "Here, try a bite of this."

"Mmm, that's really good. I never would have thought that would taste good together, but it does."

We enjoyed our breakfast and talked about the shells under the glass top table. Each table had a different design, but each displayed tiny white shells over a navy background. After breakfast we walked around to some of the shops that shared the same strip as the café. We lingered in Needful Things which held all kinds of bizarre and fun items. We also went into Sanibel Sole where Sheldon picked up a pair of flip-flops and I looked at the charms in a store called Shiny Objects.

"My parents invited us to dinner tonight. I really didn't want to share you this weekend, so I can put them off until next week if you like?" Sheldon asked as we walked back to the car.

"Dinner with your parents sounds nice," I lied. "But I'm up for whatever you want to do." I didn't lie about that. I had come to love this man, and although I would rather spend time alone with him than being uncomfortable around his parents, I knew he loved them and I wanted him to be happy.

"Okay, I'll call my mom back and let her know to plan on us." Sheldon dialed his mom after getting the car started and the air conditioning going to cool off the hot car.

After hanging up with his mom we made plans for the day. "Dinner is at 6:30. I'm going to run into the store and get a couple bottles of wine to take tonight. Be thinking of how you want to spend the day." He left the car running and I flipped through the radio stations while I waited. I landed on a station playing classic rock and watched the people as they walked in and out of the store, trying to distinguish the tourists from the locals.

When Sheldon got back in the car I gave him a list of ideas. "Swimming, biking, shelling, walking the beach . . . oh, who am I kidding? What I really want is to lounge on the beach with a cocktail that has one of those cute little umbrellas in it," I said laughing.

"Hmm, be right back." Sheldon got out of the car again and came back with a small brown bag. "Umbrellas for your cocktail, my love."

It wasn't the *I love you* from last night, but it still sent a little flutter to my heart.

"Sheldon, I was being silly, you didn't have to buy umbrellas," I grinned, glad that he had.

"Not a big deal. This weekend is all about you, whatever your heart desires," he winked. "If it makes you feel better, you can take a weekend to spoil me."

I knew he was teasing but I let my mind wander to the idea of a weekend where I catered to his every whim. *I'm sure little umbrellas wouldn't even touch your desires.* I looked over at him wondering what he would wish for if he had the chance. *Athletic competitions in the pool? No, he would probably have me in a skimpy bikini feeding him grapes.* I giggled to myself.

We lay on the chaise lounges behind Sheldon's house on the beach. He had made a tasty frozen coconut concoction decorated with the umbrellas from the liquor store and I was in heaven as I let the hot dry sun warm my body that Sheldon had slathered heavily in sunscreen.

The sun was fully overhead and I was getting too hot. "I'm getting in the water to cool off," I said, interrupting Sheldon's reading.

"I'll come too." He placed his book on the table between us and stood. Sweat was running down his chest and I followed a bead with my eyes as it trailed down his stomach. The alcohol had loosened my inhibitions and I reflexively reached out to follow the bead with my finger. Sheldon pulled me into him without warning before I had time to notice if anyone else was on the beach, but somehow I didn't care as he put his lips to mine.

My filter had apparently abandoned me along with my inhibitions as I pulled away and spoke into his chest, not daring to look into his eyes again as tears threatened to make an appearance. "I think I'm falling in love with you," I whispered.

I felt him pull me away from his chest and suddenly I felt a desperate need to hide. Instead I found an ounce of courage and braced myself to look up into his eyes, contented when I saw the way he was smiling at me. When he finally spoke I felt like I was caught in a slow motion movie clip. He pulled me in and kissed the top of my head. In a low voice filled with emotion he said . . . "I love you too."

***

Sheldon decided to call his dad while Emma was showering and getting dressed. He wanted to make sure his mom was going to be kind and welcoming to the woman he loved. His mom was one of the most giving and compassionate women, but she was also very protective of him and could come across a little harsh sometimes. Thinking back to some of the girlfriends he had introduced his parents to, he couldn't really blame her, but Emma was different.

"I know I haven't known her very long, Dad, but I'm telling you—she's the one. I don't know how to explain it, but I have never been more certain of anything in my life."

"Son, you've always had a brilliant mind and I trust your instincts, I've just never seen you fall for anyone. You were so reserved and . . . well, lacking any kind of passion with Victoria."

"I didn't love Victoria, Dad. Hell, I don't think I even liked her that much, looking back. Mom loved her, remember?" Sheldon laughed.

Bill could hear the happiness in his son's voice and couldn't wait to see him tonight and feel the situation out for himself. "I'll see you in a bit, son, and don't worry about your mother, I'll tell her to take it easy and reserve judgment until after dinner. All we have ever wanted is for you to be happy."

"Thanks, I am happy—happier than I have been in a long time."

They hung up and Sheldon heard the shower turn off. He poured a glass of Pinot Noir for himself and took a glass to Emma. She came out of the bathroom in his black robe drying her dark blond hair with a towel. She was striking and his stomach stirred with desire for her, but there was also the feeling of love and a desire to protect her that was new and exciting to him.

"I like you in my robe," Sheldon flirted. "I thought you could use a drink before we head to my parents' house," Sheldon said thoughtfully and handed me the glass of wine.

"Thank you. This might help."

"Don't worry, they're going to fall in love with you just as I did." He wrapped his arms around me and kissed me sweetly.

"What should I wear?"

"Something casual, we'll most likely eat outside by the pool."

I chose a pair of pale pink shorts with a navy-and-white-striped shirt and blow-dried my hair. I put a light coat of mascara on my eyelashes and caught Sheldon's eye. "Down or ponytail?" I asked as I held my hair into a makeshift ponytail.

"I like the ponytail—shows off that beautiful face." He winked.

Sheldon's parents greeted us at the front door but something felt different. His mom hugged me and was much more welcoming than the last time. I wondered if she had been caught off guard by us coming in while she was doing laundry or if she had chosen to give me the benefit of the doubt, assuming I was a good person. She led us inside and asked what we would like to drink.

"I brought a couple of bottles of wine. Would you like a glass?" Sheldon looked at his mom and pulled the two bottles out of the bag. "I have Pinot Noir and Pinot Grigio."

"I'll take a glass of the Grigio," said his mother as she took four wine goblets out of the cabinet.

"I'd like the same, please," I said.

He poured the two glasses of wine and handed one to his mother and the other to me. "Beer, Dad?" he asked while pulling two glass bottles out of the fridge.

"Please." Mr. Barringer took the glass bottle and thanked his son.

Sheldon put his hand on my lower back and kissed me on the top of the head. I blushed in the presence of his parents and then asked Mrs. Barringer if I could help her with dinner. She asked me to call her Helen and then handed me a cucumber to peel and chop while she assembled mixed salad greens in clear glass dishes shaped like shells.

"Emma, you seem to handle that knife well, this isn't your first chopping session, is it?" she asked with a smile.

"No ma'am, I learned to chop from watching *Barefoot Contessa* and *Good Eats* on the Food Network."

"*Good Eats* is one of my favorites. I also like *Iron Chef*, have you seen it?" she asked as she reached for a tomato.

"Yes, it's very exciting. I don't think I could create anything edible under that pressure though."

"No, me either." She smiled at me and I was overjoyed that we were getting along.

We brought the salads to the table by the screened-in pool just as the guys were coming in with steaks off of the grill.

Sheldon's dad asked the blessing before we ate and my heart warmed that I was in the presence of people that remembered to thank God for their blessings.

Helen placed her napkin on her lap and looked at Sheldon. "Son, Emma knows her way around the kitchen and I've finally met someone that loves to watch the Food Network as much as I do," she beamed.

"Yes, I've tasted a few of her creations." Sheldon smiled at me as he took a bite of steak.

"How's work, son?" Bill asked as he took a bite of salad.

"It's good. I've got another deal in the works—a place in Naples."

"Well I hope it pans out." Bill looked at me. "Sheldon has grown this business from nothing into a huge success. We're really proud of him."

I smiled, cut into my steak, and brought the fork to my mouth just as he addressed me. "Sheldon tells me you owned a gym in Tennessee. Do you plan on opening another here in Florida?"

I chewed quickly and we both smiled at the timing of his question. "I'm not sure. I have thought a lot about it. My dream would be to open something here on the island. I know the island is protected from certain businesses coming in so I'm not sure how a gym would be received. I thought about starting with some personal training at the Civic Center first just to see what the needs are. Have you been over there, Mr. Barringer?"

"Please, call me Bill," he smiled. "Yes, I have, it's really nice. I can get you started in the right direction—give you the name and number of the gentleman you need to talk to. Remind me before you leave tonight."

"Thank you, that will be a great help." I smiled warmly at his kindness.

Dinner was much more pleasant than I anticipated. The food was simple and delicious and the conversation flowed comfortably. I helped Helen take the dishes to the sink but she insisted on putting them in the dishwasher after we left. We rejoined the men on the porch to find them in deep conversation and both laughing. Bill patted his son hard on the back when we reached the table and then got up to fetch another beer, a smile stretched across his face and I wondered what had been said between the two of them.

Sheldon picked up the bottle of wine and offered to pour another glass for his mom and me. I shook my head as I wanted all my wits while in the presence of his parents. Helen allowed half a glass. We talked about their trips to Europe and I listened to them brag about their wonderful grandchildren.

I took it all in and savored the merriment, taking a moment to imagine what Nana would have thought about Helen and Bill. *I think she would have loved them, especially since they were family-oriented.* She might have said something catty about Helen's preppy tennis outfit after dinner and for my ears only, but she would have loved the way they made you feel comfortable and welcome in their home. I could hear her words now as she used to teach me some of life's most important lessons: *Always be kind to someone when they are in your home, no matter how awful they are or how much you loathe them, when they are in your home—show absolute kindness and respect.*

His parents both hugged me when we were ready to leave and I thanked them for dinner. Sheldon and his dad were making plans to go fishing in the coming week and Helen pulled me aside.

"I have to be honest with you, Emma," she started, and my heart took a dip bringing my shoulders and mood with it. I braced myself for a cutting blow. "When Sheldon called and told us how he felt about you, I thought it was too soon. Bill and I had known each other in high school and were good friends before we started dating. I thought that's how it happened for most people, but after tonight, I have changed my opinion. I have never seen my son this happy before and I have you to thank for that." She hugged me again and whispered in my ear pleadingly, "Please don't hurt him."

I was overwhelmed with feelings of joy and at the same time I felt like I had been punched in the stomach. I would never hurt Sheldon—I loved him. Couldn't she see how happy he had also made me? I increasingly understood where she was coming from as I thought about my Nana and tears threatened to sting my eyes—she loved me like that and would no doubt be saying the same thing to Sheldon if she were still here.

"Mrs. Barringer—Helen—I love him." I felt tears well up in my eyes. "I could never hurt him. He is so blessed to have you in his life watching over him. My Nana would have felt the same way."

Helen hugged me once again and everything else we wanted to say to each other was spoken through that embrace. I left the Barringer home feeling loved and accepted.

The drive home was quiet as I read the familiar signs along Sanibel-Captiva Road. A cartoon image of a raccoon, armadillo, and a few other animals asked drivers to drive slowly in three different languages. The last sign read *please* and I tried to pronounce the French version, "Sill—vows—plate."

"Are you serious?" Sheldon laughed out loud. "It's pronounced see—voo—play."

"I know, I just wanted to see if you were paying attention." I smiled.

Earlier I couldn't wait to get in the car so I could ask Sheldon what he and his father were talking about, but after my conversation with Helen I was sure I could deduce what they had shared. I let my mind replay the words she spoke to me and hung on the fact that Sheldon had called his parents to tell them how he felt about me. *Maybe that was the difference—I knew his mom seemed kinder than the last time I met her.* Sheldon reached over to turn on the CD player and the sounds of Yo-Yo Ma on the cello spilled out of the speakers, flouting my reverie.

"Did you buy this?"

"I know you used to play the cello, and thought you might like this."

"I love it—he's my absolute favorite cellist. This is called *Gabriel's Oboe*. Isn't it just lovely?" I swooned.

The elegant sounds of the cello oozed out of the stereo and graced my ears with its gift of pleasure. I closed my eyes and laid my head back to take it in. I felt Sheldon gently take my hand and hold it until we arrived in his driveway.

"I hate to shut the car off and ruin your bliss," Sheldon whispered. "Shall we sleep in the car tonight?"

"Yes, please." I kept my eyes closed and smiled.

A huge crash of thunder shook me out of my peaceful trance and I sat up straight. "Never mind, I think the house is safer," I said wide-eyed.

Once we were inside, we took turns getting into something more comfortable and decided to sit on the screened porch to watch the storm roll in over the ocean. The moon was hidden behind thick clouds and the sky was pitch black, absent of a single twinkling star. Lightning flashed and fingered out across the sky, illuminating everything below it. It was ominous and beautiful simultaneously, bringing contradicting emotions of fear and wonder.

"It's beautiful. Scary and beautiful," I said as I cuddled into Sheldon's arms.

"Mmm hmm."

The wind picked up speed and blew the rain sideways into the screened porch pelting us as we jumped up and ran inside. Sheldon shut the sliding door and we both stood there drenched and laughing. Sheldon gave me a dry T-shirt to sleep in and he changed into a pair of dry pajama bottoms. We climbed into bed and flipped the television on to check the weather. The bottom of the screen had a message scrolling: A SEVERE THUNDERSTORM WARNING IS IN EFFECT UNTIL 3:00 AM FOR THE FOLLOWING COUNTIES: CHARLOTTE . . . COLLIER . . . LEE . . .

"Just a thunderstorm—nothing to worry about," Sheldon assured me.

We lay there listening to the storm and talked until both of our voices faded away and I was sound asleep in the arms of the man that I loved.

Twenty-One

I was somewhat aware that I was in a dream state as I was surrounded by a thin blanket of fog. I tried to focus my eyes and figure out where I was when I saw that the haziness wasn't fog, but steam coming off of the ocean at sunrise. The sky was light and golden as the sun started to rise and I smiled at the angelic beauty surrounding me. I was dressed in a flowing white gown that clung to my body and made me feel feminine and beautiful. I looked down to see that I was standing on a trail of bleached-white shells that surprisingly didn't hurt my bare feet. As I walked along carefully, the shells became softer, suddenly changing into fragrant white rose petals. The sun began to rise and warmed my body making me feel glorious. An image suddenly came into focus in front of me—it was Sheldon wearing a dark suit and tie. My heart beat faster in my chest as I realized this was our wedding day. As I walked closer to him I stared into his deep blue eyes, wishing the path to him was shorter. His eyes changed suddenly, becoming dark and malicious. His face seemed to be changing more and more as I got closer to him and I squinted my eyes in confusion. When I was close enough to see his features more clearly, the sun reflected against the translucent scar above his right eyebrow and I felt the air being sucked out of me as I realized who it was—Marcus.

He lunged forward, grabbing my bouquet of flowers as I rocked back on my heels. Flower petals surrounded me and seemed to be falling from the sky as he ripped through the delicate bouquet. Panic filled my chest as he lunged toward me again and I tried to run but my legs were sinking into the sand and it took all of my strength to get one leg out while the other one sank deeper and deeper. Marcus grabbed my gown and I heard the sound of fabric ripping behind me. I was knocked down from behind into the sand which filled my nose and mouth, suffocating me as I fought the urge to slip into oblivion. The smell of liquor jolted me back to responsiveness and I rolled over onto my back. I tried to sit up but couldn't, and eventually opened my eyes to see the evil smile spread across Marcus's face. He was on top of me laughing as he held my hands above my head. I screamed and kicked with all my strength, but he just laughed and said my name over and over. Emma. . . Emma. . . "EMMA!" This time it was so deafening I opened my eyes and saw Sheldon's face over mine.

"What . . . what are you doing?" I asked as I felt hot tears streaming down my cheeks. My breathing was labored, coming in short quick pants.

"You were having a nightmare." He cradled me in his arms and was rocking me back and forth a little too hard—I felt a headache coming on. "I've got you, baby, I've got you." Thankfully he slowed down but the threat of a headache pursued.

"I'm sorry I woke you." I sniffled as tears continued to stream down my cheeks.

"You had this same nightmare on the boat, didn't you?"

"I don't know." I lied.

"You did. You screamed out the same thing on the boat as you did tonight. You were screaming "no" and pleading for something to stop. Tell me about it, babe, maybe I can help."

"I can't. I just can't. I came here to forget, I just want it to go away." A sob escaped my throat and the tears flowed again.

Sheldon got up and returned with a glass of water and two Motrin tablets.

"How did you know I had a headache?" I looked quizzically at him.

"You're rubbing your temples—dead giveaway." He nudged me to take the pills and I did. "Now, tell me about the nightmare."

"I really don't want to rehash it tonight, Sheldon." I tried to put my foot down.

"Emma"—His face was serious as his eyes bore into mine and his lips pressed into a thin line. "I love you and I can't stand to see you hurting, but this has to end. Tell me what has you so upset and let's see how we can fix it."

I could see his stubborn streak was stronger than mine and I knew that I wasn't going to win this one. I took another drink of water and set the glass on the nightstand next to the bed.

I swallowed hard as I felt the dread rising in my chest. I couldn't look in his eyes when I started telling him what happened to me on the worst night of my life.

"We had a free trial week at the gym and these two guys came in for a workout. One of them stayed back and waited for me to close up the gym—everyone had left, it was just me. Anyway, he approached me as I was getting in my car and asked me to have drinks with him that night. He was cocky and just not my type so I said 'No thank you.' Late that night I was feeling sorry for myself as my roommate was out with her fiancé and I was home alone watching *Pride and Prejudice* for the umpteenth time, so I went to the grocery to get some ice cream and stuff." I took deep breath and peeked up at Sheldon who was holding both of my hands now.

"I made it home and into the kitchen when I heard someone behind me at the back door." Tears trickled down my face again and Sheldon wiped them gently with his thumb. His hands appeared shaky and I wondered what he was thinking and feeling.

"I turned around and immediately smelled the alcohol. He was obviously drunk and smelled like he had bathed in it. I didn't know what to do, I offered to call a cab for him, but he forced his way in and grabbed me—"

Sheldon let go of my hands which stopped me in my tracks.

"Oh, God, no." He ran his hands through his hair and left them there while walked away from the bed.

"I'm sorry," I managed in a barely audible voice.

Sheldon came back to the bed and faced me. "Sorry? You didn't do anything wrong." His voice was filled with rage as his eyes became glossy and I could see tears threatening to spill over. I suddenly realized where his thoughts had taken him and I wondered if he thought I had lied to him about never having been with a man.

"I got away from him, he didn't hurt me like that, but it was his intention." I looked up to make sure he had heard me and I saw a trace of relief wash over him. "He was so strong and I have never been more afraid in my life. He hit me so hard I didn't think I would be able to move, but something inside of me powered through. After a few struggles I finally got away and ran to a neighbor's house to call the police."

"Thank God." Sheldon looked away from me and appeared to be wiping his eyes. "So the police put him in prison? How long is the bastard going to be in there?"

I hesitated before telling him that they hadn't caught him. "I think that's why I'm having the nightmares. He was sending me obscene messages and threatening to come after me again on my cell so I had to get a new number. He would use those disposable phones so the police couldn't track him."

"How hard can it be to catch this loser? What kind of police do you have in that town?" Sheldon was enraged.

"He filled out false information on the waiver I made him sign at the gym. People do that sometimes. The police had been looking for Marcus Rigsby, and that person doesn't exist." I had never seen Sheldon this angry and I wished we could change the subject. Maybe I shouldn't have gone into such detail about the nightmare.

"Now the punch in the gut when I first met you makes sense. I had no idea—"

I cut him off and squeezed his arm. "Of course you didn't know, how could you? I'm just surprised you asked me out again after that. Was your 'crazy woman' radar low on batteries or something?" I smiled, trying to break the solemnity of the conversation.

"Emma, does anyone know you are here on the island? Does Julie know?" His tone was serious—my plan had failed.

"Julie knows I'm here—she's coming for a visit a week from today." I realized my mistake in not being overly cautious about the details with her. I should have made it clear that she should not discuss her plans to visit me with anyone, but I missed her and I longed for a week with my best friend. *Besides, Marcus wouldn't come back to the gym while the police were searching for him and it's not like she's posting it on the internet—Sheldon is just overreacting.*

"You'll move your things here. We'll get them in the morning. We'll turn in the key to the rental office and tell her you had to leave sooner than you thought. You probably won't get your deposit back though."

"What? I can't do that. Plus, Julie is coming and I'm really looking forward to her visit."

"I'm not taking any chances of that monster finding you. You'll be safer here with me. Julie can stay here too. I have two guest rooms for her to choose from, unless you two want the bunk beds so you can giggle all night." He tried to lighten the mood.

"Thank you, but my answer is no. I'm not moving in with you, Sheldon," I snapped and folded my arms definitively.

"You are the most stubborn, hard-headed woman I have ever—"

I flashed a wicked grin that made him fall silent for a moment and he just stared at me. I loved him for wanting to protect me, but I was tired of Marcus ruining everything. I couldn't move in with Sheldon when we had known each other for such a short time. It was hard enough to sleep over occasionally and control the carnal urges that raged through my mind and body.

Sheldon kissed me on the forehead and took a deep breath in before exhaling. "Emma, I love you and the primal male in me needs to protect you."

I had never felt so loved and cared for than at that moment. I was sure it was written all over my face, but just to make it crystal clear I leaned over and kissed him while gently pushing him down on the bed. My lips were eager on his as I moved my hand to his chest, feeling every muscle tense under my touch. My heart was racing as desire swirled through me and I could feel Sheldon responding with matched ardor.

"Whoa, you have to stop now." Sheldon moaned and rolled me off of him.

"I don't want to wait any longer. I love you and I trust you," I said breathlessly as I traced my finger down his abdomen.

Sheldon closed his eyes like he was concentrating on finding his will power. "It's been an emotional night and I'm not convinced that you're ready for this right now."

"I am ready. . ." My words were barely audible through the exhale of breath. ". . . make love to me." I moved my hands across his chest, tracing every bulging muscle on his shoulders and massive strong arms.

Sheldon inhaled sharply and I could see by the look in his smoky eyes that his willpower was fading. My body was on fire as electricity mingled with the blood in my veins and our lips seemed to be held together by a magnetic force. I didn't need oxygen, I just needed him. The usually persistent voice in my head remained silent and surprisingly didn't argue with me. *This is really happening,* I thought to myself, and an ever-so-small pang of guilt washed over me but I quickly shook it off.

Sheldon pulled away and turned on his side to face me, breaking the spine-tingling spell. He rested his head on his hand while propped up on one elbow. "I'd like to wait for our wedding night." His cheeks were still flushed as he awaited my reaction.

Suddenly all the breath had been sucked out of me and I was left disappointed and aching for him. *How does he do that—just turn it off so easily? Does he think of something really sad or gross? Jeez, I feel so foolish now. I'm the one who wanted to wait until I was married, pushing him off of me every time he made the moves, and now HE is pushing me away? This might just be hilarious if I wasn't so irritated.* I suddenly didn't know what to do with my hands and reached for my pockets. *Good grief, there should be pockets on everything—even pajama shorts!*

"Breathe, Emma," Sheldon said as he tucked a strand of hair behind my ear, not taking his eyes off of mine. "Are you mad?" He laughed.

I inhaled deeply. "No, of course not." My voice was too high as I spoke and I knew I wasn't a good liar. "I'm just frustrated." The desire was still swirling around inside of me, but I couldn't move, I just looked into his eyes and waited for him to laugh at me.

"I love you, Emma, and even though it's killing me . . ." He closed his eyes again and fell silent for a moment. "I want to wait and make love to you on our wedding night. You *are* worth waiting for."

"Oh." My brain failed me of all vocabulary and this was the only word I could whisper as tears stung my eyes again. I played his words over again in my head and although I was left disappointed that we didn't make love, I was filled with an indescribable amount of joy at his words and repeated them in my head. *Our wedding night.*

Sheldon swung me up into his arms and carried me out of the room. I looked at the clock to see that it was four o'clock in the morning. It was still pitch black outside but the storm had settled down and the rain had stopped. "Where are you taking me?" I giggled.

He carried me through the sliding glass door toward the pool and said, "I think we could both use a swim to cool our bodies down." We both laughed before he jumped in with me still in his arms.

Twenty-Two

We slept in late after the long night. When I opened my eyes Sheldon was already awake staring at me.

"Good morning, sleepy head." He looked over at me and smiled. "I hope I didn't wake you."

"Good morning," I replied, "I'd like to go for a run this morning before the day heats up."

"I don't think it's going to heat up much." Sheldon nodded his head toward the glass doors and I saw the gray clouds that were blotting out the sun.

"Oh." I frowned. "Well, at least it's good running weather. Join me if you dare," I taunted.

"What? You really think you can outrun me, look at these little legs," he teased while tickling my legs until I giggled uncontrollably.

The familiar fragrance of gardenias suddenly filled my nose and I knew what he had done. I looked over at the nightstand on my side of the bed and saw a short glass vase filled with the blooms. There was a folded note next to it and I wondered if I should read it now or wait. "You've been up already." I grinned and held up the note. "What's this?"

"Something I jotted down. Go ahead." He nodded his head, encouraging me to read it.

It was a poem that he had written by hand and I read it slowly, taking in each word:

Hesitation, uncertainty, and
unknown futures
only compound a
problem that should not be.
"I've been hurt before..."
"I don't know what tomorrow will bring..."
Excuses, excuses.
Excuses are convenient ways
to stall happiness
and perpetuate fear.
With you, my love,
I can think of no excuse to refrain,
no sustainable arguments
to not let you in.
You are here to stay

and I trust you,
and for that I'll be forever grateful.
I love you,
Sheldon

"Oh Sheldon," I whispered. "It's the most beautiful, thoughtful, romantic thing anyone has ever done for me." We shared a soft kiss and I reread the poem. "You said you *liked* poetry, you never told me that you wrote it."

"I don't usually. I've written a few lines before but they've all turned out depressing and unfinished. But you inspired me and I thought this one was worth sharing with you." He ran a couple of fingers over my shoulder and we both watched as the goose bumps rose on my arms. "How about that run?"

After splashing some water on my face and brushing my teeth, I put on some running shorts and a tank top. I laced up my shoes and started to stretch in the living room while waiting for Sheldon to dress. My muscles were tight from lack of use and I took extra time to stretch them out.

We started out jogging down the driveway to warm up and then increased to a nice steady pace down the road. After what I determined to be close to half a mile, I turned around to head back.

"Pooped out already? I thought you were competitive," Sheldon teased.

"This is just our warm-up. I thought I would show you a CrossFit workout." I smiled.

"I'm in."

"We'll start with sprint intervals. Run to that royal palm up ahead—all out, everything you've got. Ready, go!" We both took off running as fast as we could, stopping at the royal palm to catch our breath. "Good. We'll rest one minute and run to that dolphin mailbox up ahead."

We continued the sprint intervals until we got back to Sheldon's driveway.

"What's next?" he asked winded.

"Twenty-five lunges—that should get us close to the top of the driveway." I watched to make sure he didn't let his knee go past his ankle. When we reached the top of the driveway I instructed him on proper squatting technique. "Push your butt back like you are closing the car door, then squat all the way down below parallel." I showed him a couple and then watched him. "Perfect. Let's knock out twenty-five."

We squatted together and I watched to make sure he was using good form.

"We'll finish with push-ups. What do you prefer, chest to floor or handstand push-ups?" I couldn't help wanting to show off for him.

"Handstand push-ups, are you serious? Show me."

I walked over to the side of the house, wondering if it was going to be harder in the thick Florida grass.

It was spongy but comfortable and I was able to easily go into a handstand. I rested my legs on the wall of the house and let my arms carry me down until my head rested on the green grass before pushing back up into a handstand. I could feel Sheldon's eyes on me so I decided to do three more just to impress him.

"Damn, that's impressive. I'll stick with regular push-ups—pretty sure I can't do a handstand."

"Okay, let's go back to the driveway for the twenty-five push-ups, then."

"That was great," Sheldon admitted and stretched his arms behind his back.

"Good. We have four more rounds of twenty-five each: lunges, squats, and push-ups. Let's see who finishes first." I grinned and started lunging.

"What the—?" Sheldon started lunging. "Again with the cheating!" he laughed.

We both fought hard to beat each other. I was ahead of him on the squats but he caught up to me on the push-ups. We were both lying on our backs in the driveway when we finished, trying to catch our breath.

"Great job." I raised my hand into the air and high-fived him.

"That was tough. Great, but tough."

We had a light breakfast at the bar in the kitchen and then took turns showering and dressing.

"What did you have planned for today?" I asked.

"You'll see."

Sheldon turned on the radio in his charcoal gray car as we started driving off the island toward Fort Myers. Billy Joel was singing "Piano Man" and we both helped him sing the last lines of the song while Sheldon pretended to jam out on the harmonica.

"Where are we going?" I giggled.

"You're very impatient," he smirked. "Have you ever shot a gun, Emma?" He glanced over at me to gauge my reaction.

"Yes, I have." I grinned and looked out the window to see the lighthouse as we drove over the Causeway.

"Good. I'd like to take you to the shooting range."

I took a moment to reminisce about my childhood. Papa started me out on a pellet gun in the backyard and I was shooting skeet by age nine. Handguns were never my favorite, but he wanted me to know how to handle and respect all guns, so he made me target practice at least once a month with a Ruger single-action .357 Magnum revolver. He wanted me to love pistols as much as I loved my shotgun, but nothing felt as good in my arms as my Beretta 682 over and under. He always had so much confidence in me and my ability to shoot. I was the only girl on his all male hunting trips and I could picture his wide smile as he would brag to his buddies about how I had not only shot my limit but also helped him with his.

"Sounds like fun." I beamed and decided not to tell him how well I could shoot.

Sheldon gave his driver's license and car keys to the clerk in exchange for a .22 pistol, bullets, targets, ear protection, and two pair of protective glasses.

We set up at our station, put the glasses and ear protection on, and Sheldon loaded the small bullets into the magazine. He moved slowly, instructing me in his every move and I watched him as if it was my first time to witness a magazine being loaded. He shot first and I saw that he was a great shot with a cluster of bullets hitting the center of the target.

I couldn't help myself and asked again how to hold the gun when it was my turn. Sheldon was always teasing me and I couldn't resist playing a game with him now. I had the added benefit of feeling his arms around me as he showed me how to hold the gun and aim for the target. I took a deep breath in and exhaled as I emptied the gun into the paper target. My cluster was tight with each hole in the center of the bull's-eye.

"Whoa! You hit the bull's-eye every time." Sheldon looked surprised and excited as he pushed the button that reeled the target back toward us. "Seriously—every bullet is in the center—look at this."

"Sheldon," I said giggling. "I grew up with guns. I have been shooting most of my life."

"Jeez, that's the sexiest thing I have ever heard." Sheldon grinned. "I can't believe you sharked me like that though." He shook his head as he started cleaning up our things. "Constantly cheating—*tsk tsk*."

"Are we done already? We didn't even use a fourth of the bullets." I frowned.

"No, we'll shoot more. I just want to try another gun."

Sheldon turned the gun and bullets back in to the clerk and asked to look at some of the new guns for sale. He held a nine millimeter in his hands and studied the weight and feel of the gun. He also asked to see a Walther PPK. The clerk agreed to let us shoot them both before making a decision on a purchase.

Sheldon tried both of the guns first and then loaded the clips for me to try. "Which one do you like better?" he asked as I studied the look and feel of both guns in my hand.

"I really liked shooting them both, but the Walther feels better in my hands." I preferred the sleekness of the Walther, and the way it balanced nicely in my smaller hands. The nine millimeter was more powerful than the thirty-two, but we were both good enough shots that we could easily take someone down with the smaller bullet. "I think this is the gun that James Bond uses," I said grinning.

"Only you would know something like that," he smirked.

"Which one did you like better?" I asked and watched him pick each one up again.

"Well, now that I know that James Bond carried a Walther, I definitely have to say the Walther."

After we used up all of the ammunition for both guns we returned everything to the clerk upstairs.

Sheldon held the Walther .32 back. "I'd like to purchase the Walther."

"Yes sir. You'll have to fill out some paperwork first."

Sheldon took the pen and began filling in the blanks. "Can you look around and pick out a case for it?"

"Sure," I said, and browsed the available cases until I found a brown leather one that would fit the gun nicely.

Over lunch we talked about shooting and the new gun. "Should I start calling you Mr. Bond now?" I winked and took a bite of my sandwich.

"Yeah, I like the sound of that. I'll need a hot babe to be my Bond girl, too."

"Hmm, I don't see any in here. Maybe we can find one on the beach tomorrow."

"You're funny. I don't think I'll ever find anyone hotter than that girl in the coral bikini that handles a gun better than anyone I've ever encountered, but I guess you'll do for now." He smiled, raising one eyebrow.

***

"I've had the best weekend, thank you for everything." My voice sounded small.

"I did too. It's not going to be the same tonight without you in my bed." Sheldon handed me the gun case and asked me to keep it at my bedside.

"I can't take your new gun," I protested.

"Please, I'll feel better knowing you have it."

"What about you? What's going to keep you safe?"

He looked at me and lowered his eyes, trying not to smile. "Seriously? You're worried that someone's going to get me?"

I nodded my head even though I knew it sounded ridiculous. One look at his broad shoulders and muscular arms would make any normal person think twice about picking a fight with him.

"I have another gun at home, don't you worry about me."

I took it and thanked him. "I do feel safer having a gun with me but it's only a loan. I'll get it back to you."

He walked me to the front door and waited while I unlocked the door and got the lights on. He insisted on walking through the house and checking things since I had been gone for two nights. Once he was satisfied, he came back to the living room and held me in his arms. We stood there like that for a while, neither of us wanting the night to end. Sheldon finally pulled back slightly to look into my eyes. "Goodnight, love." He kissed me sweetly and I could feel the disappointment of my choice in his body language.

Just throw me over your shoulder and take me with you! I wanted to shout, but didn't have the guts. "Goodnight." I sighed, and watched him walk to his car. I shut the door, locked it, and plopped into the big paisley chair. I desperately hoped my decision was the right one, although it felt wrong and miserable.

I pulled my phone out of my bag to call Julie and put it back down when I saw how late it was. She would be asleep already since the gym opened at six o'clock on Mondays. I exhaled a long audible groan and decided to go to bed with damp hair from the pool. I couldn't seem to fall asleep so I picked up my book and started to read. After reading the same paragraph four times, I gave up and turned out the light. Sleep came so much easier in Sheldon's arms— it was going to be a long night.

Twenty-Three

Sun-streaks made their way in through the blinds, invading my eyelids on Monday morning. My mood was melancholy after waking up from another bad dream, so I slipped on some running shorts and decided to go for a long slow run. I almost tripped over a tiny shot glass of water holding a single white gardenia bloom on my doorstep, and reached down to pick it up. A smile instantly spread across my face when I saw the folded paper underneath. I wondered what time Sheldon had dropped it off and was sad that I didn't get to see him. I breathed in the lovely scent of the flower and took the note inside to read it:

I would have preferred leaving this on your
nightstand this morning.

Thank you . . .
you have brought
taste to my dull pallet,
beauty to my blind eyes,
and silk to my rough touch.
I smell flowers where there are none,
and you are the reason.
I love you, Sheldon

I plopped into the paisley chair to read it three more times and then pressed it into my chest while I thanked God for this wonderful, romantic man. I sat the gardenia and poem on the side table before typing a quick text to Sheldon:

U R amazing! I love you!

I ran six miles at a slow pace, enjoying my environment. My curiosity lingered on the air plants, wondering how they traveled and grew on the sides of trees without soil. I admired the beautifully landscaped yards, unique mailboxes, and pastel homes. I was startled to see someone that resembled Marcus pass by in a black truck but calmed back down when I realized we had just talked about him in length the day before and I was overly sensitive.

He's not coming after you, Em—calm down and let it go already. I trained my thoughts on a girl that looked to be my age running with a yellow Labrador on a leash. She had long brown hair that swung back and forth like a pendulum. Her pace was slower than mine and I eventually passed her. "Good morning," I said, and smiled as I passed. She smiled back and returned the greeting. *That's what I need—a dog to keep me company at night.*

After my run I checked my cell and saw a text from Sheldon:

U R welcome. I love you 2 and I slept terribly w/o you. (guilt intended)

I smiled and thought of a quick comeback to type before showering:

Thinking of getting a dog to keep me company at night—maybe U should 2

I'm insulted—a dog over me?

No comparison . . . a dog won't try to make the moves :)

It also won't spoon with you and keep you warm at night :p

I thought for a moment and then replied:

Point well made! Don't you have work to do Mr. Barringer? You're going to get fired.

I'm the boss!

Well, boss—I need a shower—sweaty.

I'll be right over!

Ha! I'm definitely getting a dog—a big one that barks! xoxo

Enjoy your shower and let me work! ;) xoxo

After getting my robe on I called Julie and talked to her while eating breakfast at the small round kitchen table.

"What time are you leaving tomorrow?" I asked and then took another bite of cereal.

"I'm planning on leaving at three a.m. so I can get there in time to hit the beach with you."

I could hear the sound of barbells hitting the gym floor through the loud music and sadness filled me. I was happy for Julie, but the gym had been my idea and we were so excited to open it together. I worked day and night planning the layout, ordering equipment, and setting it up. Jake, Julie, and I laid the flooring ourselves and shared a bottle of champagne the night before opening. My dream had finally come true and I had put one hundred percent of myself into it. Now I wasn't sure what the future held for me.

"Great! I can't wait!"

"I know, me either!"

"Be careful and call me in the middle of the night if you need someone to keep you awake."

"I will. See you tomorrow!" Julie's excitement was evident in her voice and my mood quickly lifted knowing that she would be here tomorrow. I couldn't wait to hear updates on the gym while lying on the beach and having a cabana boy bring us frozen concoctions with umbrellas in it. *Cabana boy? It's Sanibel, not a cruise ship!* I laughed at myself. After hanging up with Julie I set my phone down to take another bite of cereal. It immediately dinged revealing a text from Sheldon:

This day is dragging. Wish we were on the beach

Me too. Can you take off for a bit?

I wish I could. Need to catch up on a ton of work. Cute blonde has been distracting me :)

I giggled and typed a reply: blondes are trouble!

I'll call you tonight

It was probably best that I didn't see Sheldon tonight. I really needed to get things ready for Julie's visit, including a trip to the grocery.

***

*J*ulie

One Week Earlier

The diner was noisy with the lunch crowd as Julie and Jake sat in a booth across from each other. Julie looked around at the waitresses in pink dresses with white aprons—they had really done a great job to re-create the fifties genre.

"I'd like to go see Emma next week. Can you handle everything while I'm gone? You could probably ask one of the other coaches to close up after the evening classes," Julie asked her fiancé before taking a bite of her sandwich.

"I can do that. Where did she end up?" Jake dipped his hamburger in more ketchup before taking a big bite.

"Sanibel Island. Her grandparents used to take her there every summer and holiday. She felt like it would be the closest thing to home. She rented a cute cottage near a restaurant that she likes—I can't remember the name of the restaurant, but it's on Rabbit Road, isn't that funny?"

"So let me get this straight, you want me to cover the gym while you go to a tropical paradise and sit on the beach drinking cocktails for a week?" Jake feigned displeasure as he sat back and folded his arms.

"Yup, and I know you'll do it because you love me." Julie displayed the most innocent smile she could muster and batted her eyelashes.

"How's lunch? Anything else I can bring you two?" the waitress asked as she smacked her gum and refilled their water glasses.

"No, we're great, thanks." Jake set his credit card down on top of the check she had placed on the table and turned back to Julie. "Of course I will, Jules. Have fun with Emma. I'm sure she's lonely and could really use your friendship now."

"I don't know about lonely . . ." Julie smiled. "She's met someone."

"Really? What's the scoop?"

"They met on the beach and it sounds like they've spent every day together since. I think she's really into him." Julie finished her last bite and wiped her mouth with her napkin. "I think it's moving pretty fast. I hope she guards her heart."

"A dude on the beach? That doesn't sound like Emma."

"I know, right?"

"Ready to go?" Jake stood and looked over at the three huge guys in the booth behind their table. He rolled his eyes at Julie at the sight of their steroid-induced arms. Julie smirked in agreement and they held hands as they walked to the car.

Marcus was having lunch with his buddies Jeff and Tim when he overheard Julie and Jake's conversation. "Sanibel Island . . ." he mumbled under his breath.

"What's that?" Jeff asked.

"Nothin', just thinking out loud," Marcus answered, his black eyes deep in thought.

Twenty-Four

I heard Julie's car coming up the drive Tuesday afternoon and ran out to meet her. "You're here!" I wrapped my arms around my friend and realized I had really missed her. I helped bring her bags inside and showed her to her room.

"This place is amazing, Em! I love the beach theme throughout."

"Wait until you see the fruit trees out back. The grapefruit is as sweet as an orange. So how was your drive down?"

"It was long, but it was nice to be alone with just my music. It's really beautiful here."

"You haven't seen anything yet. I can't wait to show you around. Do you feel like heading to the beach or do you want to rest?"

"Beach for sure! Let me get my suit on."

Julie changed into her hot pink bikini and we drove to Lighthouse Beach. We stopped to put our things down close to the fishing pier.

"We can either lie out here, or walk down the beach."

Julie looked around to take in the picturesque scene. The sky was blue without a cloud in sight and the water was clear emerald green. "It's just beautiful. Let's walk, and then come back and lay out."

"Sounds good, we can just leave our bag and chairs here while we walk."

"Catch me up—I want to hear all about Sheldon."

Julie and I walked down the beach toward the lighthouse while I tried to catch her up on everything. "This is where we met, Lighthouse Point." I paused to look around and then laughed, "I can't believe I thought he was such a player when we first met—he's just wonderful, Jules." I knew I was grinning like an idiot when I told her about our initial rocky encounter—how I assumed the worst when I saw the girls surrounding him on his bike. I shared all about our dinners, the time on the boat, meeting his parents, and the first time I heard him tell me that he loved me.

"Are you serious?" Julie dropped her mouth open. "You have both said the L-word? Have you lost your mind?"

"Yes, I know, we haven't known each other that long, but . . ." I fell silent as I realized how cliché it

261

all sounded. "I think he's the one, Jules. I'm crazy in love with him. When we're together it's bliss, when we're apart I feel . . . well, I'm miserable and he is all I think about."

Julie stopped walking and turned around to face me. "Oh. My. Word. You really *do* love him. I've never seen you fall for anyone so fast, and . . . so hard." Julie smiled and gave me a firm hug. "When can I meet him?"

"Tonight, if you like. He wants to take us for drinks if you aren't too tired."

"How can I think of wasting time sleeping in this paradise?" Julie smiled as she threw her head back, held her arms out, and twirled around like a little girl in a new ballerina tutu.

We continued to walk down the beach catching up. Her wedding plans were practically done except for a few minor details with the flowers for the reception tables and the decision to have a chocolate fountain alongside the wedding cake. "It's the only thing Jake has asked for, but I think it might look tacky next to the cake. I'd like to put it on a separate table."

"Either way would be fine. I think a chocolate fountain is a great idea. So what's new at the gym?"

"I put in another pull-up station and had to order more equipment to accommodate the growth. It's getting a little overwhelming actually—I had to hire someone to come in and help with the books and added another coach."

My shoulders slumped and I couldn't help feeling bummed that I wasn't part of the decisions anymore. "That's great, I'm glad you added another pull-up station, we really needed it."

"I'm so sorry—I know how much you loved it. Let's talk about something happier. What shall we do this week?"

"I have to show you all of the beaches and best sunset spots. We can watch movies, shop at the outlets in Fort Myers and the little boutiques on the island, and Sheldon said we could use his pool anytime. I can see us sipping cocktails by the pool, can't you?"

"That all sounds wonderful! We're going to have the best week."

***

Julie and I met Sheldon at the Jacaranda for drinks. I saw Sheldon's car in the parking lot so we went on in to find him at the bar. His eyes were on me as I walked toward him and I instantly smiled. I had taken extra time to get ready and straighten my hair. The pink slip dress I had chosen felt good on my skin and made me feel confident and sexy.

I loved the way Sheldon looked at me like I was the only woman on earth. I gave him a quick kiss on the lips when we reached him and then introduced my two favorite people. "Julie, this is Sheldon Barringer. Sheldon, this is my friend Julie Bristol."

"It's nice to meet you, Julie." Sheldon smiled and I watched her become flustered after looking into his eyes.

"What can I get you to drink?" the bartender asked as she set two more cocktail napkins on the bar.

"I'll have a mango mojito, please," I answered, and Julie chose the same.

"Let's get some appetizers too. I know you want the Oysters Romanoff. Julie, what looks good to you?" Sheldon asked and handed her a menu to look at.

While Julie looked over the list of appetizers I relayed every thought that was going through my mind to Sheldon by the look on my face and in my body language. I had never been good at hiding my emotions. Sheldon was wearing a pale blue button down dress shirt with his suit pants. He had obviously removed his tie and the top two buttons were undone revealing enough of his chest to draw my eyes there. "That shirt makes you look ridiculously handsome." I leaned in and displayed a flirty smile.

"Ridiculously handsome, huh?" Sheldon put his hands on my hips and pulled me in closer. "Those big brown eyes give away everything you're thinking, Emma." He winked at me and I felt the heat rush to my cheeks.

"The SanCap shrimp sounds wonderful," Julie said, interrupting our heated reverie.

Sheldon ordered the appetizers while Julie and I went to the bathroom before the drinks arrived.

"God bless America, he's smokin'!" Julie said vociferously before the bathroom door had a chance to shut. She was always bold and loud and I should have been used to it, but it surprised me and I tried to help the door shut more quickly so the entire restaurant didn't hear everything she was about to say.

"I know, right? I still blush every time he looks at me." I looked in the mirror at my flushed cheeks and tried to make them subside. "Look at me, I look like an idiot. I just might have to go on blood pressure meds like my Nana!"

"Those eyes . . . I can hardly look at him. I'm glad Jake's not here." Julie laughed. "The way he looked at you when we walked in, Em—I don't know how you've managed to sleep in his bed and keep your clothes on . . . or have you?" Julie raised one eyebrow.

I frowned. "Actually I caved and told him I was ready but he turned me down."

"What the hell?" Julie's eyes were wide with shock. "He's gay. That's the only explanation." Her arms were up in the air as she spoke too loudly.

"No, it's not like that. You wouldn't believe what he said to me, Jules." I blushed and looked down at my shoes. "He said he respected me and wanted to wait until our wedding night."

Silence.

"You're messing with me, aren't you?" Julie finally spoke, all humor gone from her face. "Okay, spill it. What's the catch, there has to be something wrong with him. Not that you're not worth waiting for, I didn't mean it like that. But he is a man, for Pete's sake."

"I told you he's different. I've tried to find something wrong with him, believe me. I have wondered why no one has snatched him up yet. He was almost engaged once, but she was very controlling and wanted him to quit windsurfing which is a huge passion of his."

"So he proposed?" She lifted my hand to look for a ring. "Are you engaged?"

"No, but it was implied that it was his intention one day. It's driving me crazy though, sometimes things get so heated that I can't shut it off. We usually end up in the pool to cool off."

"Hang in there, it will be worth it to wait. I wish that I had waited. It would have been really amazing to save myself for Jake and our wedding day."

"But you're both so happy—it can't be that big of a deal."

"We are happy, but it's a big deal and I just wish someone had told me to wait."

Julie's parents were divorced and she didn't have a great relationship with either of her parents. Although I didn't have Nana and Papa now, I was happy for the time that we did have together and the close relationship.

"I'm really happy for you, Emma. You deserve to be happy, you're an amazing woman and he's lucky to have you." Julie bumped me with her hip and laughingly added, "Since I'm already taken."

The three of us enjoyed the appetizers and a couple rounds of drinks. Sheldon held up his beer and offered a toast, "Here's to the two of you enjoying some girl time."

"Cheers to that!" Julie and I said in unison.

***

The first two days of Julie's visit we forced ourselves to get up and run together—but after that, sleep was more precious than exercise. We rented bikes from Billy's for the rest of her stay and casually biked all over the island, justifying it as enough exercise to allow us to indulge in ice cream and Key lime pie each night.

"I'm starving, let's go grab some lunch," Julie said as she propped herself up on her elbows. We had been sunning and swimming on Bowman's Beach most of the day.

"Me too. Let's go to Gramma Dots—it's my favorite so far."

We ate our lunch and then walked around the marina looking at boats. I didn't want to be obvious, but wanted her to see the boat that Sheldon had taken me out to sea on. As we walked by I casually pointed out the boat.

"Holy smokes, that's a beautiful boat. I can't believe you spent a weekend on that."

"I know . . . it was amazing." I let my mind travel down the frightening path of the unknown, my body language revealing every thought. Never perfecting the art of deception, Julie immediately picked up on it and read my mind.

"Don't go there, Em."

"I can't help it. What if I have to pick up and leave?"

"You can't keep running."

"I might not have a choice, Jules, you know that."

She looked at me with a seriousness that made me stop and listen. "They will catch him."

"I hope you're right. I don't want to leave . . . I belong here."

Julie never liked to linger on subjects that brought us down. I watched her lips curl up into a smile and awaited her predictable witty banter to lighten the mood. "Well you could at least have a very *memorable* summer." She raised her eyebrows and grinned.

"It will be memorable anyway," I retorted and began walking toward the car.

"Oh, I'm sure it will be. I hope you are journaling all of it. *Dear Diary, Tuesday we held hands and walked on the beach. Wednesday—can you believe he kissed me on the hand? It was the most thrilling experience of my life.*" She mocked me and laughed.

"Why are we friends?" I scowled and bumped her with my hip.

"You know I'm teasing." She bumped me back and laughed.

We were invited to swim in Sheldon's pool one day while he was at work and we gladly took him up on the offer. "I won't be home until after five o'clock, so stay all day and enjoy the beach and pool."

We bought ingredients to make frozen mango margaritas and a few snacks before driving to his house and using the key that he left under the mat for us. I felt uncomfortable unlocking his door and walking into his house when he wasn't there, but when we made it outside to the pool, I couldn't help feeling giddy with delight at the thought of spending the day with Julie in this paradise.

"Jeez Louise, this is amazing." I watched Julie's face as she checked out the massive home.

"I know. Let's fix our drinks and turn on some tunes." I walked to the kitchen and found the blender under one of the cabinets. We whirled up a blender full of margaritas and poured it into two large lime green cups. I led Julie outside to the pool and watched her take it all in.

"Seriously? This is who you are dating? If you don't sleep with him, I might . . . just to swim in this pool again."

"I know you are trying to be funny, but I will take you down if you say that again." I imagined her making the moves on Sheldon and fury rose inside of my chest. I knew her well enough to know that she would never do such a thing, but the anger came instantly before I could think it through.

"You know I'm joking, Em. But seriously, this is breathtaking."

I calmed myself and laughed, pretending my words were meant to be funny too. "I know, it's like the garden of Eden, right?"

I found the outdoor stereo system exactly where Sheldon described it would be and flipped through the stack of CDs sitting next to it. "How about some reggae?"

"Perfect."

We found two floats and lazily let the day waste away as we sunned our backsides and talked.

"How's Jake?" I asked and took a sip of the delicious frozen concoction that was heavily laced with mango and tequila.

"He's great. He was glad to let me spend the week with you, encouraged it actually."

"Really? That was nice. He loves you so much."

"Well, it's a good thing he has these sweet moments, otherwise I would kill him for being such a slob."

"What do you mean?"

"He's never fully grasped the concept of putting dishes *in* the dishwasher, and sometimes he spends more time with his other girlfriend . . . the Xbox."

We both laughed and finished our second cocktail. "One more?" I asked.

"Yes, please. These are so good."

We could barely walk into the kitchen to make another blender full of the tasty treat. The liquor mixed with the sun had both of us tipsy and giggling, but we were having a great time together. "It's only noon, maybe we should slow down and have some lunch."

"Oh Emma, live a little. We're soaking up the sun in a tropical paradise." She looked at me and giggled when she stumbled into the counter. "Okay, after this one we'll have some lunch."

Once we were back out by the pool we got onto the floats and decided to lay on our backs to tan our front sides. "I'm going to take off my top and get rid of these tan lines," I bravely declared and started to take off my top. I fully expected Julie to be on board, but she just lay there and grinned. *Okay, chicken, I'll be the only one with any guts today.* I was surprised, as she was usually the more daring of the two of us. "I can't believe you are such a chicken. Sheldon won't be home for hours and we're completely secluded back here." I had my hands behind my head as I lay on the float in total bliss. I looked over at her to see her body silently shaking with laughter and wondered what was so funny. I knew my bare chest was as pale as a ghost next to my tanned skin, but it couldn't be *that* comical.

"What's so funny?" I looked around, suddenly aware that we were not alone. Sheldon was leaning against the house with his arms folded in front of him and a wicked grin spread across his face.

"Agh!" I screamed and rolled into the water, covering myself with the float. *Just let me drown right now—go under the water and never come back up. Oh the humiliation!*

"Don't let me ruin the fun." Sheldon laughed and walked over to the edge of the pool.

"You could have made some noise letting me know you were here." I knew my face was cherry red.

"And wreck any chance of seeing you topless in my pool? No way, babe."

"Grrr"—I turned to Julie—"Some friend you are."

She laughed, never opening her eyes as she lay back on the float casually like nothing out of the ordinary had happened.

I splashed water on her and looked to Sheldon for help. "Could you hand me my top, please?"

Sheldon handed me the top and didn't take his eyes off of me as I struggled to get it on and fastened. *Crap, crap, crap. I was so proud to do something too daring for Julie and this is what I get. Ta-da! My name is Emma Peroni, and these are my blinding white boobs.* "What are you doing here?"

"Well, I *live* here . . . and I came home for lunch. I brought you girls sandwiches from the Sunset Grill, have you eaten yet?"

"No and we're starved. Thank you," Julie answered and rolled off of her float.

I adjusted my top making sure I was covered and took Sheldon's outreached hand as he pulled me effortlessly out of the pool. I tried to get my balance but swayed from all of the alcohol and had to hold onto Sheldon's arm until everything quit spinning.

"Whoa—how many drinks did you have?"

"I dunno." I shrugged my shoulders. "Too many, apparently."

We ate our sandwiches at one of the tables under the covered area by the pool and washed them down with much-needed water after all of the alcohol we had consumed.

"This is delicious, thank you." I took a bite of the warm turkey and brie sandwich and pretended to read the back of the water bottle, still too embarrassed to look him in the eyes.

"Yes, thank you so much for bringing us lunch. Could you point me in the direction of the restroom?" Julie excused herself, following Sheldon's directions to the bathroom and left me alone to face his torturous teasing.

"The image of you on that float is forever imbedded in my memory," he said, teasingly.

"Oh fiddlesticks, you are not going to let me live it down, are you?"

Sheldon laughed heartily. "Where do you come up with these lines? You don't have a Southern accent, but you can be as Southern as a mountain girl sometimes."

I shrugged my shoulders and relaxed a bit, eventually joining him in laughter. I didn't think the statement was funny, but watching him in hysterics made me laugh too.

"I have to get back to work." He stood and reached out for my hands as he lifted me out of the chair. "I'm glad you and Julie are having a good time, but I have missed you."

"I miss you too. Thank you again for letting us hang out here today, we're having a great time."

"You're welcome." He leaned down to kiss me and I wrapped my arms around his neck as the kiss became ardent. When we heard Julie humming loudly as she walked toward the pool we pulled away and said goodbye.

"Julie, Emma, enjoy your blissful day in the sun." Sheldon winked at me before turning to leave.

"I can't believe you didn't tell me he was standing there. What kind of friend does that?"

"The best kind. Didn't you see the way he looked at you? I doubt he will even be able to focus at work now." She smiled impishly.

"Good grief, Jules." I laughed and pushed her into the pool.

***

The week passed by too quickly. We stayed up late every night catching up and giggling like school girls. Each morning we went to the front door to find a new poem sitting under a glass of gardenias.

"He's *so* romantic." Julie over exaggerated a swoon and batted her eyelashes.

"Shut up, he's perfect." I smiled as I read another poem silently first and then aloud for Julie.

The sun may set
and the song may end.
The pearl may lose its luster
and the broken wheel may not mend...
...but as long as I feel your embrace
and the sweet rapture of your touch,
happiness will never fade,
and I will not want for much.
I love you, Sheldon

"Jeez." Julie rolled her eyes and we both giggled.

***

Marcus pulled on a pair of shorts and grabbed a T-shirt off the floor of the Sea Mist Motel room. He stumbled to the bathroom, kicking an empty beer bottle on the way, reminding him of why his head was pounding. As he picked up his keys and walked toward his truck, he thought to himself, *She thinks she's too good for me. She'll pay for that.*

Marcus drove down Periwinkle toward Emma's cottage to find her car still in the driveway. He drove down the road, pulled over, and took a swig of Jack Daniels, waiting for her silver car to pull out. The thrill of being that close to her quickly elevated his heart rate and his lips curled up into a smile. *Here we go.*

He sat in his truck watching Emma and Julie walk into the Sanibel Café for breakfast and then followed them to Jerry's Market, parking in the back of the lot to make sure he wasn't seen. *Yeah, you're smilin' now—but when your friend leaves I'll be there to step in. I'll get what I want, and you'll get what you deserve.*

***

"I can't believe you have to leave today, the time just flew by," I complained as we walked into the Sanibel Surf Shop.

"I know, I could stay here a month easily." Julie picked up a mug with pelicans on it. "I think my mom will like this. Now, what can I get Jake?"

"A shark necklace," I teased.

"Actually, I think I will, and this—Emma, are you alright?" Julie asked.

My body was trembling as I pointed to the window. "Marcus. I swear it was him looking through that window."

"It couldn't have been, Emma, there is no way he knows you are here."

"It was him, Julie. He was there in the window." Chills ran up my spine alerting me of the danger and my knees cautioned they were about to fail me.

"Stay here. I'll go check it out."

I slid down the wall into a bench just outside the store as I watched Julie pop in and out of each shop. She was in Jerry's Market for what seemed like an eternity before coming back to me. "I looked in each store and even asked if anyone had seen a man fitting Marcus's description. It wasn't him, Em, he's not here and he's not coming after you." She put her arm around me as we sat there on the bench watching the clouds bring a quick rain shower in to cool off the summer heat. "Emma, you have got to move on and let this nightmare go. You're safe here—he can't hurt you anymore."

We drove back to the house and I helped her pack the car. "Call me as soon as you get home, I don't care what time it is. Call me on the road, too—especially if you get drowsy." I sniveled and wiped the back of my hand across my wet face.

"I will. Thank you for a great week. I really have missed you. If I don't see you before, I'll see you for the wedding."

"Only five months away. I wish I was there to help you." I frowned. *Some kind of maid of honor I turned out to be.*

"There's nothing else to do except wait. Maybe you can come up a week or so early so we can hang out beforehand?"

"Absolutely." I hugged Julie once more and watched her drive away. Sadness filled me watching as my best friend left the island, and then I thought of the alone time I would have with Sheldon and typed him a text:

Hi handsome. Julie just left :(

My phone dinged almost immediately:

Sorry. Dinner and a sunset to cheer you up?

Yes please!

I'll pick you up after work. xoxo

I loved spending time with Julie, but I really missed my time with Sheldon. He joined us for drinks at the Mucky Duck once but I didn't see him outside of that. We texted and talked by phone, but I longed to feel his arms around me again and wanted to be sure that we could pick up where we had left off.

Sheldon picked me up at five thirty wearing a navy blue polo shirt that made his eyes stand out. All I wanted to do was wrap my arms around him and feel his lips on mine, but I was rendered motionless when I looked at him. Thankfully he came to me and I was rewarded with a long kiss. When we finally pulled away, I rested my head on his chest. "I really missed you."

"Mmm, me too. I'm happy that you got to spend the week with Julie, but I'm glad to have you back in my arms."

We dined at Timbers and were seated immediately on a slow Tuesday evening. Sheldon ordered a bottle of Moët and Chandon. "Champagne? What are we celebrating?"

"You know that building in Naples that I was checking out?"

"Yeah, did you get it?"

"Yes I did, and we've already turned it around. We made an insane amount of money on the deal." Sheldon's eyes lit up as he told me about the building and what they had done to get it ready for the market. We sipped champagne and feasted on blackened swordfish with a Thai chili sauce while he told me more about his business and what he deemed worthy of putting money into and what kinds of properties he would turn away.

We drove to the Causeway and pulled off to park on the left side of the road to watch the sunset. Sheldon leaned against the back of his car and pulled my backside into him. We stood there watching as two dolphins played in the sun's reflection on the water. The sunset was beautiful and understated as shades of gold danced across the sky. I felt Sheldon's soft warm lips kiss the side of my neck as the sun melted into the water, mimicking the way I felt.

Twenty-Five

I was sound asleep and dreaming about swimming in the ocean with the dolphins. There was a family of four swimming around me and one was a baby. They felt rubbery and soft, and the little one smiled at me as I rubbed his head. Suddenly the baby's face changed from a smile to a look of fear and I looked around to see what he was afraid of. The other three dolphins started to swim away and the baby looked back at me as if he was trying to tell me to run. His face looked cartoonish and I was perplexed as I tried to make sense of what was happening. I woke suddenly to a noise that seemed to be coming from outside and sat up in bed, leaving the lights off as I listened. I heard what seemed to be someone at the front door. My heart started to race with fear until I realized it was Sheldon leaving gardenias and another poem. I smiled and stretched, hoping to catch him at the door and steal a kiss before he left for work. I went to reach for my robe and caught a glimpse of the clock displaying the glowing numbers that read two forty-eight in the morning. *Why would he come over at this hour?* I grabbed my phone off the nightstand and dialed his number to be sure it was him and not someone delivering a paper or something. I could just see me opening the door and wrapping my arms around an innocent delivery person.

"Emma?" Sheldon whispered in a groggy voice.

"Are you at my door?" I grinned, but then realized he sounded like he was sleeping when he answered.

"I'm at home. Where are you? What's going on, are you okay?" I could hear the panic in his voice which caused me to panic.

"I thought I heard someone at the front door. I assumed it was you until I noticed the time. I'm sure it's just a raccoon or someone delivering the paper. I'm so sorry I woke you." I started to say goodnight and hang up the phone but Sheldon started to speak.

"No one delivers a paper to your door. Are you sure there's someone out there?"

"Yes, it woke me up. I'm sure it's a raccoon then. I'll go and look to be sure."

I tried to calm myself and keep the anxiety out of my voice as I talked to Sheldon and walked toward the bedroom door. "Emma," His voice was serious and he said my name too slowly. "Take the gun out of the case and keep it with you. I am almost to my car and I'm coming to you now. Stay on the phone with me and don't go to the door."

"Sheldon, it's nothing—I overreacted." The level of panic that washed over me was rising, threatening to push me over the edge of sanity, and my voice was shaky. I knew deep down that it wasn't a raccoon, and something or someone was trying to get inside.

"Damn it—do as I say, Emma!" His words were coarse and commanding so I obeyed, finding the case and removing the gun. I slid the loaded magazine into the gun and held it down by my side.

I decided to leave the bedroom and approach the door, my fear and curiosity taking over. I tried to look through the small round peephole when I heard the lock being worked and the knob turning.

"Oh God!" I shrieked. "Who's there?" I dropped the phone to find the safety on the gun and engaged a bullet in the chamber.

"Emma! Emma! Can you hear me? Emma!" Sheldon was screaming into the phone but I couldn't pick it back up to let him know that I was okay but someone was trying to get in.

"I have a gun!" I yelled at the door. "I will shoot," I warned. I heard the lock being worked again and then saw the knob turning in success. I thought about holding my body weight against the door but was paralyzed with fear. The door swung open in a burst and I was consumed with terror. My throat constricted and my breathing became shallow when I saw who it was.

"How did you find me?" I managed to choke out in a whisper.

I pointed the gun at Marcus and instructed him to stay put. "Don't even think about moving or I will shoot!"

Hot tears streamed down my cheeks as I tried to find some courage with the cold steel weapon in my hands, but I could see the gun shaking and couldn't make it stop. Marcus looked at the gun and then back at me, a smile spreading across his face. "Thought you could hide from me, did ya? Well I always get what I want."

I felt bile rising, the rancid taste burning as it coated my throat. I wanted to shout out every curse word I could think of as this evil pig smiled at me, but before I could comprehend what was happening, he lunged toward me, arms outstretched and his sinister eyes wide with madness.

My whole body was racked with tremors as I took aim and pulled the trigger just as he reached me. I felt the jolt of the gun as it fired, but I didn't hear the sound—only the thunderous thud of my heart beating in my ears. A small circle of blood grew larger over his right shoulder as he stumbled toward me.

Marcus knocked me down when he reached me, the full weight of his body crushing me against the hardwood floor, causing pain to shoot through the back of my head as it hit, forcing all of the air out of my lungs. The gun flew out of my hands and slid across the floor near the coffee table, out of my reach. I tried to take in enough air to scream but my lungs failed me. He suddenly relieved me of his bodyweight as he lifted up onto his hands and knees, looming over me, chuckling and then grimacing as he held his shoulder.

I took in a deep breath and screamed as I watched his lips moving but didn't hear any sound. His face became angry as he shouted into my face but I couldn't hear any sound. I tried to wriggle out from underneath his agonizing grip on my wrists but it was no use—I couldn't move. Sheldon's voice seemed to be in the distance, but he was so far away his voice was barely audible. My chest was heaving as I tried to call for him, but my voice seemed too soft and I couldn't get enough air to scream louder . . . to make him hear me.

I was caught off guard when I felt the slam of Marcus's fist hit me hard in the face. The room turned dark with little white dots floating around my head. Mind-numbing pain resonated in my cheek and tears immediately filled my eyes. Before I could make sense of what was happening I saw his fist coming down toward my face again, making my eye feel like it was exploding into my head. The pain was agonizing and my mind became fuzzy as I started to lose focus. I felt my pajama shorts being jerked down, the elastic of my underwear digging into my thighs as he ripped them off of me with one hand. My body tensed as fear overpowered the pain in my face and head. I tried to struggle but had nothing left in me and my body was uncooperative. Tears streamed down my cheeks as I gave in to defeat and braced myself for the physical and emotional pain that would soon follow, but Marcus was suddenly off of me. I tried to take in a deep breath but my lungs failed me again. My body became slack and I was unable to move or breathe. Everything around me started to darken and shrink, like a tunnel that was closing in around me . . . until I was consumed . . . in darkness and silence.

Twenty-Six

I opened my eyes and tried to blink away the fuzziness of the room. A throbbing pain concentrated on my left eye and I reached up to feel a fleshy protrusion, causing me to inhale sharply from the pain and confusion.

"Emma?" Sheldon's voice was tired and filled with concern. I couldn't see him but I could feel his hand on mine. "It's okay, baby." He stroked my hair and kissed my forehead as he spoke calmly. "You're in the emergency room, but you're going to be just fine." His words brought me enough comfort to relax into my pillow.

"My eye . . ." My throat was dry and raspy. "What happened to my eye?" I asked, panic rising in my chest as I feared the worst.

"It's going to be okay, it's just swollen. Let me call the nurse to get something for the pain."

I squeezed Sheldon's hand, not wanting him to leave my side. "No . . . don't leave me. Tell me what happened . . . did he get away?" I choked back the tears that suddenly erupted in my eyes, sending seething pain to my left eye and head. "Did he . . . rape me?" I couldn't control the sobs that followed, making my head throb as sharp pain shot through it like lightning bolts.

"Shh." Sheldon was stroking my hair again. "No, baby, he didn't do either. He'll be behind bars for a long time."

"Thank God," I sobbed and reached up to hold my head in my hands.

I heard the nurse come in and ask me how I was doing, but before I could answer her I felt the relaxing, sleepy effect of the drug she injected into my IV line. I pulled Sheldon close to me and tried to hang on to him as I slipped back into a deep sleep.

When I woke to voices around me in the room, I opened my right eye to see Sheldon talking to a doctor in mint green scrubs. The doctor was giving him orders on how to care for me after I was discharged. I swallowed hard, trying to coat my dry throat so I could speak. "Am I going home?"

The doctor walked over to my bed and sat on the edge of it, offering me a sip of water. He looked to be in his forties with light brown hair and brown eyes. Tiny lines crossed his forehead as he spoke to me, holding my chart in his hands. "Emma, I'm Doctor Statton. You received multiple blows to your face, but you are a very lucky girl. The bullet that you put into the attacker's shoulder kept him from having the strength to shatter your eye socket and cheekbone. You do have a hairline fracture on the cheekbone, but it should heal quickly. You have a small laceration in your brow line, but we glued it instead of having to stitch it so scarring shouldn't even be an issue." Dr. Statton took a few sheets of paper out of my chart. "I'm discharging you into the care of Sheldon Barringer. Do I have your consent?" I nodded my head and he handed the papers to Sheldon. "I have given him instructions on how to clean and care for your wounds." He looked at Sheldon. "If she develops a fever, starts vomiting, or her vision worsens, bring her back to the emergency room immediately."

"Yes, sir." Sheldon shook the doctor's hand and thanked him.

Dr. Statton stood and handed Sheldon a written prescription. "Here's a prescription for pain. She can take one tablet by mouth ever four to six hours as needed. You'll want to get this filled on your way home."

"Feel better, Emma." Dr. Statton smiled and left the room.

Sheldon helped me out of the hospital gown and into my clothes. All modesty had left me as I let him fasten my bra in the back and guide my shirt gently over my head. He held on to me as I stood up, balancing for a few minutes until the room stopped spinning. I glanced over toward a mirror that hung above a sink in the room.

"No, no. Let's just go." Sheldon tried to lead me to the door.

"Please, let me see."

He sighed and walked me at a snail's pace to the mirror so I could assess the damage to my face.

I gasped in horror when I saw the strange image staring back at me. My eye was massively swollen and a deep reddish-purple color spread down my cheek, mixing with colors of green and blue. There were two white Steri-Strips across my eyebrow and I gently rubbed a finger along them.

"I look like a monster," I managed to whisper and felt the burning tears well up again. The oncoming pain from the salty tears caused me to inhale sharply and I quickly found my courage before relenting to the pain that came with crying.

When we arrived in Sheldon's driveway he opened the car door and lifted me into his arms to carry me into the house. "I can walk." I tried to protest, but he ignored my pleas and didn't set me down until we reached his bed. He pulled back the covers and laid me down, putting two pillows behind my head.

"I don't want to sleep in here looking like this, please take me upstairs to one of the guest rooms." I couldn't stand for him to see me like this. Our times together were sweet and filled with love, and I didn't want to bring the memory of what happened into his bedroom.

"No, I'm not leaving your side, and it's easier to care for you down here anyway, so no arguments." Sheldon covered me up and placed a pain pill into the palm of his hand.

"Thank you." I took the pill and swallowed it down with a glass of water. It seemed too early to sleep, as the sun was still coming through the windows and I knew I had slept several hours in the emergency room, but I was so tired. I heard the sound of the ocean coming in through the glass doors and my body became so relaxed it was hard to stay awake, but I needed to know what had happened last night.

"Please tell me everything." I yawned and patted the bed for Sheldon to join me.

"In the morning—you need to rest now." Sheldon pulled the curtains closed making the room dark and slipped in beside me, resting a hand on my stomach.

"Thank you," I whispered. I wanted to tell him thank you for taking care of me, thank you for saving me, thank you for . . . but sheer exhaustion and the effect of the pain killer took my body into a deep slumber.

I woke to the smell of flowers and tried to open my eyes, but only one of them opened as the left eye was still swollen shut. I searched the bed to find it empty and then my eye focused on a large bouquet of white roses on the dresser across from me. Sheldon entered the room with a glass of juice and a pain pill.

"Are you hungry? I can pick up some lunch or make you something."

"No, thank you, I'm not hungry."

"What can I do for you? Another pillow? I closed the blinds so the sunlight wouldn't hurt your eye."

"I'm fine, really." I paused and could see the helpless look on his face. He wanted to do something for me and I couldn't think of anything I wanted or needed except for his company. I thought back to the times I stayed home from school sick and Nana cared for me. She would bring me orange juice and put in a Shirley Temple video for us to watch. Sometimes she would make chicken noodle soup and I would eat it, but I never really liked it. The video and the company were my favorite memories of being sick. "You don't happen to have any Shirley Temple movies, do you?"

"Um, no, but I'll bet I could find one online. I'll bring the laptop in here and hook it to the television." Sheldon walked out of the room before I could stop him and returned with his laptop. "I found several, take your pick."

I chose one of my old favorites and he plugged a cable from the laptop into the television.

"Will you watch it with me?" I patted the bed asking him to lie next to me and thanked him after he got comfortable. "Mmm, this is perfect. The flowers are beautiful too."

"I can't take credit for the flowers—they're from Annie and Charlie."

"They know? How much do they know?"

"Annie was working when you arrived in the emergency room, and she called Charlie. They stayed until your scans came back and knew you were going to be alright."

I was embarrassed that they were there and knew about the attack, but glad that Charlie had been there for Sheldon. He turned to face me while he told me the events from the night of the attack. He told me about pulling into the driveway and hearing me screaming his name.

"I ran into the house to find him on top of you. All I could see was blood—you were covered in so much blood." He looked away from me and I grabbed his hand, squeezing it gently to encourage him to continue.

"I thought it was your blood, Em, but it was his. You shot him."

"In the shoulder." I frowned and lowered my head. "My hands were shaking so bad, I couldn't hold the gun steady. I guess I'll never be a Bond girl after all." I tried to laugh but it hurt too much.

"You did great." He squeezed my hand.

"Go on. Did you get him off of me? What happened?" I encouraged him to finish, grimacing when I thought of Marcus on top of me and the fight that most likely ensued between the two of them.

He paused before continuing, and when he looked back at me his eyes were distant, like he was remembering something that he wished to forget. "Emma, all I can tell you is that I wanted to kill him and it's a good thing the police arrived when they did." He dropped his head and looked away from me.

I rubbed my hand along his arm, trying to comfort him. I couldn't imagine what he had done to Marcus that night, but I was grateful that he did. We lay there and watched the movie together as the throbbing of my eye faded into the background. I took Sheldon's hand in mine and my heart swelled knowing that I was with the one that my soul loved . . . the man that saved me from hell.

Twenty-Seven

A week passed before I found the courage to call Julie and explain what had happened. She was horrified to learn that he really *had* been the one I saw in the window that day at the store, but she was relieved to know he was caught and could no longer haunt my life or dreams. Due to her guilt over not being there the night he came to my cottage, I omitted most of that night's events—telling her no more than I had to.

My eye was healing nicely and it no longer hurt to be in the sun, so I planned a day on Lovers Key in Fort Myers. I was in a state of bliss as I lay there letting the hot sun wash over my body. Sheldon was snorkeling and I had to giggle every time he dove down to find a shell as only his feet stuck out above the water. His body was wet and glistening in the sun as he walked over to me holding a beautiful lace murex shell and several sand dollars.

"Wow, they're beautiful. How about some lunch?" I asked as I knelt down on the large blanket and opened the basket of food.

"Yes, I'm starving."

We ate a picnic lunch of turkey sandwiches, fresh fruit, and nuts.

"Glass of wine?" Sheldon asked as he opened a bottle of Pinot Grigio.

"Yes, please."

We ate our lunch and reminisced. "I can't believe it's been almost three months since I arrived on Sanibel," I said lazily.

"Me either. I can't believe you thought I was such a player when we met." Sheldon ran a finger down my arm and I felt the goose bumps rise.

"You had girls on both sides, it was obvious you were a player." I smiled. "But you were just too damn hot to resist." I winked at him and took a sip of the crisp white wine.

"And now?" He smiled seductively and I was tempted to laugh, but his eyes were so blue in the sun they held me in a trance while my heartbeat picked up momentum.

"You'll do, I guess." I laughed.

"I'll do? Should I find you some young chap in a leopard Speedo?" He grinned and I fell silent, wondering why my brain was failing me. I so wanted to come up with a cocky reply, but instead I was sitting there in his gaze wishing he would kiss me and wondering if my future would hold more moments like this with Sheldon.

***

Annie and I had planned a day of shopping and I was looking forward to it. I loved spending time with Sheldon but I was in need of some girl time. Annie was sweet and fun and our conversation was never dull. We seemed to have similar taste in clothes and music and never tired of talking about the men in our lives. I was getting dressed when I heard the phone ring and saw that it was Sheldon calling from work.

"I need to help my dad for a couple of hours today, want to come with me?"

"I would have loved to but Annie asked me to go shopping with her today, I'm sorry." I had gotten to know Bill and Helen over the last few months and really enjoyed spending time with them. Bill was always doing something outside, and I had learned how to properly prune several types of tropical plants and fruit trees. Helen and I enjoyed watching cooking shows, talking about food, and sometimes walking through the neighborhood. She reminded me so much of my Nana in some of her mannerisms and the way she loved me as if I were her own. I contemplated postponing my day with Annie but it had been hard to schedule our day together and I really was looking forward to it.

"That sounds like fun, enjoy some girl time. I'll see you tonight."

Annie and I were having a great time going into each shop on the island. I found a cookbook full of tropical dishes and purchased it, looking forward to trying some of the recipes.

"You like to cook?" Annie asked.

"I do. Do you?"

"I like to bake."

"I can't bake at all." I laughed. "The only dessert I know how to make is Key lime pie. I don't like to measure things, so my desserts never turn out."

"Aren't these cute?" Annie held up martini glasses rimmed in lime green. I nodded and smiled. She set them back down and we made our way out and to the next store.

"So how are things going with Charlie?"

"Great. He seems to want to spend more time with me now that Sheldon's not as available to him."

I felt terrible for taking Sheldon away from him and wasn't aware that I had come between them. I would have to fix it as soon as I could and encourage him to spend more time with Charlie. "I don't want to take him away from his friends. He must be forming quite an opinion about me." I couldn't contain my worried expression.

"No, believe me, Charlie thinks you're great and he's happy for Sheldon. I'm just saying, the two of you meeting has been really good for me and Charlie." She held up a red dress to her body and looked in the mirror. "Every girl should have a well-fitted cocktail dress, don't you think?"

"That will look amazing on you. Try it on," I encouraged.

"I'll wait for you to find something." She flipped through the rack with me and pulled out a black dress in my size. "Here, try this one." I found another one and decided to try them both on.

"Ooh, I really like this one," Annie said, and I peeked out of my dressing room to see her in it.

"It's stunning on you—you have to get it."

I didn't care for the first dress that I tried on so I hung it up and slipped on the second one. "What do you think?" I asked as I stepped out of the dressing room.

"Wow. If you want to render Sheldon speechless, then you have to buy that dress."

"I don't know if I will ever have an occasion to wear it." I studied myself in the mirror and loved the way it clung to my body. I did want to look stunning for Sheldon and wondered where I would be able to wear it.

"I'll make sure we have an occasion. We *have* to get these dresses." Annie smiled.

We both found shoes to go with our dresses and made our purchases. I immediately regretted spending that much money not knowing if I could find a job soon. I had a very comfortable cushion after selling my half of the business, but without money coming in I didn't feel at leisure to spend it on frivolous things.

"I'm sick of shopping," Annie admitted. "Want to take a break and have a drink?"

"That sounds so good, my feet are killing me."

We drove over to Doc Fords and enjoyed mango mojitos and great conversation. "Anything exciting happen at work lately?" I asked. I loved hearing her crazy stories of the emergency room and hoped that my visit didn't make the list of stories she talked about with other friends.

"Always. We had this guy come in the other day that was recently diagnosed with diabetes. His doctor had shown him how to administer insulin injections by using an orange and had the patient practicing on the orange. He came in wondering why his blood sugar was still so high and we finally figured out that he was injecting the insulin into the orange and then eating it."

"No way!" I joined Annie's laughter and begged her to tell me more.

After another ridiculous story, Annie threw her head back and laughed hard. I had to concentrate on swallowing the sip of margarita that I had just sipped so it wouldn't come out of my nose when I laughed. "Let's do this again soon."

"Absolutely." Annie and I paid the bill and she dropped me off at home. I grabbed my bags out of the trunk and waved goodbye before going inside. The air-conditioned living room felt so good on my skin, I set my bags down and took a seat in my paisley chair to phone Sheldon.

"Hi, love." He answered. "Did you have a good time?"

"I did. Annie's great. How is your dad? Did you get everything done?"

"He's good—said to tell you hello. We got a lot done, but with my dad there will always something to fix or build."

"I'm sure he just likes your company." I smiled into the receiver.

"I'd like to take you out to dinner tonight. Are you up for it?"

"Sure, I'm always up for spending time with you."

"Good answer. I'll pick you up at six o'clock."

"What should I wear?"

"I'd like to take you somewhere a little nicer."

"I bought a dress today that I think will work." I smiled. "See you at six."

I took my bags into the bedroom to dress, silently thanking Annie for talking me into the purchases. I slipped on a black lace bra and matching panties just in case tonight was THE night. The black dress hit just above the knee and hugged my body just right. I brushed out my hair and applied a little more makeup before putting on the black heels that I purchased. I looked myself over in the mirror and hoped Annie was right about Sheldon's reaction.

He arrived promptly as usual and handed me a large bouquet of flowers filled with lime green cymbidium orchids, birds of paradise, lavender dendrobium orchids, and delicate white ginger. "Oh Sheldon, these are really gorgeous. Thank you."

"You look—stunning." I watched as Sheldon looked me up and down with admiring eyes and everything inside of me was cheering. He was wearing a black suit, white shirt, and a light blue tie that made him look like a Special Forces Agent. His long dark eyelashes framed his eyes that stood out next to the light blue tie. "Wow, you clean up nicely." I smiled and kissed him, lingering a bit longer than I had planned. I had a few inches of added height with the heels and it was nice to look straight into his eyes.

We dined at the Mad Hatter and were seated at a table in the back corner. A waiter poured water into our glasses and Sheldon ordered a bottle of Pinot Noir.

We sipped our wine and looked over the menu and the restaurant. I chose the black truffle sea scallops and Sheldon ordered rack of lamb.

"I'd like to catch the sunset after dinner, there are still a few clouds, but that usually makes for the best sunsets."

"I would love that."

Sheldon lifted his glass for a toast: "Here's to us." I clinked my glass gently to his and we took a sip without taking our eyes off of each other. I loved this incredible man sitting across from me and felt like the luckiest woman on earth. Our entrées arrived and we ate slowly savoring every bite.

"Try a bite of this." Sheldon offered me a bite of his lamb. It was encrusted with a walnut and cherry pesto, pan seared, and finished off in the oven until it was medium rare. It rested on a rosemary and port wine demi-glace that was rich and silky and melted in my mouth.

"Oh my, I think that is the best lamb I have ever had." I went over the ingredients in my head so I could duplicate it.

"Here, now try mine." I ran a bite of scallop through the beurre blanc and offered the forkful to his mouth.

"That's delicious. Now tell me what I have just eaten."

"A scallop tossed in panko crumbs laced with grated black truffles. The sauce is called beurre blanc, which is a butter sauce with cream, white wine, and in this case caramelized shallots."

"I'm impressed. You're hired," he teased.

"You know I would love to cook for you anytime." I really did love cooking for him and especially enjoyed preparing food in his kitchen. It was a chef's dream kitchen, not that I was a chef—just a wannabe.

"I'm going to take you up on that. I can just picture you now cooking, naked, in my kitchen."

"Sure, sure. I mean, why risk getting my clothes dirty." I held his gaze. He was constantly teasing me and I was ready to play his game.

The waiter returned and set a black leather folder on the table containing the check. Sheldon slipped his credit card inside and handed it back to the waiter before he walked away.

"Let's catch the sunset behind the restaurant."

We walked outside into the warm air and Sheldon held me steady while I took off my heels to walk barefoot in the sand. There was already a crowd of people on the beach as we made our way through the sand to find a spot for viewing the sunset.

"It's beautiful already," I said as the billowing clouds seemed to catch on fire as the sun started its descent.

Sheldon took me in his arms. "Let's dance." He started leading me around and I could feel the soft sand between my toes as we moved.

"There's no music, silly." I giggled.

Sheldon cleared his throat and began to sing softly in my ear. His voice was rich, deep, and masculine as the smooth melody filled my ears and sent chills down my spine. "More than anything in this world, I just want you to be my woman. More than anything in this world, I want to be your man."

I could feel the stares of the people around us but I didn't care, I only wanted to concentrate on how good this moment felt. I hugged him tighter in response to the lyrics. *I am yours, completely and indubitably,* I thought to myself as he continued singing the lyrics of Lenny Kravitz in my ear.

"I'd walk through fire, stand in the rain. I'll go to hell and back . . ."

I listened to his voice and put my head on his chest. My heart felt so full I couldn't imagine being any happier than I was at this very moment.

When he pulled back to look me in the eyes, I got the feeling that he actually meant what he was singing to me. I was rendered speechless and could only stare into his intense azure blue eyes. I silently thanked God for this wonderful, smart, funny, thoughtful, and romantic man. "I love you," I whispered, and kissed him.

Sheldon held both of my hands when he began to speak. He was serious and his words seemed too slow as they left his mouth. "Emma." My name rolled off of his tongue and it felt like it was the first time I had ever heard the word. "I love you. I was drawn to you the first time I saw you on the beach and once I got to know you, I immediately fell in love with you. I know that sounds passé, but it's true. You're beautiful, smart, fun to be around, and you are the sweetest person I have ever known." He kissed the inside of my right wrist before he continued. "I can't think of a life without you, I feel the need to protect you and I want to take care of you." He kissed the inside of my other wrist. "Emma, I have never loved anyone the way that I love you. Yes, we've only known each other for a few months, but I know this is right and I don't want to spend another day without you beside me."

Tears stung my eyes as I looked at him and let his words sink in. I couldn't make my mouth speak to convey all that I wanted to say back to him. That I felt the same way about him and would gladly wrap myself up in his arms and stay there forever. That I would do everything that I could to stay on Sanibel just to be near him and I had already talked to a man about offering personal training sessions at the Rec Center. I could find an apartment in Fort Myers until I built up my clientele and then maybe I could find a condo on the island. He squeezed my hands, interrupting my rambling thoughts and I looked back into his eyes. He seemed to be nervous about something and I wasn't sure why.

"Emma Olivia Peroni . . ." He dropped to one knee.

Oh—my—God! I slapped my hand over my mouth a little too hard and felt the bite to my top lip. I didn't see this coming and was overwhelmed, wondering if I was dreaming.

"Will you marry me?" The words came out of his mouth and convened in my ears. I couldn't feel my feet touching the sand and hoped I didn't suddenly float away.

I realized I was holding my breath and took a deep gulp of air. I knew this was too soon, no one got engaged after just a few months of knowing each other, but it felt so right. When I was with him I felt amazing, comfortable, and safe. When we were apart I was thinking about him constantly, wishing I was with him. I had thought about what our kids would look like and saw us growing old together, sitting on the back porch, and riding those big tricycles with large baskets on the front all over the island. I tried to blink away my tears as I looked into his eyes but couldn't control them when I suddenly realized that this strong, beautiful man was mine. I loved him so much, and as the deluge of emotion consumed me all I could whisper was "Yes."

He smiled up at me and I dropped to my knees, throwing my arms around the man that I loved unequivocally. I vaguely heard clapping in the distance as our lips met and I assumed the sun had made its bow into the sea. *Who cares about the sunset—all of my dreams are coming true and I am so happy I could die* I thought to myself as I lost myself kissing Sheldon on the sand.

"Hold on, babe." He guided me off of him for a moment to retrieve something out of his pocket. In his hand he held open a small velvet box displaying the most exquisite round diamond set in a platinum setting with tiny diamonds wrapping around the band.

I gasped when I saw the ring. "Oh, Sheldon, it's stunning." It was more exquisite than anything I had ever seen. I wiped the tears that continued to flow with the back of my hand. "I can't believe this—I'm so happy, I love you so much."

"I love you too, babe." He slid the ring onto my finger and it fit perfectly. I wrapped my arms around his neck again fisting one hand in his hair as I kissed him with every bit of passion inside of me, ignoring the crowd that still surrounded us.

Twenty-Eight

The scent of gardenias filled my senses as I awoke in my room at the rental cottage. I stretched my arms and legs, keeping my eyes closed to block the invading sunlight a bit longer. The smell in the room was delightful and I finally opened my eyes to see where it was coming from. Gardenia blooms were on both nightstands and several were spread across the dresser. I sat up to see that there were petals in a trail on the floor leading out of my bedroom so I pulled on my robe and fastened the tie around my waist. I couldn't believe he had come in so early to put this all together without waking me. I paused to lift a bloom to my nose and inhaled deeply, taking in the glorious scent. My ring sparkled on my finger and I studied it for a moment, smiling as I remembered last night's romantic proposal. I was blissfully happy and couldn't wait to share the news with Julie and Annie. I looked around the bedroom for a poem, but didn't find one until I reached the door. A loose piece of paper lay in front of the door amongst the petals, so I picked it up and read it.

JOY
Let Columbus have his America
Let Franklin fly his electric kite,
and let Edison shine his iridescent light.
For nothing will ever compare to the
JOY
I have discovered in you.
I love you,
Sheldon

After reading the poem twice more, I opened my bedroom door and followed the smell of coffee to the kitchen where I saw Sheldon drinking a cup and reading the *Island Reporter*. He looked up when he heard me coming toward him and I couldn't help a wide grin.

"Good morning, my beautiful fiancée."

Oh, I like the sound of that. "Good morning, my sneaky future groom." I found my spot on his lap and wrapped my arms around him, suddenly wishing I had stopped to brush my teeth. I took a swig of his coffee and wrinkled my nose as I swallowed. "The flowers and poem are awesomely wonderful." I kissed his forehead. "It's early—don't judge my choice of vocabulary," I warned with a smirk and then kissed him on the cheek before snuggling into his shoulder and taking another look at the exquisite ring on my finger.

"I can't quit staring at this ring, it's beautiful." I smiled into his shoulder.

"I'm glad you like it." He kissed my hair and then patted me. "Hop up . . . I made you some tea and breakfast."

"Breakfast?" I secretly hoped it was cereal as I recalled the last time he attempted eggs.

"Yes, this morning I searched the internet and made you a gourmet breakfast." He sat a bowl of yogurt topped with granola and blueberries in front of me and I giggled.

"Master Chef overnight—who knew?" I teased and we both laughed. "Why are you up so early and why are you spoiling me so?"

"I couldn't sleep." Sheldon took another sip of coffee and set it down. He was wearing a pair of olive green cargo shorts and a faded brick red T-shirt. His hair was messy and I wondered if he had the windows down when he drove over. I must have been zonked when he came in as I don't remember even stirring.

He cocked his head and grinned. "You think I have a hidden agenda? Don't you know me by now?"

"Yes, I do." I raised one eyebrow and smirked. "So what's up? You should know me well enough to know that I'd do anything for you with or without flowers as persuasion."

"Hmm, I'll have to remember that." He shifted in his chair to face me. "There is something that I want to talk to you about."

When he looked at me I saw a grown man with the eyes of a child that wanted something desperately. I smiled and encouraged him to continue, "Okay, what is it?"

"A big storm is coming in this week. The waves are going to be stellar—a windsurfer's dream condition. Charlie and I would like to be out there early Tuesday morning."

It didn't sound dreamy at all to me, swimming in the ocean during a storm sounded miserable, cold, and probably scary. "You don't have to ask me—of course you should go if you want to." I smiled and took a bite of my yogurt. "Is it dangerous in a storm? What about the currents?"

"It's not the first time I have windsurfed in a storm, babe. Charlie and I have chased storms all over the coast just to get in those waves. It's not dangerous if you are experienced." Sheldon took a sip of coffee. "Maybe you can come and watch? Annie is going."

"Does she windsurf too?" A surge of jealousy washed over me and I was surprised by it. I really liked Annie but the thought of her having the love of windsurfing in common with Sheldon made me feel like an outsider and I wanted to be a part of it too. I needed to learn how to windsurf quickly so I could be out there with him, although the thought of being on the water in a storm frightened me and a shiver ran up my spine.

"No, she just comes to watch." Sheldon laughed. "I can see that competitive streak flashing in your eyes."

"Humph." I crossed my arms and feigned irritation.

"I have no doubt that you could windsurf and be great at it, but this storm is not the right time to teach you."

"No, I know that. I would love to come and watch you. Maybe I can take some shots? I'll have to pick up a rain guard for the camera first."

"I would love that, and the next sunny weekend I'd like to teach you how to windsurf. I really think you'll love it." Sheldon poured a fresh cup of coffee and refilled my tea cup. We sat there for a moment looking outside into the backyard and watched a cardinal preen itself on the porch railing. I thought back to last night, the most wonderful night of my life to date, and wondered if Annie was in on the whole thing. She was the reason I bought that black dress and had something nice to wear last night. I smiled and shook my head before taking a sip of tea and it didn't go unnoticed.

"What?"

"Did Annie know about last night?"

"Yes, she took you shopping to make sure you had something to wear."

"I thought so! She was adamant about me getting that dress. How did you know my ring size?"

"I had some inside help from Julie. I know you would have liked to tell her the news yourself, but I didn't have any other options. I tried to measure your finger on several occasions but it was just impossible." I smiled at my clever man and could see there was something else on his mind.

"I have one more question for you," he said.

"Sure, what?"

Sheldon motioned for me to sit on his lap and I gladly complied. He pushed my hair around to rest on the opposite shoulder and planted small sweet kisses on my neck. I felt the goose bumps rising on my neck and a shiver ran right through me. The feeling of his lips ever-so-gently touching my neck instantly sent desire swirling through my stomach. I couldn't believe something so sweet and gentle could affect me like that.

"Mmm." Sheldon groaned into my ear, obviously enjoying the heavenly torture he was putting me through. "Marry me this weekend," he whispered into my ear and my body melted as it caught on fire from his breath on my ear.

"Sheldon . . ." I moaned his name as the feeling of his lips on my earlobe sent me into another dimension.

"Is that a yes?" he whispered and I would have agreed to anything at that moment just to make sure he didn't stop what he was doing to me.

"You're a wicked man asking me like this," I managed to exhale. "How. Can. We . . ." Each word came out in a pant.

"Just you, me, and a minister on the beach behind the house." He stayed at my ear, and I felt my hands dig into his thighs as my body tightened, desire building deep inside of me. "I don't want to wait any longer. Cold showers can only do so much. Marry me this weekend."

I smiled at the thought of him stepping into a cold shower. "What about your family and friends? Your parents will be devastated." I was suddenly hit with the realization that I wouldn't have anyone to walk me down the aisle and my side of the church would be bare compared to his. Julie and Jake would come, and a handful of friends and a cousin might make the trip, but it was a long way to drive and a lot to ask.

Sheldon seemed to read my thoughts and kissed me on the forehead—it was a soft lingering kiss implying that he knew what I was thinking. He had obviously considered all of this already, knowing that I would be thinking about my family and wishing Papa was there to walk me down the aisle.

"I've already talked to my parents. They want us to be happy and do whatever we want. The only thing my mom asks is that she can throw us a huge reception after our honeymoon. She's eager to show you off to her friends, and I can't blame her so I agreed—I didn't think you would mind."

I took a moment to linger on the thought of our honeymoon. A week alone with Sheldon on the beach filled me with butterflies that had been charged with electricity.

"I would love it." His parents' generosity was too much but I had come to love them as my own. Bill treated me like the daughter he never had and Helen was so sweet and loving.

"Yes, this weekend—I can't wait." I snuggled into Sheldon's chest as he wrapped his arms around me and kissed the top of my head. I couldn't believe that I would be Mrs. Sheldon Barringer so soon and that I would start a new wonderful life with this man and never have to sleep in that huge bed alone again. I inhaled deeply into his neck to take in his clean masculine scent and felt the muscles in his back through the soft T-shirt. *Mine—he is all mine.* I smiled and looked at the ring on my finger once again, eager to call Julie.

***

"Tell me every detail," Julie commanded.

"Oh Jules, I have never been so happy in my life." I held the phone in one hand and pulled my knees up to my chest, wrapping an arm around my legs. I would miss this overstuffed paisley chair after I was married and living with Sheldon. I told her every detail—dinner, the song, proposal, and ring.

"He sang to you?"

"Yes and he has a magnificent voice. I had no idea."

"Go on, what happened next?"

"He told me how much he loved me and didn't ever want to be apart from me. I was shocked—I just didn't see it coming. I actually thought he was wining and dining me for our first night together." I dropped my head in embarrassment even though I was alone in the house. "I shaved my legs twice and put on my sexiest bra and panties."

"Oh, that's hilarious, Em!" She laughed out loud and I joined her until we were both out of breath.

"I know, I'm such a dork."

"So have you set a date?"

"Yes, and don't be mad but we're getting married this weekend."

Silence.

"We just can't wait, Jules, surely you can understand. Papa isn't here to walk me down the aisle, I have no family except for you, so we're just going to elope on the beach behind the house."

"I understand, Em. I'm so happy for you. I just really wanted to be there. Make sure you have pictures to show me, at least."

"Of course." I told her about the reception that Helen and Bill wanted to have after the honeymoon.

"Do you know where you are going for the honeymoon?"

"I assume we are staying here. What could be better than a week on the beach?"

Julie grinned. "Yeah, I doubt you will be spending any time on the beach, Em. I'll bet you a hundred bucks you don't even see sunlight for a week."

"You're so crass, Julie." I laughed and wondered if she was right. "I will decline on that bet and hope that you are right." I wanted to ask her for any tips that might help me seem less inexperienced, but every time I tried to speak total humiliation took over and I fell silent.

"Call me as soon as you are able, I want to hear everything about the wedding and honeymoon—well, not everything, I just want to know that you are happy and okay."

"I will. Bye, Jules." I hung up the phone in time to hear Sheldon pulling up the gravel driveway with our lunch. We had decided to waste a Sunday cuddled up on the couch to watch a movie. Sheldon was having some work done to the outside of the house so we had to settle for the smaller television at the rental.

"Hi babe, what movie did you get?" I greeted him at the door and took the bag containing our lunch to the living room.

"*The Princess Bride*." He smiled at me and walked over to the DVD player to insert the movie.

"Yay, I can't wait to see it. 'Hello, my name is Montigo Ayoyo . . . prepare to die.'" I swung my arm around pretending to strike him with a sword and he threw his head back rolling with laughter.

"It's Inigo Montoya."

He didn't stop laughing until the movie started and we settled in next to each other on the couch eating out of the to-go boxes prepared by the Key Lime Bistro. I loved the movie and laughed every time he quoted some of the more famous lines along with the characters.

We were both too restless to stay on the couch for the rest of the day like we had planned, so we went for a long bike ride and let the cool breeze blowing in from the upcoming storm wash over us.

"Oh, I can't believe I forgot to tell you this!" I said as we stopped along the path for a drink of water. "So I made an appointment with Mr. Faber at the Rec Center—remember the man that your dad told me to call?"

"Sure, I remember, and?"

"Well, he posted my name, number, and credentials on the wall as a personal trainer. I can start booking clients immediately."

"That's great news, congratulations!"

"Thank you. I just hope I can book a full schedule to keep me busy during the day. I can't just sit around and think about my handsome new husband all day after we're married." I winked.

"That doesn't sound so bad to me. I think about you all day now. We are usually hand-in-hand walking along the beach, or sometimes we're kayaking and swimming with the dolphins . . . oh, and you're naked."

"That's my man—wasting all of his brain power on inappropriate and improbable thoughts." I grinned.

"I don't know about that. You agreed to marry me, didn't you? And I haven't given up on the thought of having you naked in the pool. In fact, once you see how freeing it is to not be clothed, I probably won't be able to take you in public anymore."

"Hmm . . . I'm sure I could get more clients to train with me that way." I gave him a flirty wink, and got back on my bike. I was sure that comment got him and I wished that I could have seen his face.

As we biked along the path headed home, we talked about windsurfing and the wedding, but mostly we were quiet. I wasn't sure what had Sheldon deep in thought, but I was thinking about what I was going to wear when I promised him in front of God to love him until the day I died. I smiled to myself and then let my thoughts wander to the wedding night . . .

Twenty-Nine

"Hi Annie, this is Emma." I was looking through my closet for something to wear when I called her. "I'm so glad I caught you—are you busy?"

"Hi. No, I'm good. Charlie told me that you're going tomorrow, I'm so glad."

"Yes, it should be fun . . . right?"

"It's really exciting to watch them. They're really good. Just make sure you dress warmly and bring a poncho. An umbrella won't do—you need a poncho."

"Thanks for the heads-up. Listen, I'm calling to see if you have time this week to go dress shopping with me? The earlier, the better." I found a pair of khaki shorts and a white shirt to wear and set the outfit on the bed while I finished our conversation.

"I'm free today actually. I was just finishing up some laundry. Have ya'll set a date, then?" I heard the excitement in her voice and I was sure she was picturing a big wedding and waiting for me to ask her to be a bridesmaid. If things were different, she would have definitely been in the wedding.

"Um . . . yes. We are eloping this weekend." I scrunched my nose and waited for the uncomfortable silence that was sure to follow.

"Sounds perfect—I'm excited for you." Annie sounded genuine and I replaced my scrunched face with a smile.

"Thank you. I'll just need a few minutes to finish getting ready. Want me to pick you up?" I asked.

"No, I'll come get you. I know where all the right shops are. Is thirty minutes enough time?"

"Yes, plenty." I thanked her before hanging up and finished getting ready.

Annie and I looked for dresses in three shops before finding my dress. It was a simple white organza spaghetti-strapped gown that hugged my waist and flared at the bottom into a sweeping train. The ruched bodice was accented with a diamond brooch, and I looked myself over before stepping out to face Annie. "What do you think about this one?"

"Oh Emma, you look beautiful. You are going to take Sheldon's breath away."

I smiled and looked at myself in the dress—my wedding dress. I loved the way I looked in it and couldn't believe this was happening.

I purchased the dress and made an appointment to try it on once more after the alterations were finished. The alterations lady looked at me incredulously when she heard how quickly I needed the dress back and I had to pay extra to have them rush it. I wanted to tell her "No, I'm not pregnant—just desperately in love and impatient," but decided to just let it go. "What about shoes and jewelry?" Annie asked, picking up a pair of dangly diamond earrings.

"I have the pearl necklace and earrings that my Nana wore on her wedding day. I planned on wearing those. I think I'll go barefoot since we will be in the sand."

"You're right, I hadn't thought about the sand. How sweet to be married in your Nana's pearls." Annie exhaled and smiled at me. "Let's grab some lunch."

We ate at the Blue Giraffe and sat for a long time catching up and laughing. Annie looked at my ring several times, commenting on how beautiful it was and how thrilled she was for us both.

"I just can't imagine being any happier than I am right now, Annie. I don't think my heart could handle it. I'm crazy in love with him—I just hope I can make him as happy as he makes me."

"I know you will, you already do. His face lights up every time he sees you."

I was so glad that I had met Annie—she had become a really good friend and I enjoyed her company. I just hoped Charlie opened his eyes and realized what he had in her. He was a good-looking guy, but he really couldn't do better than her, in my opinion. She was beautiful, sweet, and loving, and she brought out the best in him.

"How are you and Charlie?"

"Really good, actually. He asked me to move in with him." She beamed.

"Wow, what did you say?"

"I said yes. I'm over there every night anyway."

"I'm so happy for you. You two are really good together."

Annie nodded in agreement and took a sip of her water. "You'll need to have your nails done before the wedding. I'd like to treat us to pedicures and manicures later in the week."

"That sounds wonderful, thank you. Let's go dutch, though—that's expensive."

"No way, my treat."

***

I was dressed and ready Wednesday to go watch my man on the waves when I heard the phone ring.

"Hi, babe, I'll be there to pick you up in ten minutes. Don't forget your poncho and rain cover for the camera." Sheldon sounded like a kid brimming with excitement over windsurfing in this storm.

"I'm all ready and have my things by the door."

I had on a sweatshirt and jeans with tennis shoes and my hair was French braided to keep it out of my face in the wind. I checked over my camera bag making sure I had everything I needed to get some great shots of Charlie and Sheldon. I watched out of the window in the living room for Sheldon's truck and wrinkled my nose at the weather outside. The sky was dark gray and ominous, bringing strong winds that blew the palm tree fronds sideways. The rain was pelting against the window and I remembered how it felt on my skin when we were caught in the rain on Sheldon's porch. I didn't understand how he could enjoy being out in this nasty weather so much, but I loved hearing the enthusiasm in his voice and was looking forward to watching him on the water with his board. He was so passionate about windsurfing and talked of it often, but this would be the first time I got to see him in action.

As we pulled in next to Charlie's truck I saw Annie in the passenger side. I waved to her and unbuckled my seat belt. "I'm going to sit with Annie while you get ready."

Sheldon kissed me hard on the lips and I felt the excitement raging through him. I was delighted that he was so happy. "Sure. It will take us awhile to get set up. I'll come to you before we head out."

I grabbed my camera bag and pulled the poncho hood over my head before racing over to Charlie's truck to slide in next to Annie.

"Man, it's ugly out there. I can't believe Sheldon's so excited about being out in this."

Annie nodded her head in agreement. "I'll never understand it, but Charlie's like an excited little kid on Christmas."

"I know, Sheldon too." We both laughed and watched them get their boards and sails ready. They walked toward us with broad smiles and it looked like something out of a movie scene. They were both very handsome men and the image of them walking toward us as the wind swept their soaking wet hair sideways would forever be embedded in my mind. I cracked open the door and was immediately assaulted with the wind and rain. I quickly stepped outside of the truck so the inside didn't get soaked and tried to shield myself from the rain but it was no use.

Sheldon held my face in his hands and kissed me hard, making my lips sting a little. My body instantly warmed and the pelting rain ceased to irritate me.

"Get some good shots—I fully intend on showing off for you." He winked.

"I will. Have fun out there." I tried not to crinkle my nose as I became aware of the pelting rain again. "And please be careful."

"I will," Sheldon assured. "I love you."

I didn't think I would ever get used to hearing him say those words to me. My chest filled with the sensation of sparklers as little electric shocks tapped my insides.

"I love you too," I said as I watched my soon-to-be husband walk away from me in his tight black wetsuit. I was sure my cheeks would have flushed if it wasn't so cold.

I climbed back into the truck with Annie and got my camera ready, taking the rain cover out of the new package and fitting it to my camera and lens.

"You might want to wait a few minutes before you get out of the truck, they'll do some practice runs before they attempt anything camera-worthy."

After their practice runs Annie gave me a nod. "Okay, it should be getting good soon. I'll join you outside." She pulled her poncho hood up and tightened the string so only her eyes and nose were exposed.

I set up the tripod and attached the camera to it. The rain cover seemed to be working well to keep my camera safe so I found Charlie through the lens and zoomed in to snap a few shots for Annie. I quickly found Sheldon at the end of the lens and snapped a few shots of him standing on the surfboard holding onto the bar that controlled the sail. I saw a huge wave coming and wondered if it would knock him over. I kept my camera zoomed in on him and fought the urge to close my eyes as he turned into the wave. His board got a decent amount of air and he came back down on the water still standing. "That was amazing!" I gasped. "I think I got a good shot of that."

Annie looked at me and laughed. "You just wait."

Charlie's board got air and I snapped more shots for him and Annie. Another good-sized wave came in and I saw Sheldon brace himself for it. He whipped the board around into the wave and got enough air to flip completely upside down and land perfectly. "Holy smokes! I got it!" I squealed with delight.

Annie laughed out loud. "I told you it was going to get good." She clapped even though it was just the two of us standing there and the guys were too far out to hear it.

They made several more jumps and I joined in the clapping for them after getting the shot on camera. Sheldon let go of the sail with one hand for a moment to wave at me and I was so proud of what he was able to do out there. I knew it took a lot of strength to hold the sail against the strong wind and wondered how hard it was and how long it took him to learn how to flip into the air. I had a dozen questions that I wanted to ask him and couldn't wait for my private lesson as soon as the storm passed and the sun graced us with its presence again.

I readied my camera for more shots and waited for the right moment. A massive wave was coming and I could see both men preparing to take it. I kept my camera focused on Sheldon as he whipped into the wave first. He pulled the board up into a flip while spiraling in the air. I was in awe of him and his impressive skills as I watched through the camera lens, holding the button down to capture every second of the jump. I heard Annie scream something next to me and I whipped my head around to look at her. She had both of her hands over her mouth as she looked out to sea. The next few moments seemed to go in slow motion as I followed her eyes to Sheldon and Charlie. Sheldon was still in the air and seemed to be held there by a string while time stood still and all of the breath left my body. Charlie had begun his loop into the air way too close to Sheldon and a crash was inevitable.

I couldn't move, I couldn't breathe. All I could do was watch as the two boards collided, crumpling the sails and crashing back down into the water in one heap. I silently prayed that they had somehow gotten lucky and avoided injury, but they hit so hard and fast it would have been a miracle to come out of it without a scratch. Annie called an ambulance immediately while I looked for them to appear above the water.

Nothing. Suddenly Charlie's head popped up out of the water and he grabbed onto his board. It appeared that he was looking around for Sheldon. I tried to run toward the water but my legs refused to comply and I was paralyzed as I watched Charlie dive back into the water.

"Oh please, please let him be okay . . . God, please let him be alright." Tears streamed down my face and the feeling in my legs returned. I knocked the camera and tripod over by accident and ran as fast as I could toward the raging sea. I swam against the waves, taking in water each time I cried out for Sheldon. I could barely see Charlie in the distance when he came back up out of the water with Sheldon under one arm, swimming toward his board while holding his head out of the water. Sheldon's body looked limp and motionless as I got closer and I feared the worst.

"Sheldon!" I shouted through sobs.

Charlie reached his board and spotted me in the water. He yelled for me to go back to shore and wait. "I've got him. Go back and call an ambulance."

I kept swimming toward them, ignoring his order to go back, knowing that Annie had already made the call.

"Emma, damn it, go back! I can't hold on to both of you."

I stopped, suddenly conflicted between my desire to reach Sheldon and the reality that I couldn't do anything to help and might make matters worse. I felt completely helpless as I treaded water. "Is he okay?" I shouted over the sound of the wind and waves.

"Yes. Go back!"

I swam back to shore, slightly contented with Charlie's promise that Sheldon was okay and saw the lights from the ambulance coming toward us. "Oh thank God," I cried out as I reached the sand and fell over on my knees to pray.

The emergency team arrived just in time to help Charlie drag Sheldon out of the water and onto a spine board. I watched in horror as one of the paramedics squeezed a large round rubber device forcing air into Sheldon's lungs. They lifted him onto a stretcher and into the ambulance, never stopping the squeezing of the bag of air. I followed closely, not wanting to leave Sheldon's side.

"She's his fiancée," Annie told the paramedic who then offered me a hand to help me into the vehicle.

"We'll be right behind you," Annie informed me, helping Charlie to the car.

Sheldon looked lifeless as he lay on the stretcher. I looked to the paramedic for permission to hold his hand and he nodded while squeezing the air repeatedly into Sheldon's lungs. He remained unconscious the entire ride to the hospital and I felt helpless as I sat there and watched the man that I love slipping away from me. I held his lifeless hand to my cheek. "Don't leave me, Sheldon. Please don't leave me." My words came out staccato between sobs. "You promised you would never let me go. Fight . . . fight hard." My sobs had turned to hiccups by the time we arrived at the emergency room. The paramedics quickly lifted Sheldon's stretcher down out of the ambulance, giving the doctor his vitals.

"Unresponsive, thready pulse . . ." My head was spinning and I felt the urge to vomit as my body was wrenched with hiccups and sobs. I didn't know where to go or what to do. I was frozen in place, watching the doctors wheel Sheldon into the emergency room.

Annie and Charlie pulled in behind us and Annie got a wheelchair for Charlie. He grimaced when she helped him out of the truck. "I'm pretty sure you've cracked some ribs."

I followed Annie and Charlie into the emergency room and sat with Charlie while Annie checked him into triage. He kept repeating the same lines over and over, "I'm so sorry, Emma. I'm so sorry." I wished that I could tell him it wasn't his fault, but all I could do was pray that Sheldon would be okay and concentrate on not vomiting between sobs and hiccups.

Annie rubbed my back as we sat there waiting for the doctor to return with any news. She had given me something to help me calm down after helping me change into a pair of dry scrubs since my clothes were drenched and wrapped a blanket around my shoulders. I wasn't cold but my body was shivering so I pulled it tighter around my body and hugged it tightly. After vomiting twice, my body was racked with dry heaves. She said it was shock due to the overwhelming surge of emotions. When my body had finally calmed down, the tears began to stream steadily down my cheeks and I let them flow not taking the time or energy to wipe them away.

"Someone should call Bill and Helen," I whispered.

"I've been trying, they must be out. Don't worry, I'll keep trying."

Annie was so calm and seemed to have everything under control. I was thankful that she was there next to me and thankful that she was smart enough not to try to talk me out of my feelings of despair. She just rubbed my back and met any needs that I had without me even being aware of them myself. A man that looked to be in his fifties with salt-and-pepper hair, glasses, and bluish-green scrubs walked over to us and Annie stood to greet him before sitting back down to hold my hand as the doctor spoke. Miss Peroni, I'm Doctor Ogilvy." He smiled sympathetically at me as I waited for him to give us the update on Sheldon. The look on his face let me know that Sheldon was okay, but I still wasn't sure what the extent of his injuries was. "Sheldon's accident caused a lot of trauma to his body but we have been able to repair the damages thus far. He has several broken ribs. One of those ribs punctured his left lung causing it to collapse. Thankfully he was knocked unconscious before he went under water which prevented too much water from entering his other lung. While he was having a CT scan of his lungs done, he became tachycardic, hypotensive, and his air pressure rose quickly. He—"

"What does that mean?" I interrupted.

"I'm sorry, it means that his heart rate was too high and his blood pressure was too low. It's a sign of a tension pneumothorax, which is a progressive build-up of air within the pleural space. When a lung is punctured it allows air to escape into the pleural space but doesn't allow any return of air. We inserted a chest tube to relieve the pressure and he will have to keep that in until his lung heals. Now let me be clear that Sheldon is stable, but still in critical condition."

I had watched enough emergency room television and movies to know that he was trying to give me a peace and calm before he relayed the bad news, so I braced myself and concentrated on breathing in and out. I watched his lips move and did my best to understand his medical terminology. "When pressure builds in your pleural space it pushes the mediastinum—or the space in your chest that contains the lungs and heart—to the opposite hemithorax—the other side and obstructs blood return to the heart. This leads to instability of the heart and, in Sheldon's case, cardiac arrest."

"Oh God, no." I covered my mouth with my free hand as Annie squeezed the other one in hers and tried to comfort me.

"He's okay now, Em," she said and I wiped the tears from my eyes, calming myself so the doctor could finish.

"Yes, we were able to revive him and, like I said, he is stable but in critical condition. We have transferred him to the Intensive Care Unit where he will be monitored very closely."

"When can I see him?"

"You may go in now, but he is heavily medicated and shouldn't wake before tomorrow. Annie can show you where the ICU is." He looked to Annie and she nodded.

I looked at the doctor and forced my lips upward into a weak smile. "Thank you."

Annie led me to the ICU and I looked Sheldon over. It seemed like he had tubes coming out of every body part. I walked over to his bedside and held his hand in mine while assessing the tubes. He had an IV line in his left hand, a blood pressure cuff attached to his right arm, a tube coming out of his side just under his armpit, an oxygen tube in his nose, and something attached to his right index finger. I looked at it as I held his hand in mine, curious to know what it was for.

"It's a pulse oximeter," Annie answered my unspoken question. "It measures the oxygen in his blood. The monitor over your head shows his percentage of oxygen, blood pressure, pulse, and heart rhythm. Everything looks good."

***

I woke up the next morning with a crick in my neck. I had slept in a chair that I scooted up next to Sheldon and fell asleep with my head on his bed. I felt the warmth of a blanket over me that wasn't there before and slowly lifted my sore head and neck up to look at Sheldon. My hand had slipped out of his so I reached over and gently took it again, kissing the top of it gently.

"The doctor said there hasn't been any change," I heard Sheldon's dad say behind me and I turned to look in his direction. He was holding his wife into his side on a small pink loveseat as she sobbed quietly.

"I'm sorry I fell asleep—Annie gave me something and it must have knocked me out. What did the doctor say?"

"He didn't say much—just that there was no change and it was a waiting game from here." Mr. Barringer's eyes look tired and bloodshot.

Annie wheeled Charlie to the door of Sheldon's room but didn't come in all the way. Charlie's nose was bandaged and he had two black eyes. He looked melancholy as he looked from Sheldon to me and finally to Sheldon's parents. "I'm so sorry . . ." he started and then fell silent.

Bill gently lifted Helen away from him and stood up from his spot to walk toward Charlie. "Charlie, it wasn't your fault. You saved my son's life . . . thank you." He squeezed Charlie's shoulder gently and I watched Charlie grimace and try to stifle a groan.

"Charlie, how are you?" I asked, trying to convey concern in my voice. I did care about him and was thankful for how he fought to save Sheldon, but my world had been turned upside down and it took all of my effort just to breathe in and out.

"Just a few fractured ribs and a broken nose. Emma, I would give anything to trade places with him. I'm so sorry."

I couldn't put another sentence together so I just nodded my head and turned back toward Sheldon, stroking his hand with my thumb.

Bill came over to me and I squeezed his hand as he stood there for a moment and stroked my hair to comfort me. "You should go on home and get some rest. A hot shower and a bite to eat would do you some good."

"No, I'm not leaving. Please don't ask me to—I need to be right here." I laid my head back down on the bed and kept Sheldon's hand in mine while Bill found his spot again next to Helen on the couch and I prayed silently until I fell asleep.

Thirty

The high-pitched shrieking of an alarm jolted me upright in the recliner next to Sheldon's hospital bed. I was met at the door by a nurse who assured me it was nothing. "His pulse oximeter has come off of his finger, that's all."

"Oh." I exhaled and looked him over.

The nurse clipped the gauge back onto his index finger and watched the monitor until everything was as it should be again. Sheldon's eyebrows twitched and his face grimaced before he groaned and blinked his eyes open.

"Sheldon?" I took his hand and squeezed his fingers. "Are you in pain?"

He nodded his head once, every movement seeming to cause more pain. I looked to the nurse for help. She was as round as she was tall. "I'll get something for the pain," she said and quickly strode down the hall.

Relief washed over me when I saw Sheldon look at me. His eyes were pale and lacked their usual luster, but he was alive and I was filled with renewed hope when our gazes locked. "You're going to be just fine, my love," I said, stroking the top of his hand.

"What hap—?" he tried to speak but winced in pain.

"Shh, just relax. The nurse will be here soon to give you something for the pain. You and Charlie collided on the water while windsurfing." I saw the startled look on his face and knew he was worried about Charlie. "Charlie's fine—a broken nose and a few broken ribs, but he's just fine." Once Sheldon settled down and relaxed, I continued to tell him what happened and how Charlie had pulled him out of the water. He fell asleep shortly after the nurse returned and injected something for pain into his IV line.

Sheldon was heavily medicated the next two days for pain. Dr. Ogilvy explained that since he was young, healthy, and athletic, his recovery time should be half as long as usual and he should be able to go home in a couple of days with some physical therapy sessions scheduled for the next two weeks.

I had gone back to the cottage to shower, change clothes, and give Bill and Helen some time alone with their son. When I came back, I could hear Charlie and Sheldon's laughter down the hall.

He's going to be okay, I thought to myself. *Thank God, he is going to be just fine.*

***

The last three weeks had been busy with physical therapy for Sheldon and a jumble of wedding details for me. I debated hitting the snooze button one more time as my body desperately wanted to stay in bed, but decided to get up and get moving instead. Julie and Jake had driven down and surprised me with a visit so we had stayed up late—too late for a wedding the next day.

Since the scare with Sheldon's accident, we decided to allow our closest family and friends to attend the ceremony and I was so glad that we did. Sheldon remained compassionate about my family not being there, but I reminded him, "Your family is mine now too. We will be surrounded by the ones who love us both, and that's how it should be."

Julie was there to help me get ready for our sunset wedding on the beach behind the house. She curled my hair in long loose curls, sweeping the front section back off of my face, and helped me get into my dress. I added Nana's pearl necklace and earrings last and stood in front of the full-length mirror to check myself over, running my hand down the organza and straightening the diamond brooch. The dress fit perfectly and made me feel beautiful and feminine. "I can't believe this is happening, Jules, I'm about to marry the man of my dreams."

"You look radiant, Em. I'm so happy for you."

We hugged gently, trying not to ruin the hard work she had put into my hair and makeup, and I had to blot a tear gently with a tissue. I heard a soft knock on the door and saw Annie peek in. "Come in." I waved my hand motioning her to join us.

"Sheldon wanted me to give you this." Annie handed me a bouquet of beautiful flowers—white roses, stephanotis, and gardenias that were tied together by a wide white ribbon.

"Gardenias . . ." I breathed in the sweet scent and smiled. He thought of everything. I stood in front of the mirror again to see the full picture of my dress while I was holding the bouquet.

"You look beautiful, Emma. I can't wait to see the look on Sheldon's face." Annie kissed me on the cheek, said hello to Julie, and left to take her seat with Charlie. Julie followed behind her and blew me a kiss on her way out.

Annie, Charlie, Julie, Jake, Sheldon's parents, and both of his brothers were sitting outside sipping on champagne while we dressed in separate rooms. Sam and Grant's families were unable to attend but it had been so nice to meet the two of them the night before.

Sam was tall and thin with blue eyes and short dark brown hair. Grant was also tall, had lighter brown hair and blue eyes. He was muscular and exuded more confidence than his older brother Sam.

We had dined together at Timbers and I watched Sheldon's face light up as he and his brothers talked about their childhood escapades. They teased Sheldon relentlessly as big brothers usually do, and I laughed when they told me about his goofy stage in elementary school. "He used to collect toothpicks from restaurants and glue them together. He wanted to make the world's largest raft and actually thought he could sail out to sea on it. Mom would get so embarrassed when he would empty the toothpick dispenser at the hostess stand."

I stood there alone in the room where I was dressing and took a sip of the champagne that Julie brought me earlier, trying to calm myself before I walked down the path to the beach. I started to tear up when I thought of my Papa holding out his arm to take mine, but shook it off quickly as this was the happiest day of my life and sad tears were not welcome.

I took a deep breath as I heard the elegant sounds of a cello playing Canon in D Major. I opened the door to find Sheldon's dad, Bill, standing there. "I was wondering if you would allow me to walk you down to the beach."

Tears filled my eyes and I quickly blinked them back before they had a chance to spill over. "I would be honored, thank you so much."

"You look beautiful, Emma." He offered me his arm and I took it. "Thank you for making my son so happy. We're thrilled to have you as part of our family."

"You and Helen have been so kind and loving to me. I am very blessed to have you in my life."

He guided me down the sandy path that led to the beach. I walked with my head down, carefully stepping with my bare feet through the path. It was so hard not to look up as I heard the sound of the waves crashing gently on the shoreline and the elegant sounds of the cello drawing me closer to my beloved. I was almost there, just a few more steps through the path onto the beach. When my feet touched the thick, powdery sand, I looked up to behold the most glorious image . . . the man that I loved.

Sheldon's eyes were a smoldering blue against his clean-shaven face and white shirt. When our eyes met I saw his mouth break into a breathtaking smile. He was wearing a black jacket that was tailored to fit him, and a crisp white shirt that had the top two buttons undone because he knew it drove me wild. He stood there with his hands clasped behind his back waiting for me. I didn't notice our friends and family sitting in the white chairs ready to witness our vows, only

Sheldon—his captivating eyes and smile drawing me to him.

Bill kissed me on the cheek and placed my hand in Sheldon's before taking his seat next to Helen. The warm, dry October breeze blew gently over my bare shoulders as the sun started to dip down behind a few wispy clouds. It was a beautiful evening—more perfect than anything I could have planned.

Sheldon exhaled slowly as he looked me over and whispered, "You are stunning, my love."

The love that I felt for him shone back at me in his eyes and I was overwhelmed with emotion. We were the only two people on the beach and in the world while we gazed into each other's eyes and exchanged our vows. When the minister pronounced us husband and wife, Sheldon took my chin gently in his hand and whispered, "Finally, you're mine." He kissed me with such gentleness that I felt like one of the delicate flowers in my lovely bouquet. I wanted more so I wrapped my arms around him, bouquet and all, and kissed him deeply, forgetting the witnesses and the need to breathe. All I could focus on was the fact that I loved this man with every fiber of my being and he loved me—I was his and he was mine.

Our guests enjoyed glasses of champagne while the photographer took a few pictures of Sheldon and me on the beach. When we returned to the house, Helen and Bill were the first to make their way over and congratulate us. Helen smiled sweetly as she held my hands in hers. "Welcome to the family, Emma. I couldn't have chosen a better woman for my son if I had tried, and I thank God for bringing you to us."

"I feel very blessed to be a part of your family. Thank you for making me feel so comfortable and loved." I hugged her and watched her eyes fill with tears as she looked at her son. He was her last born—the baby. Even though he was a grown man that towered over her petite frame, she would always see him as her little boy.

Sheldon was so gentle with her as he hugged her and asked her not to go overboard with the reception planning.

Sam welcomed me to the family before rustling Sheldon's hair and hugging him hard like brothers do. "I'm happy for you, little brother. She's seems like a great girl."

Grant shook my hand awkwardly and smiled before addressing us both. "Congratulations. I'm happy for you both."

"Thanks, bro, and thanks for flying down last minute."

"Wouldn't have missed my baby brother's wedding, plus I had to see it for myself. I thought you were going to be a bachelor for the rest of your life?" Grant glanced at me. "That's what he vowed the last time we were together—just a few months ago . . .

Easter, I think. I wish I had put money on the table over that bet." He laughed and I joined him.

Sheldon smirked. "Yeah, yeah, laugh all you want. But can you blame me?" He put his arm around my waist and I flushed from the compliment.

"No, little brother, I can't."

Jake and Julie made their way over and I breathed a sigh of relief. I liked Sheldon's brothers, but I didn't know them well enough to feel comfortable around them yet. Jake shook Sheldon's hand as Julie whispered in my ear, "We're staying two more nights at the Inn, but I don't expect to hear from you—enjoy your hot husband." She winked at me and I laughed, looking around to make sure no one else had heard her. Julie had never been good at whispering.

I hugged her and smiled, "If everyone would go ahead and leave, maybe I could."

"Do you want me to get them out?" she offered.

"Good heavens, no!" I knew she would and could but I would never live down the embarrassment.

Charlie and Annie were the last ones to tell us congratulations and leave the house. I wanted to toss my bouquet to her but didn't know if she would find it funny or insulting so I thought better of it. "Thank you for everything, Annie. You've been such a great friend to me." We hugged and watched Charlie hassle Sheldon. I wondered what he was telling him and got the feeling some of what he was saying was not meant for a lady's ears.

Charlie hugged me tight and congratulated us once more before looking at Sheldon with a wide grin. They had obviously shared something that wasn't meant for me or Annie to hear. I was dying to know what it was, but doubted I would remember to ask him about it later.

When they finally left, Sheldon and I shared another glass of champagne on one of the chairs that hadn't been taken away yet. I was sitting on his lap as he leaned in. He let his breath linger on my ear a moment before whispering, "I can't wait to get my beautiful bride out of this dress." My body tensed at the sound of his voice, low and husky. He took my empty glass of champagne and set it down in the sand. His eyes were ablaze as he moved to meet my mouth with his, so soft and tenderly. I wrapped my arms around his neck pulling him in closer, and deepened the kiss with a passion of my own. He scooped me up into his arms and carried me to the house, pausing in the kitchen to offer me more champagne. I shook my head, unable to speak, and searched his face for comfort. My heart was racing and my body began to tremble lightly as Sheldon carried me to the bedroom.

He set me down so we were facing each other. Holding his gaze, I felt the heat rising in my body, stirring and building my desire for him. His eyes locked on mine while he reached around and slowly unzipped my gown, pausing to kiss my shoulder and neck before sliding the thin straps off of my shoulders and letting the gown slide into a pile on the floor. Standing there in my new white lace bra and panties, I waited for my groom's reaction. Sheldon inhaled sharply as he backed up to look me over. My body began to respond with tiny jolts of electricity charging through me and my body felt like it was on fire. I closed the space between us and started unbuttoning his shirt, taking my time to trace my fingers over his chest before sliding the shirt off of his arms, and letting my hands glide over every muscle. I had always been hesitant to touch him too much as it always ended with a cold shower or a quick plunge in the pool, but now I wanted to explore every inch of his body. He pulled me into him and kissed me with a wild passion and hunger that nearly took me over the edge. I knotted my fingers in his hair and I couldn't seem to get close enough to him to satisfy my need.

Sheldon finished undressing himself, never breaking the seal between our lips until he removed my lacy undergarments and stepped back to look at me. "You are so beautiful."

We were inches apart and I could feel the magnetic pull of our bodies wanting and needing each other. He planted kisses up my neck and nibbled my earlobe until I moaned his name, "Sheldon."

His hot breath washed over my ear sending chills up my spine as he whispered, "I love you." I tilted my head back and groaned with pleasure at the sheer rapture of his words. He lifted me up in his arms and guided me onto the bed.

"This is all mine," he whispered as he took his time tracing every inch of my body with his hands and lips. I was breathless and greedy as I felt my hands slide over his back and feel the contours of each muscle. His arms were flexed as he held himself over me kissing and nibbling until I couldn't take it any longer.

"Sheldon . . . please . . ." I exhaled.

We were lost in each other, completely consumed in the ecstasy and harmony of our bodies becoming one.

Thirty-One

I awoke to Sheldon's finger softly trailing down my cheek to my neck, then down my shoulder and arm. I slowly opened my eyes to the invading light in the room. Sheldon was propped up on one elbow and holding a champagne flute full of orange juice.

"Good morning, Mrs. Barringer. How are you feeling?" He offered me the juice and I sat up to take a long drink, letting the words *Mrs. Barringer* sink in. I looked up at my husband—my gorgeous, wonderful husband who has made all of my dreams come true—and I was filled with a tremendous feeling of love that warmed me all the way to my soul.

"Good morning to you, Mr. Barringer. I feel divine." I couldn't contain the smile that spread across my mouth.

Sheldon grinned. "Are you hungry?"

I should have been as I wasn't able to eat much yesterday due to nerves and excitement over the wedding. Dreams coming to fruition didn't allow for much need of nourishment. I set the rest of the juice on the nightstand and looked into those mesmerizing blue eyes. Aftershocks reverberated through my body when I recalled the events of last night. "Very," I answered as I pulled him down toward me and kissed him hungrily. I felt him respond immediately and he pulled back to look at me. "You are insatiable, Mrs. Barringer." He ran his hand up my leg and whispered, "Damn, I'm a lucky man."

We spent most of the day in bed except for a quick swim in the pool. "My dreams have all come true now." Sheldon grinned mischievously. "I finally got you swimming naked in my pool."

"I don't see the point of clothes—you just keep stripping them off of me. Besides, someone once told me that you could swim faster naked," I said, giggling.

Sheldon chased me through the pool and I instantly became weak with laughter making it too easy for him to catch me. I couldn't believe how natural and good it felt to be naked around him.

"What was going on between you and Charlie last night?"

"What do you mean?"

"I saw the way he was grinning at you like you two had a secret."

"You'll find out soon enough, Ms. Impatient."

"Don't call me that—I like Mrs. Barringer much better." I grinned.

"But you are so impatient."

"Then I shall call you Mr. Secretive." I swam away from him and lay on a towel to soak up some sun.

"Fine. Pack your things and we can go tonight."

"Go where?" I popped up and whipped my head around to look at him. "I thought we were staying here all week."

"No, I have big plans for you, baby." He got out of the pool all male and muscle without an ounce of shame as he walked over to sit down next to me.

Jeez, his body was fantastic. "Do tell," I encouraged.

"No way. I want it to be a surprise."

I leaned in and kissed him, tugging seductively on his bottom lip. Pulling away, I gave him my best impression of bedroom eyes. "How about a little hint?"

"Damn, you're a filthy cheater." He leaned down and kissed me back, sending chills up my spine. "Okay, I can't wait. Get dressed and pack so I can show you where we're going to start our honeymoon."

"What should I pack?"

"Just a small bag—swimsuit, change of clothes. We'll only be gone a couple of days."

I jumped up and dressed quickly, eager to see what surprise he had in store. I packed enough to get me through three nights while Sheldon made a phone call. It couldn't be far since we didn't pack much and I wondered if we were going to stay in a nearby resort on the island. I didn't see the point of that when we had our own tropical paradise with more privacy than any place could offer, but as long as I was with him I would be happy with whatever he chose.

We drove down Periwinkle toward the lighthouse. *Are we staying in the lighthouse? I didn't think it was available to rent, doesn't the caretaker live there? However, knowing Sheldon, anything is possible.* It wasn't very romantic, but I could see his thought process since that was where we had first met. Sheldon slowed the car down and turned left into the Sanibel Marina and I knew instantly that he had borrowed the boat from Bob again. My heart skipped as I loved our time on the boat and couldn't wait to experience it all again. After Sheldon parked I smiled a knowing smile at him and he took my hand. We passed the *Sea Oar Knot to Sea* and kept walking down the dock. Sheldon gave my fingers a squeeze and I looked at a boat very similar to the one Bob owned. That's when I saw it. The name was scrolled in navy across the back of the boat . . . *Island Girl*.

Sheldon was giddy as he watched my expression. He lifted me up into his arms and carried me onto the boat. "Well, are you surprised?"

I was stunned and couldn't find my words. I knew he had wanted this boat, but when did he have time to make it happen? "I can't believe you finally got it! When did you—?" His lips found mine before I could finish.

"Charlie was a great help and made it happen while I was in therapy. We had a lot of time to talk and plan while I was in the hospital." He shrugged his shoulders.

"I'm so happy that you finally have your boat," I beamed.

"Our boat. Do you like the name?"

Our boat. It would take me some time to get used to the fact that I was a wife and that we shared everything. My world had been turned upside down with the loss of Nana and Papa, the attack, and leaving my business and friends. I had started to slip into a deep depression and thought a mediocre life of working and breathing in and out would carry me through the rest of my life, but instead I was blessed with the man of my dreams who loved me immeasurably and wanted me to be a part of his world. I was in a state of euphoria and hoped I wouldn't come down anytime soon.

"I love it, and I love you." I cupped his face in my hands and kissed him before looking around. "I think I'm going to have to lock the bedroom door again though." I grinned wickedly.

"I don't think so." He looked at me sternly.

"Oh yes, I'm locking us both in there until morning." I grinned as he carried me down the two steps leading to the bedroom. I shut the door with my foot and we spent our second night of marriage on the *Island Girl*.

***

The smell of hot Earl Grey tea filled my nose and I awoke with a smile. "Come, sit with me." He led me out of the bed and onto the couch, pulling me onto his lap. "Our flight leaves the day after tomorrow, will you have enough time to get packed?"

"Flight?! Mr. Barringer, you are full of surprises. Where on earth are we going now? This is blissful enough for me, being on the sea with the most dangerously handsome man . . . what more could a woman possibly want?" I giggled when I saw the predatory look in his eyes.

"*Dangerously* handsome, huh? I promise I'll be gentle with you."

I was rewarded with a mischievous grin when he noticed me wearing the shirt he let me sleep in months ago during our first overnight on the sea.

"I remember that shirt."

"I still love it." He handed me the tea and I took a sip.

"I'll need to wrap some things up at the office before we leave and then it's just you and me babe—no more interruptions for the next two weeks."

"Two weeks? When will you tell me where we are going? I do need to know how to pack."

"Give me a kiss and I'll give you a hint."

I reached over and playfully gave him a peck on the cheek and grinned widely.

"It's an *international* flight."

"Hmm . . ." I kissed him sweetly on the lips.

"They speak another language where we're going."

"Really!" I was getting excited now.

I scooted around and straddled myself on his lap, looking into his eyes while running my hands through his hair and kissed him with everything I had.

He groaned out each word, *"Sei cosi bella, amore mio."*

"Italy? We're going to Italy!"

He smiled and pulled me in close. "Yes, and I know you're going to want to see and experience everything, so I plan on savoring that fine body every chance I get until we leave." He grinned wickedly and the tingling sensation instantly swept through my body as he guided my head down on the cushion.

I couldn't believe how my life had changed since arriving on Sanibel in June. I had dreamed of living on the island since I was a little girl. It was more than just a pretty place, everything about it called to me and made me feel safe and free. I had thought it was a place I needed to run to—to escape the nightmares and pursuing demons, but I suddenly realized this was where I had always belonged. I wasn't running *away*—I was actually running home.

Epilogue

We walked on the sand with our heads down, carefully stepping through the path of the thick sea grape hedge toward the beach. It was hard not to look up as we heard the sound of the waves crashing gently on the shoreline, but this had become a tradition, something I had done since coming here as a little girl with Nana, and now I was trying to carry on the tradition with my own daughter.

"Don't peek, keep your head down," I said to Channing as we held hands.

"We're almost there—just a few more steps and then you can race to the water! Let's count to three. Ready? One . . . two . . . three!"

Channing squealed with delight as she ran toward the water. Her long and heavily sun-streaked hair flew wildly in the ocean breeze. I took a moment to adjust her pale pink ruffled bathing suit, and then squatted down to snap a few shots of my blue-eyed little girl as she stood there searching for her daddy's kayak.

My love for Sanibel had not diminished after living here. Every day the sunrise was new and beautiful, and every evening the sunset painted bold colors across the sky. I still clapped every time I watched the sun melt into the sea.

My reverie was interrupted by a small sandy hand with bubblegum pink fingernails placing a lettered olive shell on my leg. "Here, Mommy, I found a pretty shell."

"Thank you, these are my favorite. Can you find more?" I watched as she rushed to the water's edge and looked intently for another. She bent down and scooped something up into her hand and ran back to me. "Do you like these?" She held out her hand to reveal a tiny orange shell.

"Yes, I do. These are called kitten paws. See how they look like a tiny foot from a kitten?" Her eyes lit up as she traced it with her small finger. "These are *my* favorite."

The sky was blue and cloudless as the sun shone down on the clear water. There was a slight breeze coming off of the ocean that kept us from getting too hot on the sand. I laid a large blanket down and watched Channing.

"There he is!" I heard and looked to where she was pointing. Together we watched as he rowed, each stroke bringing him closer to the shore. Channing danced around as she eagerly awaited her daddy's arrival.

Sheldon pulled the kayak onto the sand and laid the oar inside. He grabbed Channing up into his arms and swung her around, making her giggle. When he set her down she put her hands on her hips and declared she was too big for that.

"You're four, Chan, and you'll always be my baby girl." He smiled at her and she rolled her eyes.

"Hello, my beautiful island girl," Sheldon said and looked at me with those blue eyes that still caused me to blush.

"Hello to you, my handsome husband."

"How are you? Are you comfortable?" Before I could answer, his lips were on mine with a sweet, loving kiss.

"I'm just fine," I said, smiling. "I'm not a fragile china doll, you know." I giggled as he shook his wet hair over me, misting my hot skin with water. I ran my hands through his hair as he leaned down and placed his hands on either side of my round belly.

"And how are you, son?" he asked before planting a kiss right above my belly button. We watched Channing play in the sand, shoveling it into a bucket and dumping it out for the base of her castle.

"What a perfect day." Sheldon closed his eyes.

I beamed as I took a deep breath of the sweet salty air. "Yes, another gorgeous day in paradise."

"Channing, come over and get settled in the sand for a good story." Sheldon scooted closer, taking my hand while reaching out for Channing's little fingers. "This is where your mother and I first met . . . Lighthouse Point."

Soul Full Eyes

Glimpses are fleeting,
and glancers don't care.
Ours is the love
of a meaningful stare.
For we were young when
that beauty first caught my eye,
and it's yours now,
I pray,
till the day that I die.
and as we hold hands one day,
when memories are old,
you are the woman
I long to behold.

~Kiley Murphy

To the Reader

I hope you enjoyed *Lighthouse Point* and were swept away as Emma and Sheldon discovered each other and what their summer together would mean for their "happily-ever-after." Though the characters were fictional, the setting is a very real and magical place for me.

Sanibel Island, located on the Gulf Coast just off of Fort Myers, Florida, was where I spent my summers and long weekends with my Nana and Papa. Now that I have a family of my own, we carry on the tradition of keeping our eyes closed as we walk toward the water, eagerly awaiting the splendor before us.

Just twelve miles long and two miles wide, you'll find the quaint island absent of stoplights, chain restaurants, and tourist-type shops. The laid-back atmosphere, world renown shelling beaches, and delectable restaurants will capture your soul and have you longing for Sanibel year after year.

For pictures, more information, and upcoming book titles, please visit the links below.

www.lisapostonmurphy.com

https://www.facebook.com/SanibelEscapes

Made in the USA
Monee, IL
01 November 2020